# FIREBALL

## a J.T. Ryan Thriller

A Novel
By

## Lee Gimenez

RRP

River Ridge Press

# FIREBALL
by
Lee Gimenez

Printed in the United States of America.

Published by
River Ridge Press
P.O. Box 501173
Atlanta, Georgia 31150

First edition.

Cover photos: Copyright by Zoom Team and Sit Photography used under license from Shutterstock, Inc.

Cover design: Judith Gimenez

ISBN-13: 978-0692132333
ISBN-10: 0692132333

# Other Novels by Lee Gimenez

FBI Code Red

The Media Murders

Skyflash

Killing West

The Washington Ultimatum

Blacksnow Zero

The Sigma Conspiracy

The Nanotech Murders

Death on Zanath

Virtual Thoughtstream

Azul 7

Terralus 4

The Tomorrow Solution

Lee Gimenez

# FIREBALL

## a J.T. Ryan Thriller

Lee Gimenez

# Chapter 1

*Billings, Montana*

**At** precisely 2:15 a.m. a powerful electric current surged into the vacation home's breaker box, causing it to overload and explode. The violent sparks from the explosion ignited the wooden structure and the fire quickly spread throughout the house. The intense flames reached the master bedroom a minute later, where the carpet, drapes and furniture immediately caught fire.

Startled awake from a deep sleep, the Chief Justice of the Supreme Court tried to rouse his sleeping wife. But he began coughing and was quickly overcome by the acrid, black smoke that filled the room.

The flames engulfed the bedroom and the Chief Justice and his wife were burned to death in a matter of seconds.

Their charred remains were found later by firefighters.

## Washington, D.C.

At the same time, a sophisticated military-grade drone flew toward its intended target at high speed. Reaching it moments later, the drone hovered over the large, extensively landscaped home in Georgetown, a wealthy community of D.C.

The craft landed on the pitched roof and emitted a series of whisper-quiet clicks. The clicks came from the drone's electronic igniter. Also attached to the drone was a brick-sized quantity of C-4 explosive.

Seconds later the igniter set off the bomb which immediately blew off the roof and destroyed the upper floor of the house.

The Senate Majority Leader, his wife, and his two children were asleep at the time and were killed instantly by the immense explosion.

The fireball from the blast lit up the night sky and echoes from the detonation were heard miles away.

## Atlanta, Georgia

The semi truck barreled down the quiet street at 70 miles per hour. It was 2:30 a.m. and there was no other traffic on the road.

The driverless truck quickly reached the end of the street, jumped over the curb, and after narrowly missing the Catholic church building, rammed into the church residence at the back of the property.

The speeding semi easily broke through the home's wall and continued smashing into the bedroom. Cardinal Baker, who was asleep, was crushed to death instantly.

The cardinal's body was found later among the ruins of the home.

# Chapter 2

*The Oval Office*
*The White House*
*Washington, D.C.*

John (J.T.) Ryan had only been in the Oval Office once before. That had been years ago when he had received the Medal of Honor for saving his Green Beret unit during the Afghanistan War.

But this visit was different. Much different.

He, along with his boss at the FBI, Erin Welch, had been called to the emergency meeting without explanation. They had been told to drop everything and fly to D.C. immediately.

Ryan glanced around at the other people in the room as they waited for the president to arrive. Sitting next to him was Erin, an attractive brunette in her mid-thirties. In the other wingback chair that fronted the president's desk was Alex Miller, a senior CIA officer who Ryan had worked with on other assignments.

Also in the room was Mike Corso, the Director of National Intelligence. Ryan had never met Corso before, but had seen him on TV during news casts.

Just then the door to the Oval Office opened and President Harris strode in, flanked by two brawny Secret Service agents. The meeting's attendees stood in unison as the president made his way around his desk and sat behind it.

President Harris turned to the agents. "That'll be all, gentlemen. You can wait outside."

"Are you sure, Mr. President?" one of them asked.

Harris nodded. "Yes."

Although the meeting's attendees had been thoroughly vetted and searched before entering the Oval Office, the agents still seemed unsure. Reluctantly they filed out of the room and closed the door behind them.

President Steve Harris placed his hands flat on his desk. "Please sit," he began. "And thank you for coming on such short notice."

As the group sat, Ryan studied Harris. The president was an imposing man, well over six feet, almost as tall as Ryan's own 6'4". Like himself, Harris was powerfully built, but unlike Ryan, the president had a paunch, no doubt a result of constant campaigning. Harris had a full head of jet black hair, a square jaw and blue eyes. He reminded Ryan of photos he'd seen of J.F.K.

"I'm sure you're all familiar with the recent tragic events," the president said gravely. "In fact, that's the reason you're all here."

There was a thunder clap from outside and Ryan glanced out the three tall windows of the Oval Office. Dark storm clouds were building over D.C.

Harris looked over his shoulder as well, no doubt jumpy about the deaths of the three leaders. He turned back and faced them again.

"We've suspected for some time that people," the president said, "possibly from within the government, have made it their mission to see that the United States is brought down." Harris paused and lowered his voice. "These rogue, deep-state elements have done their best to block our policies from the start. And the three tragic deaths, murders actually, confirm that they will stop at nothing to destroy the U.S. government, regardless of the cost."

"Sir," Erin Welch said, "do you think the deaths are connected?"

"I do. And the evidence we have collected so far appears to confirm this," Harris continued. "It's very difficult to kill a president of the United States. The security is extraordinary. So these rogue, treasonous anarchists did the next best thing. They murdered the Senate Leader, the Chief Justice of the Supreme Court, and Cardinal Baker. Three of the most prominent U.S. leaders. Men with only one thing in common – they are all patriotic men, men who love the United States. Men who believe deeply in America's role to advance freedom and democracy in the world."

Ryan spoke up. "So the murders were a signal? A warning to others?"

Harris nodded. "I believe so. As does Mike Corso, my DNI." The president motioned toward the other man. "That's why I'm appointing him as the White House liaison on this. You'll be working with him directly."

Ryan exchanged questioning glances with Erin and she said, "Mr. President, you're assigning us to this investigation?"

"I am, Erin. Effective immediately. I'm setting up a special task force to handle it. You, John Ryan, Alex Miller, and Mike Corso are on the team. Top secret. My eyes only."

Erin waved a hand, as if to encompass the whole room. "One question, sir. You have the resources of the whole government at your disposal. Why assign such a small group to something this big?"

Harris's lips pressed into a thin line. "That's very true. I have the entire government at my disposal." He paused. "Unfortunately, there's not many people I can trust," he added, his voice grim. "I know each of you personally. Erin you did an excellent job on several FBI assignments recently, and that's why you're here. And I know Ryan helped you on those cases. That's why he's here."

The president faced Alex Miller next. "Alex, we believe there's an international component to this conspiracy. As head of the CIA's Special Operations division, you are perfect for ferreting out those connections."

"Of course, Mr. President," Miller replied. "And I'd like to bring in one of my best agents to work on this."

"Someone you trust?"

"Implicitly."

"All right." Harris turned back to Erin Welch. "Erin, since you're an Assistant Director of the FBI, I'm putting you in charge of the team. Don't let me down. The stakes are too damn high."

"Yes, sir."

The president gave J.T. Ryan a stern look, then glanced back at Erin. "Ryan's good. Very good at what he does, no doubt about it. But he's also a cowboy at times. His Rambo tactics sometimes cross the line. I expect you, Erin, to keep him on a tight leash."

Ryan chuckled at this and Erin jabbed him in the ribs with an elbow.

"Of course, Mr. President," she said.

"Mike Corso has compiled the details of the murders," Harris said, "and the information from the preliminary investigations that have taken place by the local authorities. Mike, hand out the information we have. Those local investigations will continue. But what I need for this team to do is figure out who's behind these treasonous acts."

The Director of National Intelligence reached into his briefcase, took out several file folders, and handed them to the people in the room.

Ryan quickly scanned the documents in the folder, which were sparse.

Just then a red light began flashing on a device resting on the president's desk.

Mike Corso stood abruptly. In an alarmed voice he said, "They've broken through, Mr. President! They're listening to us now."

President Harris grimaced. "Damn it! Can you tell who's doing it?"

"No, sir, I'm afraid not. But whoever it is, they've been able to bypass all of our security measures."

The president shook his head slowly in disgust. Then he rose from his chair and stared at the team. "This meeting is over. You have your marching orders. Remember. Trust no one. Suspect everyone."

# Chapter 3

*An undisclosed location*

"This meeting is over. You have your marching orders," the man heard over his headset. "Remember. Trust no one. Suspect everyone."

Then the man heard no more voices for the next three minutes, just the rustling of papers, the shifting of chairs, and a door opening and closing. He knew they'd traced his intercept.

The man picked up the handset of his encrypted desk phone and tapped in a number he'd memorized long ago.

When the call was answered, he said, "This is 27. I was able to record the end of a conversation."

"Not all of it?" the woman on the other end replied.

"I'm afraid not. They detected the intercept."

"Damn. That's bad," she said, acid in her voice. "Do better next time."

"Yes, ma'am. Should I transmit what I have?"

"Of course, you idiot! That's what I pay you to do."

Then he heard a click and knew the woman had hung up.

# Chapter 4

*FBI Field Office*
*Atlanta, Georgia*

Erin Welch was pacing her large office when J.T. Ryan knocked on her open door. Erin waved him inside and said, "Close the door."

She stopped pacing and perched on a corner of her desk, folding her arms in front of her. "Did you take care of your other cases?"

Ryan sat on one of the visitor chairs and looked up at the attractive, slender brunette, who today was wearing a stylish Ralph Lauren business suit with a dove gray blouse.

He grinned and gave her a casual salute. "All done. I gave them to my associate, Lisa Booth. She'll handle them."

"Good. I trust you didn't tell Lisa about the case we're working on? You remember what the president said, 'Suspect everyone'."

Ryan's grin faded and he nodded. "I trust her. But to answer your question, no, I didn't tell her about the case."

"Listen," Erin said, "I trust Lisa also, but we have to be extremely careful." She rubbed her temple with a hand. "Someone broke through the security measures of the Oval Office, for Christ sakes. Whoever it is, they're using very sophisticated technology."

"That's a fact," Ryan said. "By the way, I assume I'll be paid my usual rate on this?"

Ryan was a private investigator who did security work for the FBI and other law-enforcement agencies like the Department of Homeland Security. He was a tall, rugged, and good-looking man in his late thirties.

"Yes, J.T. Your usual rates." She frowned. "High as they are."

Ryan smiled. "I'm worth it. Admit it. I'm your best investigator," he joked. "Better than those 'Special' Agents you have on staff."

She pointed a stern finger at him. "Try to muzzle your humorous side for once. This is serious business. Remember what President Harris told us – that I needed to corral your Rambo tactics."

The PI flashed another grin. "It's those tactics that get the job done. Kind of why you hire me."

Erin was about to argue the point, then simply sighed and shrugged her shoulders. "Fine. Enough about that. Let's talk about next steps."

Ryan sat up straighter in the chair. "Got it," he replied, the levity gone from his voice. "Since one of the murders took place right here in Atlanta, I thought I'd tackle that first."

"The cardinal. Did you know the man?"

"Not personally, Erin. I know Cardinal Baker was very prominent in the Catholic Church. A lot of people thought he could become the next Pope."

Erin nodded. "I'd heard that too. You're Catholic yourself, aren't you?"

"I am. Somewhat anyway. I was raised Catholic, although I haven't been to church in quite a while." He paused. "Anyway, I'll focus on that murder first. And you?"

"I'm still debating that, J.T."

"Are you going to assign any of your agents to this case? Since you run this office, you have a large staff to pick from."

Erin shook her head. "No. We're supposed to keep this investigation to as few people as possible."

"How about the FBI Director? Does he know about all this?"

"Negative."

"That's risky, Erin. Not telling your boss."

"I agree. But I have no choice. I got a call this morning from Mike Corso, the DNI. He told me in no uncertain terms to keep this case confined to a tight group. We'll add people only when there is an absolute need. Corso suspects the conspiracy has a lot of deep roots, probably involving government employees. He, like the president, doesn't know who to trust."

"Roger that." Ryan stood. "Unless there's something else, I'll get going and get to work."

Erin nodded. "Where's your next stop?"

"The morgue."

# Chapter 5

*CIA Station*
*Paris, France*

Rachel West unlocked the front door of the building and stepped inside. It was only 6 a.m. and she was the first one to arrive.

Rachel flicked on the lobby lights and tapped in the code to the security system to turn it off. That done, she strode to her office, went inside, and stared at the stack of progress reports her field agents had left for her to read.

*Damn*, she thought for the thousand time. *That's all I do these days. Read reports.* She shook her head in frustration. Taking off her windbreaker, she draped it over the back of her desk chair and sat down. In her mid-thirties, Rachel was a tall and curvaceous woman. With piercing blue eyes, long blonde hair, and striking good looks, her appearance was more like a model than a covert agent. As usual she was dressed casually in jeans and a black polo shirt, and her long hair was pulled into a ponytail. Holstered on her hip was her favorite weapon, a 9 mm Glock 43.

She booted up her laptop and was about to scroll through her emails when her desk phone rang. The info screen read 'CIA Headquarters' and she instinctively knew who was calling.

Picking up the handset, she blurted out, "Alex, you've got to get me out of here!"

"What's wrong, Rachel?" Alex Miller said. Miller was highly-intelligent but also a very reserved man, and he seemed taken aback by her outburst. He was her boss and the director of the CIA's Special Operations Division.

"I'm suffocating here, Alex."

"What do you mean?"

"All I do is assign cases and read progress reports."

"When I promoted you to station chief, I thought you'd be happy. Running the French operation is a big deal."

"Don't get me wrong, Alex. I appreciate what your did. But it's not a good fit for me. I should be out knocking down doors, kicking butt, and taking names. Like I said before, I'm suffocating here. I need to be a field operative again. It's what I do best."

"All right."

"All right what, Alex?"

"All right. I'm putting you back in the field."

Suddenly suspicious it had been so easy to convince him, she said, "Just like that. I ask for something and I get it right away. What's the catch?"

"Well it so happens that I've been assigned to a new case. A very important case. That's why I called you today. I need your expertise."

"That's great, Alex. Tell me about it."

"Not over the phone. It's too sensitive. We need to meet in person. I need you back in Langley. ASAP."

Rachel glanced at her watch. She knew there was a flight from Paris's de Gaulle Airport to Reagan National every morning. "There's an Air France flight at 10 a.m. I can take."

"Be on it," Miller replied and hung up.

# Chapter 6

*Fulton County Morgue*
*Atlanta, Georgia*

The county morgue is located on Pryor Street, just south of downtown Atlanta.

After navigating through heavy traffic, J.T. Ryan drove his Tahoe SUV into the lot and parked in front of the nondescript building. He strode inside, showed his credentials at security, and was led to the M.E.'s office by one of the morgue's technicians.

Ryan had been here on numerous occasions, and although his profession dealt with death often, he always dreaded coming to the morgue. It was the stench that bothered him the most. The antiseptic scent of ammonia that overlaid, but could not erase, the pungent odor of death and decay. The Fulton County morgue processed an average of 2,500 cadavers a year and there was no way the nauseating reek of decomp could be eliminated. Ryan knew he'd have to scrub himself later with lemon juice to remove the smell.

Ryan followed the technician along the white-tiled corridors and was shown into the medical examiner's cluttered office.

After shaking hands with the M.E., he sat in one of the chairs fronting his desk. Doctor Mallory was a tall, gaunt-looking man with white hair, oval wire-rimmed glasses, and a pallid complexion. Ryan had met with him many times before and was always struck by the paleness of his skin – it was obvious the man spent little time outdoors.

"I'm sure you're here about Cardinal Baker?" Mallory said, taking off his eyeglasses and resting them on the desk.

"I am," Ryan said.

"Tragic, what happened. The cardinal was revered. He worked tirelessly for the homeless, the poor, and our veterans. He will be greatly missed in the community."

Ryan nodded, knowing this to be true. "I read the police report. It was inconclusive. Could this have been an accident?"

"It's possible. The semi that crashed into the home obviously veered off the road and plowed through several rooms, killing the cardinal instantly. As you would expect, a 70,000 pound truck does an incredible amount of damage. Every bone in his body was crushed and all his organs ...." He didn't finish the sentence.

"What about the driver of the truck, Doctor? Was he killed also? There was no mention of him in the report."

Mallory shook his head slowly. "That's the odd part. There was no other body found at the scene. The truck cab was damaged of course, but it was clear there was no one driving it."

"How's that possible?"

"From what I can piece together and from what the CSI tech at the scene told me, it was probably a driverless vehicle. One of those high-tech things you hear about these days."

Ryan frowned. "So the truck was piloted remotely?"

"Yes, it appears that way. It's possible, J.T., that it could have been an accident. That something went wrong with the electronics and the truck veered off the road."

The PI thought about this a moment and knew that was improbable, considering what the president had told them in the Oval Office. It was clear all three deaths that night were connected somehow. But he had to keep this to himself. Even though he'd known the M.E. for years, he had to keep the investigation confidential.

"You're right, doc. It could have been an accident. Do you have any information on the truck itself?"

"I do," the man said, reaching into a drawer. He pulled out a file folder and handed it to Ryan. "I can let you read this, J.T. It's a preliminary report, but the pertinent facts are there."

Ryan quickly scanned the M.E.'s notes, paying particular to the make and model of the semi and a few other details. He handed the file back to Mallory and he put it away.

"Do you need anything else, J.T.?"

"I'd like to see the body."

"Are you sure? It's ... gruesome."

Ryan nodded. "I understand."

"Okay, then. Come with me."

He followed Mallory down a long corridor and they stepped into a cavernous room at the end of the morgue. This room, the PI knew, was referred to by the technicians as the 'meat locker'. It was the place the cadavers were kept after the autopsies. The bodies would eventually be transported to mortuaries or, in cases of the destitute, to the crematory.

The room was kept at a frigid 36 degrees and Ryan zipped up the jacket he was wearing.

At the computer workstation in the room, the M.E. typed in some numbers on the keypad. Finding what he needed, he strode past a long row of stainless-steel freezer lockers. Stopping in front of one of them, he pulled out the metal shelf. He removed the sheet from the corpse and stood aside so that Ryan could see.

The PI had witnessed numerous dead and wounded years ago during combat in Afghanistan. Yet, all that didn't prepare him for what he was seeing now.

The cardinal's body, what remained of it, resembled raw hamburger meat. The cracked skull, crushed chest cavity, and bloody, shredded legs were barely recognizable.

Although Ryan was not a religious man, he crossed himself and said a silent prayer for Cardinal Baker. Then he swore to himself that he was going to find the killers responsible and make them pay.

# Chapter 7

*Tektronn Industries*
*Sandy Springs, Georgia*

As Ryan drove around the extensive property of the technology company, he mused that the wooded setting looked more like a college campus than a high-tech firm.

Along the winding, two-lane road he spotted at least ten glass-and-steel structures nestled among the park-like setting. The complex was located in Sandy Springs, a suburb of Atlanta.

Moments later he found the main administration building, parked his Tahoe, and strode inside.

"I'm John Ryan," he told the receptionist, handing her his card. "I'm conducting an investigation for the FBI. I need to speak with the person in charge."

The young woman read the card and made a phone call. She spoke briefly and replaced the receiver. "If you'll have a seat, Mr. Ryan, Ms Williams will be right out."

He sat in one of the plush sofas and gazed around the glass-walled atrium. By the expensive decor, the company appeared to be very profitable.

A moment later he heard the clicking of heels and looked up to see a plump, middle-aged woman with frizzy auburn hair walk up to him. The woman was wearing a blue dress with a white lab coat over it.

"I'm Amanda Williams," she said, "I'm Vice-President of Public Relations." She extended her hand and he shook it.

"Good to meet you. I'm J.T. Ryan." He took out his cred pack and showed it to her. The billfold included his FBI Contractor's ID and his PI license.

The woman scrutinized the credentials closely. "You told the receptionist you're conducting an investigation?"

"That's correct. May we talk in private?"

"Of course," she replied. "We can use the conference room over there." She led them into a glass-walled room adjacent to the lobby and closed the door behind them.

"What kind of products does Tektronn make, Ms Williams?"

"We're a high-tech firm – we're involved with a multitude of projects. Most of them have to do with robotics."

"And that includes driverless vehicles?"

"Yes it does, Mr. Ryan." She gave him a sharp look. "Why are you asking these questions? Is Tektronn being investigated by the FBI? If so, I'll need to have our company lawyer present."

Ryan held up his palms and smiled, hoping to disarm her suspicions. He knew that once attorneys were involved he would find out little from the woman.

"It's nothing like that, Ms Williams. I just have a few simple questions."

She still looked nervous, but nodded. "All right. Go ahead and ask."

"One of your trucks, a large semi was involved in an accident recently. There was a death involved."

"It was? One of our self-driving trucks was stolen about three weeks ago. We reported the theft to the police of course, but have heard nothing since."

"I see." Ryan studied the woman closely, looking for any 'tells', physical indications that she was lying. He'd been a PI for years and had developed an uncanny ability to spot liars. He saw no evasiveness in her manner.

"You said someone died?" she asked.

"Yes. The truck veered off the road and crashed into the residence of Gerald Baker, the Catholic Cardinal."

She covered her mouth with a hand, and her face paled. "Oh, my God! I read about that in the paper. I can't believe it was one of our trucks." She collapsed onto one of the conference room chairs.

If she was lying, thought Ryan, she was a hell of an actress. The woman seemed genuinely distraught. The PI sat across from her and gave her a moment to compose herself. Then he said, "There was no one driving the truck. So it was piloted remotely. How is that possible, if your company didn't do it?"

She shook her head slowly. "I don't see how it could have happened. Self-driving technology requires sophisticated computer software programming. Only a few organizations in the world have that capability."

Ryan thought about this, then recalled what the president had told them – that he suspected rogue elements within government were part of the criminal plot.

*Trust no one*, the president had said. *Suspect everyone.*

# Chapter 8

*Billings, Montana*

It felt good to be out in the field again, Erin Welch mused, as she drove the rented Toyota Camry out of the Hertz lot at the airport.

Since Erin's promotion to Assistant Director in Charge, she'd run the Atlanta FBI Field Office with clocklike precision, managing the day-to-day aspects of the large unit with a firm hand. Her case closing ratio was one of the highest in the Bureau. Her biggest obstacle from day one had been the resentment harbored by the mostly male agents in her unit. The FBI, like most law-enforcement organizations, was male dominated. Especially at the top. There were 56 Bureau field offices in the U.S. and she was still the only female ADIC. But she had been single-minded in her efforts to succeed. She put in more hours than anyone on her staff, giving up any semblance of a social life to get the job done.

Still, it felt good to be back out in the field, working a case, just like she'd done after graduating from the FBI's Quantico years ago.

Erin took the exit ramp out of the airport and merged on to Interstate 90 toward the mountainous region north of Billings. She tabbed down her window and breathed in the cold, fresh air. It was an azure blue, cloudless day and the sky seemed immense over the mostly desolate, unpopulated region. *No wonder they call it Big Sky country*, she thought.

A half-hour later she located the entrance to a sprawling, upscale community. The residences were mini-mansions constructed to look like log homes. Obviously very expensive, each of the houses sat on wooded, acre-size properties.

Erin drove deeper into the residential area until she found the correct address on the mailbox. She turned into a gravel driveway and drove the Camry toward the home. When she reached it moments later, she stopped her car, got out of the vehicle, and gazed at the scene.

There wasn't much left of the house. The intense fire had burned the structure literally to the concrete foundation. A large stone fireplace, blackened from the flames, remained as did the charred remnants of what appeared to be the home's appliances and a large SUV. It was clear that any evidence of the murder had been erased by the blaze.

***

Erin Welch surveyed the open bullpen of the Billings PD office, looking for Detective Carter. She'd called the Chief of the department earlier and was told Carter was working the case. She spotted the detective and walked over.

After flashing open her cred pack, she sat in the visitor's chair next to his desk. "I'm ADIC Welch, FBI. I understand you're the detective working the murder of Chief Justice Rogers and his family."

Carter gave her a long look. "We haven't classified those deaths as murder. We're still investigating." The detective was a short, squat man with a scraggly mustache. He was wearing a rumpled white shirt and a blue striped tie which was dotted with food stains. His desk was littered with crumpled hamburger wrappers sitting atop stacks of case folders.

"You think this was an accident?" she asked.

"It could be."

"Tell me, Carter, how long have you been a detective?"

"Five years. And ten before that manning a patrol car."

"I see. Five years. You don't think it's suspicious that the Chief Justice of the Supreme Court died after a powerful electrical surge caused a fire at his vacation home?"

"Like I said, we're still investigating," he replied, seeming annoyed at her questioning. "Can I see your creds again?"

Erin pulled out the billfold, opened it, and placed it on his desk. He stared at it carefully. "This says you're an Assistant Director in the Bureau," he said with a leer, giving her a long up-and-down look, obviously taking in her attractive face and shapely curves. "What's a pretty girl like you working at the FBI anyway? Shouldn't you be barefoot, pregnant, and in the kitchen?"

Erin saw red. She hated being called a 'girl', and she hated being insulted by this clown. She reached over, grabbed his tie with both hands, and slid the knot tight against his throat.

His eyes got big and his face flushed red. He tried to pull away, but she kept tightening the knot even further.

After a moment she let go and he loosened his tie knot and began coughing.

Several of the other cops in the bullpen noticed what had taken place and chuckled.

"Sorry about that," she said to Carter. "I got carried away."

The detective massaged his throat and pushed his chair a foot away from her. Then he realized the other cops in the room had seen the incident and his face turned red again.

"I was the one out of line, Ms Welch. I apologize."

"No hard feelings. Let's start over, okay?" She extended her hand and he shook it, although it was tentative on his part as if he expected her to blow up again.

"Now that that's behind us, Carter, why don't you tell me what evidence you have on the case."

"All right, ma'am. By the way, there's a reason me and my boss are in no rush to classify this as murder. We get a lot of rich people buying expensive vacation homes in Billings. People like the Chief Justice. These rich people bring a lot of money to our community. We'd hate to scare them off if they think we're not a safe area."

Erin rolled her eyes. "Let's just focus on the facts of the case."

"Yes, ma'am."

"I understand from the original police report that a high-voltage surge of electricity caused the home's breaker box to overload which ignited the fire."

"That's correct, Ms Welch."

"What was the cause of the power surge?"

"Unknown."

"Okay. Did the electric company give you any helpful information?"

Carter opened a desk drawer, rummaged through it, pulled out a sheet of paper and handed it to her.

Erin read the incident report from the power company. It said that a computer software malfunction caused the electrical surge. There was no further explanation. She wrote down the name of the power company engineer who had prepared the report and handed the paper back to Carter.

"Did you talk with the power company engineers?" she asked.

"Of course."

"And?"

"They had no explanation. But."

"But what, Carter?"

"They said that their software system may have been hacked. They suspect someone could have broken through their security and programmed the high-voltage surge."

"Could they trace it back to the origin?"

"No ma'am. They said whoever hacked into their system was very sophisticated. They left no trace behind."

# Chapter 9

*Washington, D.C.*

J.T. Ryan slowed the rented Chevy Impala and veered right to avoid running into a large group of people milling on the street.

"What the hell is going on?" he muttered.

Erin Welch, who was in the passenger seat, said, "Protesters."

Ryan gazed over the people holding up signs and chanting angrily. "What are they protesting?"

"Who knows. Different day, different protest. You notice the signs they're holding up are all professionally printed. Looks like this group was hired from Rent-a-Rioter."

Ryan chuckled at her joke as he slowed the Impala to a stop. "With all this going on, I don't think we'll be able to drive the rest of the way to the White House."

"I agree, J.T. Find a place to park and we'll walk the rest of the way."

"Okay."

Ryan spotted a nearby lot, parked the car, and they began walking along Pennsylvania Avenue toward their destination. He had to push past the angry-looking men and women who seemed intent on blocking their way.

A few minutes later they reached the outskirts of the White House grounds and neared the gated security checkpoint to the West Wing.

Just then three masked men dressed in black ran up to them. The men were carrying baseball bats, which they brandished menacingly. One of them grabbed Erin and yanked her to the ground, while the other two thugs charged Ryan, ready to swing their bats.

Instinctively the PI went into a martial-arts fighting stance and side-kicked one of the thugs in the solar plexus, sending his baseball bat flying. The man staggered back and fell as Ryan faced the second attacker. He punched him hard with a right hook and followed that with an upper cut. The PI was powerfully built, with a weightlifters physique, and the black-dressed thug crumpled to the ground.

Ryan picked up the bat and began chasing down the third thug, who was dragging Erin behind him, obviously intent on kidnapping her. The PI caught up to the man and smashed the bat across his torso. The guy screamed, let go of Erin, and fell to his knees.

As Ryan knelt next to Erin to check her condition, he noticed a flurry of activity around him. A group of Secret Service agents had rushed out of the security gate and began arresting the thugs and several of the protesters who had been cheering them on.

Ryan hovered by Erin, who sat up on the ground and began massaging her forehead.

"Are you okay, Erin?"

She nodded. "Yeah. I got a hell of a headache from the fall. Otherwise I'm fine."

"Good to hear." He noticed the rips on her Donna Karan dress and the damaged Louboutin heels. He pointed to her shoes. "Those are expensive. What did they set you back? A grand?"

She sighed. "About that. Help me up, will you?"

Ryan pulled her up to her feet.

Erin smoothed down her dress and hand combed her long brunette hair. After taking off her broken high-heel shoes, she pulled out her cred pack and flashed it open for one of the Secret Service agents that were nearby. "I'm Erin Welch, FBI. We have a meeting scheduled with Mike Corso."

The agent scrutinized her ID and said, "Yes, Ms Welch. We were expecting you. Follow me."

The Secret Service man led them through the security checkpoint onto the White House grounds and brought them to the entrance to the West Wing. After Erin and Ryan were frisked they were allowed into the building, where another Secret Service agent took them to a small conference room. The man left and Erin faced Ryan.

"Thanks," she said.

"For what?"

"For back there. For taking care of those thugs."

Ryan grinned. "Part of my job description."

She returned the smile.

"And my wit, charm, and good looks are no charge," he added with a chuckle. "I throw those in for free."

Erin shook her head slowly and her smile faded. "I'm glad you brought up your wit, J.T. I understand and *sometimes* appreciate your joking around. But this is serious business. And I know Mike Corso doesn't have a sense of humor. So when we meet with him, no jokes. Got it?"

He turned serious and gave her a half salute. "Got it. By the way, what do you know about this Corso guy?"

"I know he's got the president's full confidence. He's the DNI, the Director of National Intelligence, which means technically all of the intelligence agencies like the CIA, FBI, NSA, and Homeland Security report to him."

"What do you mean 'technically', Erin?"

"Just because those agencies report to him on paper doesn't mean they tell him everything. Washington D.C. is a town full of secrets, full of liars and double-crossers. Take my word for it – I worked here for a while. I know."

Ryan nodded.

The door to the conference room opened and Mike Corso strode in. He closed the door behind him and said, "Please have a seat and we'll get started."

After sitting around the conference table, Corso turned to Erin. "I heard from the agents about your scuffle outside. Sorry about that. I'm glad you're okay."

"Does that happen often?" Erin asked.

The DNI let out a long sigh. "I'm afraid so. Someone's busing people into the area, paying them to protest, create havoc, and even riot. We arrest the ones that commit crimes, but new ones show up the next day."

Ryan leaned forward in his chair. "Who's paying them to do it?"

"We don't know," Corso said. "But we do know that whoever they are, they're well-funded. Okay, enough about that. Let's review your progress on the investigation."

Erin nodded. "Yes, sir. I was in Montana, looking into the death of the Chief Justice. My findings confirm your theory that he was murdered. It appears that the power company's software was hacked, causing the electrical overload and resulting fire. Whoever hacked the system left no digital fingerprints. Which means the intruder was very computer literate."

"I see," Corso replied.

"I found a similar situation," Ryan added, "in the death of Cardinal Baker in Atlanta. The semi that rammed his home was a driverless vehicle. I questioned personnel of the tech company who owns the truck. It appears their software was also hacked."

Corso nodded. "Any possibility it was an inside job? That people within that company programmed the truck to crash?"

"I'm still following up on that, sir. If there's a link I'll find it."

"Okay," the DNI said. "What about the Senate leader's death. Have you investigated that?"

"That's our next stop," Erin replied. "Ryan and I are going to the scene after this meeting."

"Good." Corso leaned back in his chair. "I'll inform the president of your progress. And I'll keep you in the loop as I learn more information on our end. We've found an interesting lead with an international connection. I'll be notifying the CIA so they can pursue that angle."

The DNI seemed ready to conclude the meeting, then said, "While you're here, I want you to meet my Deputy DNI, Samantha Lowry." He pressed a button on the desk phone that was on the table and a moment later a very thin, mousy-looking woman with frizzy hair entered the room. She wore a plain black dress and a frown that seemed to be a permanent fixture on her face. The Deputy DNI looked more like a librarian than a high-level government official.

After introducing everyone around, Corso said, "If you can't get a hold of me, Erin, or have an emergency situation, call Samantha. She'll find me and arrange a meeting."

"Yes, sir," Erin replied. "One question. When we met with the president, he suspected there were rogue elements within the government that are involved in the conspiracy. Have you had any success in tracking that down?"

The DNI grimaced and his shoulders slumped. "I'm afraid not. I just hope we do ... before it's too late."

# Chapter 10

*An undisclosed location*

The man removed his headset and rested it on the surface of his workstation. What he'd just heard was disturbing. Very disturbing.

He picked up the receiver from his desk phone and tapped in a number. When the call was answered, he said, "This is 27."

"Yes?" the woman replied.

"I picked up some chatter a few minutes ago and I wanted to alert you."

"What do you mean by 'chatter'?"

"Just pieces of conversation," he said. "Random words here and there, nothing I could record."

"Why the hell not?"

"Please understand, ma'am. The White House is a big place. Over 1,800 people work there. It's impossible to break through the security measures in every room. I believe this conversation took place somewhere in the West Wing."

"Just get on with it, damn it," the woman shot back, her voice harsh. "Tell me what you heard."

"They appear to be investigating the three murders and ...."

"And what, damn it?"

"They also seemed to know there was an international connection."

"You heard that?"

"Yes, ma'am."

"Fuck."

He heard nothing for a long time, then the woman said, "Stay on it, damn it! Work around the clock if you have to. We need to know everything. We *have* to know everything. Am I making myself clear, 27?"

"Yes, number 3. I understand."

"Remember. There's no turning back from this. We're in too deep. *You're* in too deep."

Then he heard a click and knew number 3 had hung up.

# Chapter 11

*Oslo, Norway*

The woman known as number 3 sat at her desk a long time, staring at her phone. Acid began to churn in her stomach, the nauseous sensation pushing bile up her throat.

*Should I inform the others?* she wondered, as she thought through what 27 had just told her.

She looked up from her desk and gazed toward the wide windows that overlooked the half-frozen lake. It was snowing outside and a fierce wind buffeted the two-story chalet, causing the snow to pelt and rattle the glass windows.

After another few minutes of brooding, she came to a decision.

*No. I won't tell the others. I'll handle this problem myself.*

# Chapter 12

*Special Operations Division*
*CIA Annex Building*
*Langley, Virginia*

Alex Miller was at his computer reading a status report when he heard a rap at his door. Looking up he saw Rachel West with a radiant smile on her face.

"Come in Rachel," he said. "Have a seat. You look awfully happy."

"I am, boss." She pulled up a chair and sat. "It feels good to be back at the Factory." The Factory was the nicknamed used by Agency personnel for the Special Operations Division of the CIA.

"You're just glad you're not in Paris," he said.

"Oh, I don't mind Paris. I just hate being station chief."

Miller nodded. "I know. You like to —"

"Be in the field," Rachel said, finishing his sentence. "Kicking ass and taking names."

Miller noticed what the good-looking, blue-eyed blonde was wearing today. Blue jeans, a gray polo shirt, and a black windbreaker. On her hip was her holstered Glock 43.

"We have a dress code at the Agency, young lady. And that applies to everyone. You are not exempt."

Rachel glanced down at her clothes and suppressed a grin. "Oh, yeah. Guess I forgot."

Miller frowned. Then he said, "Let me tell you why I needed to meet with you."

The CIA woman turned serious. "Sir, before we start, I have a request."

He sighed, used to her impetuous manner. "Yes?"

"I want to be permanently assigned back to the field. I'm not cut out to be an administrator, pushing paper all day."

"I'll take that under advisement, young lady."

"But, sir, I'm your best covert agent."

"One of my best, Rachel."

She smirked. "I have the most commendations. And the best closing ratio on my assignments."

"You are good, I grant you that."

"So you agree to put me back in the field on a permanent basis?"

Miller drummed his fingers on his desk as he mulled this over. "I'll tell you what, Rachel. You do a good job on this new assignment and you'll get your wish."

"Really?"

"Yes, really."

She gave him a radiant smile. "Thank you, boss."

"Don't thank me yet. You haven't heard the details of the mission."

Rachel shrugged. "Doesn't matter – I'll solve it."

"You seem pretty sure of yourself."

"Have I ever let you down, Alex?"

Miller thought about this a moment. "You did disobey a direct order when you were in China with that Ryan guy."

She looked pensive. "Oh, yeah. That."

"Yes," he replied, his voice hard. "That."

"I promise, I won't screw up again."

"You better not, Rachel. I saved your job that time. Even though the Director of Central Intelligence wanted me to fire you. Lucky for you, I still have a lot of pull here. But if you screw up again ...." He shook his head slowly. "I won't be able to save you."

Rachel looked unsure of herself for the first time since she'd come into his office. "I understand, sir," she said, her voice contrite.

"Good. Now let me fill you in. I've been assigned to a secret task force. I'm adding you to that task force."

"Okay. How many people are in this group?"

"From the CIA – two people – you and me."

"That's it?"

"That's it."

"What about your boss, the CIA Director?"

"What about him, Rachel?"

"Isn't he the person that assigned you to the task force?"

"Negative. He doesn't know about this operation."

Rachel appeared puzzled. "So who ...."

"The president."

"The president of the United States?"

"One and the same. President Steve Harris."

Her eyes grew large. "I see."

"We met in the Oval Office recently. He gave us our marching orders. Besides us, there are three other people on the task force. Mike Corso, the DNI, and two people from the FBI. Erin Welch, who heads up the Bureau's Atlanta office, and someone you know well. His name is Ryan."

"As in, John Taylor Ryan?"

"That's correct, Rachel."

A stunned expression settled on her face.

"Is this going to be a problem for you, young lady?"

"Absolutely not, sir."

"Good. And one other thing. I know you've had a personal relationship with this Ryan character in the past." Miller spoke his next words slowly and emphatically. "This is a very important and very secretive mission we're undertaking for the president of the United States. The country's national security is at stake. Which means you and Ryan are not, I repeat, not to have a personal relationship until this mission is complete. Am I making myself perfectly clear, Rachel?"

"Crystal clear, sir."

He gave her a stern look. "Good. Now that I've established that ground rule, let me tell you the specifics of the operation."

Miller spent the next thirty minutes briefing her on the details of the assignment. When he was done, he said, "This morning I got a call from the DNI, Mike Corso. He's found a lead to a possible international connection. That lead originated in Denmark. I've booked you on the next flight to Copenhagen."

"Yes, sir."

Miller handed her an envelope. "There's more details about the case in here. Any questions?"

"No, sir."

"In that case, Rachel, get to work."

# Chapter 13

*Washington, D.C.*

J.T. Ryan pulled the rented Chevy Impala to the curb and stared out the windshield.

"Not much left," he said as he surveyed the charred ruins of the Senate Majority Leader's home. The whole second floor of the house had collapsed onto the first floor. Burnt pieces of the roof and walls were strewn over the large property. Yellow crime scene tape roped off the whole area.

Erin Welch, who was in the passenger seat, nodded. "The police report says the explosion was caused by a bomb."

"Could they tell what kind, Erin?"

"The forensics lab believes it was a military-grade explosive. Most likely C-4."

Ryan glanced at Erin, and then back at the scene. "C-4 is highly regulated. You have to have a government license to buy it."

"That's right."

"Let's get a closer look," he said, turning off the car and climbing out.

They strode over the charred grass, went underneath the crime scene tape, and walked up to what was left of the blackened structure. Although the explosion and fire had taken place a week ago, a strong burnt smell still permeated the area.

Ryan pointed toward the ruins. "The explosion took out the roof first, which probably means the bomb was set off there. The question is, how did it get up there? Did someone climb up there, attach it to the roof, leave the area, and set it off remotely?"

Erin shook her head. "No way of knowing. And there was no trace evidence left, no evidence of any kind telling us who planted the bomb."

"Just like the other murder scenes, there were no clues left behind. Everything appears to have been handled electronically."

"That's true, J.T."

"I just had a thought. Didn't the senator have surveillance cameras at his house and property? They would have picked up an intruder planting a bomb."

"That's correct, the senator did have security cameras," she replied. "The video camera footage stored in the home's system was destroyed. But that footage was also kept by the senator's security monitoring company. The police viewed that and didn't spot any intruders. And the home's alarm system showed no intrusion whatsoever."

Ryan rubbed his jaw as he mulled this over. "What if ...."

"What if what?" she said.

"What if the bomb was flown in on a high-tech device."

"Like a drone?"

Ryan nodded. "Yes. A drone could have landed on the roof undetected and been exploded remotely."

"You may be on to something, J.T. That would fit with what happened at the other crime scenes. All the murders were committed using high-tech, remote access methods. A driverless truck in Atlanta. An electrical surge in Montana. And now this."

Ryan gazed back toward the charred ruins. "The murders were carried out using highly-sophisticated technology. Technology only available to a select few."

"This reinforces the president's suspicion," Erin replied, "that people inside the government are involved. Everything we've uncovered points to that. The problem is, they've left no clues behind. We're at a dead end right now."

Ryan recalled his visit to the morgue where he'd seen the cardinal's bloody corpse. That day Ryan had sworn to himself he'd find the killers responsible and make them pay.

"We'll find them," he said, his hands forming into fists. "We have to."

# Chapter 14

*Atlanta, Georgia*

J.T. Ryan drove north on State Road 400 and ten minutes later took the Sandy Springs exit. Soon after he was winding his way through the campus-like grounds of the Tektronn Industries complex. He'd called earlier in the day and had arranged to meet Mr. Parker, the Chief Technology Officer of the firm.

Finding the right building, he parked his Tahoe in the front lot and went inside. He was escorted to the office of a tall, stooped man with balding hair and bushy eyebrows. The man wore a white lab coat over his regular clothes.

"I'm J.T. Ryan," he said as they shook hands.

"Yes, Mr. Ryan. Our VP of Public Relations told me you'd be coming to see me."

"Did she explain what I was investigating for the FBI?"

"She did. A tragic thing. To think one of our vehicles was ... involved in a death. I hope our company's reputation isn't tarnished by this event."

"I'm not really worried about your 'company's reputation'," Ryan replied testily. "I'm trying to solve a damn murder. The murder of a revered man."

Parker raised his palms up. "Of course. Of course. I didn't mean to minimize the cardinal's death."

Ryan took in a deep breath to calm his anger. "All right," he said after a moment. "The truck was stolen and its self-driving technology was hacked. Have you been able to determine who could have done this?"

Parker blinked rapidly a few times, then said, "Since we learned what had happened, I've been researching that exact thing."

"And?"

"Well, unfortunately, Mr. Ryan, we haven't been able to determine that."

There was something about the man's tone that made the PI suspicious. "Aren't you the Chief Technology Officer of this company?"

"I am."

"Then why can't you determine what happened?"

Parker shifted uneasily in his chair. "The truck was heavily damaged during the crash, so neither we or the police techs were able to salvage the electronics of the vehicle."

"Okay, I'll buy that. For the moment. But I'm sure you can tell me if the computer software of the truck was hacked."

"Yes, Mr. Ryan. That I can tell you. We monitor all of our vehicles software from our headquarters here. The truck's software stopped 'communicating' with our mainframe soon after it was stolen. Then it went 'live' the night of the crash. It's clear someone tampered with the software and guided the truck to crash."

"Who did this?"

Parker shook his head. "We don't know. But it would take an expert in computer programming."

"You're sure you can't determine who it could have been?"

"That's right," the man replied. But he looked slightly away from Ryan when he responded.

After asking Parker more questions, the PI left his office ten minutes later. But he couldn't shake the feeling the man wasn't telling him the whole truth.

When he got back in his SUV, Ryan pulled out his cell phone and pressed a number on speed dial.

"It's Ryan," he said to Erin when she picked up. "What can you tell me about this Parker guy, the Tektronn CTO."

"I did a full background check on him, J.T. Like I did for everyone at that company. Parker's clean. Nothing pops on the NCIC database. No history of arrests, not even a parking ticket."

"How about his bank records, Erin? Anything unusual?"

"Nope. Nothing about him raises a red flag."

"Too bad. Something about his body language when he answered my questions makes me not trust him ...."

"Okay, J.T. I get that. You're good at sniffing out the bad apples. Part of the reason I hire you. What's next?"

"I've got one more stop to make. By the way, on my next expense report you'll notice a large cash expenditure. With no receipt."

"What's it for, J.T.?"

"Don't ask."

She said nothing for a long moment, and he visualized the FBI agent grimacing as she mulled this over.

"All right," she finally said. "I won't ask. As long as you get results."

"Don't worry, I will." He hung up before she had a chance to change her mind.

Next he stopped at the nearest Bank of America branch, withdrew $1,000 in cash from his account, and left. Twenty minutes later he parked his Tahoe in the lot of the 'Gentlemen's Club'. He eyed the seedy exterior of the strip joint, it's blinking neon sign looking even more decrepit than last time he'd been here.

He climbed out of his SUV, paid the cover charge at the door, and walked inside the strip joint. He was instantly assaulted by the ear-splitting music and momentarily blinded by the flashing strobe lights that bathed the stage. On the stage a group of tired-looking naked female strippers danced and gyrated on poles. A crowd of men sat at tables and at the bar leering at the women and cheering them on.

The whole place reeked of stale beer, cigarettes, and vomit, and the air was thick with cig smoke. Ryan found an empty table and flagged one of the semi-nude waitresses, who came over.

"I'm looking for Candy," he yelled at her, trying to be heard over the din of the ear-splitting music. The woman nodded and moved away.

Moments later a tall, statuesque brunette wearing only pasties, a tiny G-string, and high heels sashayed over. The waitress had tired eyes, a pockmarked face, and a haggard look. But when she saw Ryan sitting at the table, she broke into a broad grin, exposing her crooked teeth.

"Well, if it isn't John Taylor Ryan, my favorite customer!"

Ryan returned the smile. "Candy Cane. I bet you say that to all the guys."

She placed her hand sensually on his shoulder and leaned over, giving him a real good look at her double-Ds. "See something you like, honey?" she asked in a throaty voice.

He tried not to stare at her huge breasts nor the rest of her almost nude body. Although Candy was not a pretty woman in the traditional sense, she exuded a raw sexuality that was difficult to ignore.

"This is business, Candy."

"Ha, shucks. That's too bad." She batted her fake eyelashes and grinned. "One day you're going to come in here, propose to me, and carry me off on a white stallion like Prince Charming."

"I'm looking for information."

"You're no fun, J.T. You're always looking for information. Did you bring cash? I don't take plastic, remember."

He patted the breast pocket of his blazer. "I brought cash."

"Good." She glanced at her cheap Timex. "I got a break in fifteen. I'll meet you in the parking lot. You still driving the Tahoe?'

"That's right."

"Okay. See you in a few." She waved to him, blew him a kiss, and moved on to another table.

Ryan got up and exited the strip club, glad to be out of the noisy, foul-smelling place. Then he climbed back in his SUV to wait for Candy. She had been one of his confidential informants for years and was probably his most reliable. She knew a lot about what took place among the seedier elements in Atlanta.

Ten minutes later he spotted her coming toward his SUV, now dressed in black leggings, a fake-fur jacket, and flats. She got in the passenger seat and turned to face him.

"God, I'm tired," she said with a sigh.

"You should quit that dump," he replied. "You're too smart to work there."

"I know I am. But I'd make a fraction of what I earn here if I was working as an office clerk somewhere."

"How's your daughter, Candy?" he asked, noticing the woman had put on strong perfume.

Her tired face brightened. "She's getting great grades at school. I'm so proud of her!"

Ryan smiled. "I'm glad for you."

Candy reached out with a hand and caressed his face. "You're so sweet. You're a real gentleman, J.T. Not like all the schmuks I see every day. All they try to do is grab my tits or ass, wanting a quick fuck out in the parking lot. It takes a lot of energy to fight them off ... thank God we have a good bouncer here."

Ryan nodded. "Like I said before, I'm looking for info on someone." He handed her a sheet of paper. "His name is Parker. He works at a high-tech company called Tektronn, which is located here in the Atlanta area. There's additional details about him on this sheet. I'm looking for anything you can find out about this guy."

She quickly read the paper, unzipped the top half of her fake-fur jacket and tucked it in an inside pocket. "Okay. I'll start working on this when I get off work."

"Good. How much?"

"It'll cost you two grand."

"Bullshit. That's too much, Candy."

"All right. One grand."

"Still too much. I may be a gentleman but I'm not a sucker. I'll pay you 500 bucks. Half now, half when you deliver."

She crossed her arms over her ample chest. "$750."

"I'll give you $600. And that's final," he said tersely.

"Okay, sweetie. You got a deal."

He took cash out of his jacket, counted out $300 and gave it to her. She snatched the money and quickly tucked it into her pocket.

Then she gave him a wide smile. "Now that we've got business out of the way, tell me what's happening with you." She glanced at her Timex. "I've got time before my break's over." She caressed his shoulder with a hand. "I heard a rumor you'd broken up with your long-time squeeze, Lauren what's-her-name."

"It's more than rumor," he said. "It's true. Lauren broke up with me a while ago. She wanted a husband who wasn't in a dangerous profession like mine."

Candy scrunched her face. "Stupid girl. She should have realized you're the real deal. Maybe," she added with a purr, "now that she's out of the way, the two of us can finally get together." She slid her hand off his shoulder and rested it on his lap. With her other hand she unzipped her fake-fur jacket all the way, fully revealing her ample breasts, which he noticed, were now not covered by the pasties.

Once again he was attracted by her raw sexuality and he became aroused.

Candy began stroking his pants, making his hardness harder still.

"I have someone else, Candy."

"Oh, baby ... don't say that. Who is she?"

"She's a very special woman."

"Darn it," she pouted. "I was hoping ... you know ...."

"I know. Is that why you took off your pasties and put on perfume? To entice me?"

She gave him a wicked grin. "Of course." Then she looked down at his lap, saw his bulging crotch and began stroking his pants again, making him harder still.

"Candy, please ... don't ...."

"Just relax and enjoy the ride, baby. You don't always have to be such a proper gentleman."

"You've never ... done this before ...." he said, his voice hoarse.

Her eyes bright with excitement, she kept massaging him and he knew it was just a matter of moments before he climaxed.

"In case your new girlfriend doesn't work out," she said with a purr, "I want you to remember I'm still here."

Although he was enjoying every stroke of her touch, he needed to be honest with her. Calling on every ounce of willpower he had, he grasped her hand and pulled it away from his lap. "Please Candy. You need to stop."

"What's the matter, honey. Don't you like it?"

"Of course I do. I'd be crazy not to. But you need to know. We're not going to get together. Not now. Not ever. We're just not right for each other."

She frowned, bit her lip, and her shoulders sagged. After a moment her eyes glistened with tears.

He gently pulled her hand to his lips and kissed it. "I'm sorry, Candy."

# Chapter 15

*Copenhagen, Denmark*

Rachel West's SAS flight touched down at Kastrup Airport at 10 a.m. By noon she had cleared customs, rented a car, and had driven the eight miles to the city center.

Rachel drove the Volvo along Copenhagen's Tietgensgade Avenue, passing the central train station and the impressive Christiansborg Palace. The palace was once the seat of royalty but now served as the home of the Danish parliament. As a CIA operative Rachel had been to Denmark several times before and was familiar with the layout of the city. It was a beautiful place, she had always thought, with its Renaissance era architecture and brightly painted townhouses overlooking the canals.

A half-hour later she reached her destination, a small home in the outskirts of the downtown area. The house was bordered by similar small homes, separated by quaint white-picket fences.

Rachel parked in front of the home and pulled her suitcase from the back seat onto the passenger seat. Clicking open the bag, she rummaged through it and found her weapon. Because of Denmark's tight gun control laws, she hadn't been able to carry it on the flight over. She removed her Glock 9mm handgun, checked the load, racked the slide, and tucked the weapon at her hip, underneath her windbreaker.

That done, she climbed out of the Volvo and strode to the front door. It was much colder outside than she had expected and she zipped up her jacket, knowing she'd have to buy a warmer coat.

Using the ornate brass knocker, she rapped on the door and waited. There was no response and she knocked again several more times with the same result. She found that odd, since Alex had arranged the meeting in advance.

After glancing at the neighboring homes to make sure she wasn't being observed, she pulled out her lock-pick set, intent on getting inside. But instead of picking the lock, she tried turning the knob first, and to her surprise found the door unlocked.

Rachel slipped inside, shut the door behind her and called the man's name. There was no response as she peered into the home's dim interior. After calling out his name several more times, she pulled her Glock and held it at her side, then went through the small living room and kitchen. Both were vacant so she proceeded further into the house.

The lights were on in a room at the end of the corridor. She called out again, and hearing no response, stepped into the bedroom. Seeing blood stains on the wood floors, she immediately tensed and gripped her gun tightly. Training the Glock in front of her she crouched and slowly advanced.

The signs of a struggle were everywhere. Glass and a broken lamp lay on the floor by the bed, and blood stains covered the torn bedspread. Pictures had been knocked off the walls and the mirror over the dresser was cracked.

Then she spotted the body which was sprawled on the floor on the other side of the bed. Blood was everywhere. Kneeling by the inert man, she felt his neck for a pulse. There was none.

Getting to her feet, she quickly searched the other parts of the home. Finding it vacant, she went back to the bloody corpse. She crouched next to it and inspected the wounds, which had not been caused by gunshots, but rather a large knife. Deep cuts lacerated the man's neck and torso. The smell of gore hung in the air.

She reached into the man's back pocket and removed his wallet. From his driver's license she confirmed he was her contact. She also noticed the wallet contained cash and credit cards, signifying this hadn't been a robbery. Rachel searched his other pockets for a cell phone. When she didn't find it, she rummaged through the rest of the house but couldn't locate a phone, a laptop computer, or an electronic tablet. She suspected the killer had taken those.

She glanced at her watch. It was 1:30 p.m. local time which meant it was six hours earlier at Langley. Figuring Alex Miller was already at work, she pulled out her compact satellite cell phone and tapped in a number.

"It's me," she said when her boss picked up. "I'm at the location."

"Have you talked to the informant?" Miller asked.

"No."

"Why?"

"He's dead, Alex."

The man said nothing for a moment. "You're at his house? You're sure it's him?"

"Affirmative on both counts."

"Damn. Give me the details."

"Murder. Multiple stab wounds to neck and chest. He bled out after a scuffle."

"Did you find his computer?"

"Gone, Alex. Along with his phone. Whoever killed him has them I'm sure."

"Christ. We're batting zero."

Rachel stared down at the bloody corpse. "The vics not having a good day either."

"Spare me the lame humor."

"Yes, sir." She gazed around the room, realized she'd stepped on the gore – her shoe soles were leaving bloody prints on the floor. She'd have to clean up after herself – wipe off her fingerprints and shoe marks. "Should I sanitize the place and get the hell out of here?"

"No, Rachel. We can't take the chance someone spots you leaving a murder scene and thinks you're the killer. We need the Danish authorities cooperation on this."

"Okay. It's your call. You'll contact them?"

"I'll take care of it," he said. "I'll call our State Department and explain what happened and they'll contact the Danish police. Stay where you are. The cops will show up soon." There was a pause. "Are you armed?"

"Always."

"Then unload it and hand it to the cops when they get there. They have strict gun laws in Denmark."

"Will do, Alex."

"Call me later."

She hung up and put her phone away. Then she unholstered her Glock, ejected the clip, and removed the round from the chamber. She placed the gun on the living room floor by the front door.

Twenty minutes later she heard the high-low wail of European police sirens approaching the home. She stepped outside and saw two Danish police cars pull into the driveway. Four uniformed men, their guns drawn, climbed out and slowly advanced toward her.

She held her hands up in the air. "I'm Rachel West, American CIA," she stated in Danish, a north Germanic language similar to Norwegian and Swedish. "I have ID in my jacket."

"We received a call," one of the cops said. "We were told you would be here and that there has been a murder. Show us your ID."

Very slowly she removed her cred pack and held it open for them to see. One of the police officers inspected it and said, "All right, Ms West. Are you carrying a weapon?"

"It's inside on the floor by the door."

The man nodded. "I will keep it until the detectives and forensics people show up. Then you will get it back."

"Okay."

"Is the body inside?"

"It is."

"Show us," the man said.

Rachel led them inside and recounted what she knew. When she was done, she heard more vehicles pulling to the curb of the property.

She spent the next two hours at the scene as the forensic techs gathered evidence, and two more hours at the police station answering questions. It was clear to her that the Danish police didn't fully trust her and didn't appreciate her conducting an investigation on Danish soil. She refused to tell them the nature of her covert operation, which further antagonized them. They finally released her with an admonition not to carry her weapon while in the country. She nodded, fully planning to ignore the request.

Rachel left the station and drove the Volvo to the Ibsen, a French-style boutique hotel where she'd previously stayed. It was located in central Copenhagen, on a cafe-lined street close to Nansensgade Avenue. After checking in, she called Alex, then at his suggestion called a CIA agent based in the city. She didn't know the man personally, but since she had no other leads, decided to meet with him and see if could be useful in the investigation. They agreed to meet for dinner at a restaurant she knew in the Tivoli Gardens.

\*\*\*

One of Copenhagen's most famous attractions, the Tivoli Gardens was an entertainment park. The park featured elaborate gardens, fairground rides, open-air concert venues, amusement arcades, and a multitude of restaurants. Rachel walked past the Ferris wheel and the rollercoaster and made her way through the gardens to her destination. It was well-past dusk and the gardens were lit with thousands of tiny lights. It was a festive, party-like atmosphere, with throngs of young people and families strolling among the music and entertainment venues.

She found the restaurant and saw a man at an outdoor table motioning to her. Walking over, she sat opposite him.

"I recognized you immediately," the man said in slightly accented English. "After we talked, I looked up your file." He was a tall, distinguished-looking man in his mid-fifties with graying temples. He was dressed in a three-piece suit with a striped tie and a pocket square. She was still wearing her blue jeans, long-sleeve polo shirt, and a windbreaker, and she now wished she had changed into something more appropriate.

They shook hands and he said, "Hans Frederick at your service." He smiled. "Your reputation precedes you, Ms West."

She didn't return the smile. "May I see your identification."

His smile dampened a bit as he handed her his ID. "Of course."

After scanning his CIA cred pack she returned it. She was about to pull hers out, but he waved her off.

"No need for that, Ms West." He gave her a long up-and-down look. "You look identical to your Agency photos. Long-blonde hair, sparkling blue eyes, classic high cheekbones." He grinned again. "A ravishing beauty, I may add."

Rachel frowned. She was used to being hit on by men of all types, including agents within the CIA. She was one of the few female NOCs, the CIA term used for covert operatives working without official cover. But just because she was used to being hit on didn't mean she enjoyed it.

"I'm here on business," she said.

He smiled again. "I am sure you are. Would you like some wine?"

She nodded and he flagged down a waiter and ordered a bottle of Bordeaux. As he was doing this she surveyed the scene and noticed the patrons sitting at the other tables were not close by, giving them plenty of privacy to talk. She also scrutinized each of the people in the outdoor cafe, trying to determine if any appeared to be a security threat or if she was being monitored. On the walk to the restaurant from the parking lot she had been just as vigilant, making sure she wasn't followed. It was called 'situational awareness'. The constant alertness to your surroundings was something drilled into them at the Farm, the Agency's training center. And it was something she practiced religiously. A practice that had saved her life several times.

The waiter brought the bottle of wine, poured out two glasses and moved on to another table.

Frederick raised his glass. "Cheers, as you Americans would say." He downed his glass in one gulp as she took a sip of hers.

"There is one thing I do not understand, Ms West. On the phone you said you were in Denmark conducting an operation. You are Station Chief of the Paris office. You must have agents that you can send here to conduct the investigation."

She took another sip of wine. "This is a special assignment."

"I see. How long will you be in our fair city?" He waved a hand as if to encompass all of Copenhagen. "I would love to show you around." He grinned again.

She knew exactly what he meant. Scowling, she unzipped her windbreaker and pushed the flap aside so he could see her holstered weapon. "It's locked and loaded, my friend. I said I was here on business."

Frederick stared at the handgun and nodded. "I understand. I did not mean to offend you in any way."

Rachel zipped her jacket back up. "Let me tell you why I'm here. I'm on a covert assignment. A very sensitive one. I was supposed to meet an informant today. Unfortunately he was dead when I got there." She told him the name of the informant and his particulars. "Do you know this man? Or anything about him?"

Frederick shook his head. "No. But I will make inquiries. I have been in Copenhagen a long time. I have many contacts."

"Good."

The man drank down his second glass of wine. "May I ask what the operation is about? That would be helpful to know."

She studied him closely, trying to gauge his trustworthiness. She had checked out his file and knew he had a good reputation at Central Intelligence. But she recalled what Alex had told her: Trust no one. Suspect everyone.

"It concerns national security," she said.

"Everything we do concerns national security. That is not very helpful."

She mulled this over, knowing she had to share some information. "True enough. There's a conspiracy within the U.S. government. A plot to destabilize the current administration and the country as a whole. There's an international connection, one that appears to originate in Denmark."

His eyes grew big. "That sounds ominous. Are you implying that U.S. agents are plotting to overthrow the government?"

"It appears so."

He picked up the bottle of Bordeaux and refilled their glasses. Then he downed his wine in one long gulp.

"Do you know where in the U.S. government this plot originates, Ms West?"

Rachel shook her head. "No. And I urge you not to share this info with anyone else."

"Not even my Station Chief? He is based in Norway."

"Not even him."

"That is highly irregular, Ms West."

"Yes, it is. But it's for your own safety, as well as for the integrity of the operation. Now, shall we order dinner? I'm starved."

# Chapter 16

*Atlanta, Georgia*

J.T. Ryan strode through the tree-lined path, found a bench and sat down to wait. He had picked the time of day and location for the meet deliberately. It was broad daylight and Centennial Park in downtown was one of Atlanta's most public places. He didn't want a repeat of what happened at their last meeting.

The bench he was on faced south and from it he could see the nearby CNN building and the rest of the city's skyline.

Ten minutes later he spotted Candy as she strolled toward him. She was wearing the same clothes as at their previous meeting, the fake-fur jacket, black leggings, and flats.

Candy sat down next to him, a contrite expression on her face. "I'm sorry, J.T. for what I tried to do last time. It won't happen again. I promise."

"Okay," he replied. "When you called me you said you'd found some information?"

"I did." She glanced around to make sure no one was nearby, then lowered her voice. "Parker, the Tektronn guy, is married as you probably know. He's also an elder at his church. All in all, a highly respected man in the community. A straight arrow. On the surface."

Ryan nodded. "Yeah. Erin ran a background check on him, found he had no arrest record, not even a parking ticket. So what did you find?"

"Is our deal still good?"

"It is, Candy." He patted his blazer. "I brought cash."

"All right, then. A friend of mine is a madam who runs a high-end prostitution operation over in Buckhead. She found out Parker likes hookers. Rents them frequently. In fact, gets his ashes hauled twice a month."

"Is your source reliable?"

"My friend's never been wrong, J.T. In fact, she told me the name of the hooker Parker prefers. A seventeen-year-old that goes by the name of Tanya."

"Good work," he said. "If you were able to find this out, someone else may have also. And that someone may be blackmailing Parker."

"That's what I thought too. Since this guy is highly respected, I'm sure he doesn't want his wife or his church to know he hires hookers."

Ryan nodded and he pulled out an envelope from his jacket. He handed it to her.

Candy counted the cash quickly, then looked at him with a puzzled expression. "This is $400. You only owe me $300."

"I know," he said. "Take the extra hundred and buy your daughter dinner at a nice restaurant. You told me she's getting good grades – she deserves a treat."

She smiled. "You're such a sweet man, John Taylor Ryan." Then she glanced at her Timex. "Got to go. My shift at the club starts soon."

They said their goodbyes and the woman strolled out of the park. Ryan sat there for several minutes as he processed what Candy had told him. Then he walked toward his SUV which was parked nearby.

An hour later he was back at the Tektronn Industries headquarters in Sandy Springs.

Parker initially refused to see him, informing Ryan through the receptionist that he was too busy. The PI made it clear he wasn't leaving, implying he'd have the technology officer arrested if he refused to meet.

Soon after he was shown into the man's office.

"I've told you everything I know," Parker said haughtily, standing behind his desk.

"Not everything, Parker. You're holding something back." Ryan sat in the chair fronting the desk.

"Are you calling me a liar? I won't be insulted in my own office. Get out now or I'll call security."

Ryan pointed an index finger at him. "Sit down."

The technology chief seemed about to protest again, then shrugged and slumped onto his executive chair. "What to you want, Ryan?"

"The truth."

The man's eyes flashed anger. "I told you everything. Our truck's computer system was hacked."

"By who?"

"I don't know. There's no way for me to trace who did it."

Ryan stared hard at the man, sensing the same evasiveness he'd noticed last time they'd met.

The PI stood, leaned forward and placed his hands flat on the desk. "I think you do know. You're lying to me."

"I am not," Parker replied indignantly.

"You're a happily married man, aren't you?"

"Of course. What does that have to do with it?"

"You're also an elder at your church."

"Yes, Ryan. And proud of it. But how is that relevant to our conversation?"

"Does your wife or your church know about Tanya, your seventeen-year-old hooker?"

The man's faced turned bright red and he pushed his chair back on its rollers, distancing himself as much as possible from the PI. He opened his mouth to reply, but no words came out.

Ryan sat back down and said, "You're being blackmailed to keep quiet."

Parker lowered his head and covered his eyes with a hand. "I am."

"Look," the PI said. "I'm not here to cause you trouble. I'm just trying to get the truth."

The other man raised his head and stared at Ryan, a pained expression on his face. "It's true," he said, his voice shaky. "I am being blackmailed. After we found out our truck was stolen, I received a call here in my office. The guy who called said that no one could find out who had tampered with the vehicle's software. He also told me he knew all about my dealings with Tanya."

"Who was the man who called you?" Ryan demanded.

"I don't know. The voice was altered. All I could tell is that it was a man's voice."

"Who hacked into the truck's software, Parker?"

"I don't know the person's name. The only thing I know is their location."

"Where is that?"

"A small town in east Georgia, near the South Carolina border."

"What's the name of the place?"

Parker told him and then said, "Please, can you keep my dealings with Tanya secret? If my wife or church finds out ... God, my life would be ruined." He gave Ryan a pleading look.

The PI felt sorry for him. "I won't tell anyone. But we're dealing with murders. It's a good bet that the people responsible will eventually be caught and put on trial. Your 'dealings' with a teenage hooker are likely to come out then. If I were you, I'd try to get your house in order now."

The man nodded sadly and his shoulders sagged.

Ryan stood and left the office.

# Chapter 17

*FBI Field Office*
*Atlanta, Georgia*

"So the Tektronn guy was being blackmailed to keep quiet," Erin Welch said.

"That's right," J.T. Ryan replied.

The two of them were meeting in her office on the top floor of the building.

Erin leaned forward in her executive chair and steepled her hands on the desk. "Good work on getting the lead, J.T. I assume your next step is to check out this town in east Georgia?"

"It is. I'm going to my office first to check on things, then I'll go home and pack. I'll probably be gone a few days."

"Okay."

He pulled out a sheet of paper from his blazer pocket and handed it to her. "This is my expense report for the last week."

She scanned it quickly and tapped one line item with a finger. "You've got a large cash expenditure here. To a Candy Cane. As I recall, she's one of your informants. Did you get a receipt?"

Ryan shook his head and smiled. "Sometimes in my line of work, I don't get receipts. I get results."

She frowned, then shrugged. "Fair enough."

The PI stood. "I'll be on my way." He gave her a half-salute and left her office.

He located his Tahoe in the underground parking lot and drove north on Peachtree Street until he reached his own office in midtown.

When he went inside the office he found his young associate Lisa Booth working at her laptop. Ryan had hired her a year ago to help handle the growing case load for his private investigative firm.

"Hi Lisa," he said, as he poured himself a cup of java from the coffee maker on the cabinet. "What are you working on?"

She looked up from her computer. "Hello, boss. We just got two new cases. One from Atlanta PD and the other one from the Department of Homeland Security."

Ryan grinned. "That's good news."

"It is," she said in her usual earnest and cheerful tone. "I told you my marketing ideas would pan out."

"And so they have." Ryan studied the 25 year old. She was short, slender, and cute, with an aura of innocence that made her appear much younger than her age.

"Maybe one day soon, J.T., you'll make me a partner in your firm. Instead of Ryan Investigations we could be Ryan and Booth Investigations."

Ryan shook his head slowly and suppressed a smile. "I gave you a raise a few months ago. Now you want to be a partner? I'm surprised you don't want to call it 'Booth and Ryan Investigations'."

She nodded and grinned. "Even better!"

Ryan pointed to her laptop. "Get back to work, young lady."

"Yes, boss."

He went to his desk, rummaged through his drawers, found the files he was looking for and packed them in his satchel. Standing, he said, "I'll be gone for a few days. If you need me, Lisa, call my cell phone."

She stopped tapping the keyboard of her computer. "Where you going?"

"I can't say."

"Can't say or won't say?"

"Same difference, Lisa."

"You've been awfully secretive since you came back from Washington, D.C."

He nodded. "That's true."

"C'mon, J.T. Fill me in. You can trust me. I'm your partner, remember?"

"Actually you're not my partner. Not yet anyway. And even if you were I couldn't tell you what I was working on." He hated keeping Lisa in the dark, but President Harris had given them strict orders to keep the operation secret.

Ryan approached her desk and sat on a corner of it. "I'd love to tell you what I'm working on, Lisa. But I can't. It involves national security. I gave my word I'd keep it confidential."

"Okay, boss. I understand."

"Good." He stood and grabbed his satchel from his desk. "I'll be on my way. Call me if you need help with any of the cases."

"Got it, Chief," she said cheerfully.

"I told you not to call me chief," he replied as he turned to go. "Call me that again and I'll start calling you Nancy Drew, Junior Detective."

She snickered and went back to working at her computer.

Ryan left his office and drove to his apartment where he packed some clothes in an overnight bag. Then he got back in his SUV and drove south on I-75 and then east on I-20.

Three hours later he was in the town of Darton, Georgia. As he drove through the main street, he realized the term 'town' to describe the place was an overstatement. The village had one traffic light, one gas station, and one small motel. The main street consisted of two blocks of business establishments. There were two places to eat: a Cracker Barrel Old Country Store and a quaint little restaurant called Leburda's Grits N' Gravy.

Driving past this, he took a dusty county road east for four miles until he reached the address he'd obtained from Parker, the Tektronn guy. It turned out to be a nondescript, metal-sided warehouse about a half mile from the county road. The rusting, aging building was not the high-tech operation he had expected to find. The place was nestled in a heavily-wooded, desolate area which he reached by a single-lane gravel path. Driving well past the building, he parked his Tahoe among the heavy vegetation, and doubled-back on foot.

He stopped when he was a hundred feet away, pulled out his mini-binoculars, and peered through the trees. There were no cars parked in the small lot that fronted the place and no lights visible from the roof skylights, which were the only windows of the structure.

Listening for sounds of machinery or voices, he heard none. The warehouse appeared to be vacant.

Ryan kept up the observation for another half-hour, and seeing no one go in or out, decided to get a closer look. He pulled his Smith & Wesson .357 Magnum revolver from his hip holster, and holding it at his side, advanced slowly along the gravel path until he reached the metal front door. He noticed the sturdy padlock hanging from the door handle and a thick metal bar which ran across the door. A second padlock hung from the metal bar as well. He also noticed a security camera attached to the roof beam, pointing toward the entrance.

Though he didn't expect anyone to answer, he repeatedly pressed the buzzer by the door. After several more minutes of knocking, he stopped and mulled over the situation. Without heavy cutting tools he knew he'd never be able to break the locks. He also considered shooting off the locks, but didn't want the sound of gunfire to alert neighbors.

Ryan circled the building, looking for another entrance. He found a garage-style mechanical rolling door at the back, but it too was heavily padlocked. He glanced toward the roof and got an idea. Using the garage door's metal grooves as hand grips, he pulled himself up and climbed the wall of the building until he was on top of the roof. Crawling on his hands and knees, he reached one of the skylights.

He peered through the clear Plexiglas into the dim interior below. Although it was still afternoon, the heavy canopy of trees and the lack of lights inside the building prevented him from seeing much.

Pulling out a penlight from a pocket, he shined the light through the skylight, illuminating the inside of the warehouse. He saw two vehicles, a green, four-wheel drive Jeep, and a black Ford pick-up truck. He also saw several large tables on which he spotted at least three or four desktop computers, printers, and more tech gear he couldn't identify. There were no people inside.

After spending a few more minutes scanning the interior, he retraced his steps, climbed down from the roof, and walked back to his SUV. He'd have to come back again and this time bring heavy cutting tools to access the interior of the warehouse.

Ryan drove back to town and checked into the motel. He inquired about the nearest hardware supply store and was told there was a Home Depot twenty miles away. After driving there and back it was nighttime. Deciding to tackle the break-in early the next morning, he had dinner at the Cracker Barrel and went to bed.

After placing his Smith & Wesson on the chipped wooden night-table, he turned off the lights and laid on the lumpy bed. Although the bed springs creaked and groaned each time he moved, he fell asleep in minutes.

Hours later he awakened and sensed something was wrong. Quickly getting out of bed, he heard a metal cracking sound and knew his room door was being jimmied.

The door flung open and two big men burst inside.

Ryan grabbed his gun from the night-stand, but before he could aim he felt a blinding pain on his arm and his pistol clattered to the floor. A second blow struck Ryan's head and he staggered back, falling to one knee. He was stunned by the blow, but managed to get on his feet and faced the attackers. He clubbed one of them in the neck with his elbow, then punched the second man in the gut. One of the attackers was holding a crowbar and Ryan grabbed it from him and struck him on the chest. The thug howled in pain and ran toward the door.

The PI turned toward the second guy, who likewise was sprinting toward the exit. Ryan retrieved his weapon from the floor and chased after them. As the men raced into the nearby woods, he stopped his chase realizing he'd never find them in the dark of night.

His head and arm still throbbing from the blows, Ryan went to the motel office and reported the attempted robbery. Going back to his room, he closed the door behind him, pushed a wooden desk against the entrance, and gulped down four Excedrin to alleviate the pain. After placing his revolver underneath his pillow, he laid back on the bed and fell into a fitful sleep.

When he awoke the next morning, he showered, shaved, dressed, and applied a bandage to the cut on his temple. He took more Excedrin, had breakfast at the Cracker Barrel, and drove out to the warehouse. After observing the place closely to make sure there was no one inside, he approached the front entrance. From his backpack he removed the bolt-cutters he'd bought the day before and cut off the door locks.

He pulled out his handgun and stepped inside. Flicking on the overhead florescent lights, he was stunned to find nothing. The building, which just yesterday had been full of equipment and vehicles, was now completely empty.

As he walked around the large vacant structure he realized the break-in of his motel room hadn't been an attempted robbery. The men had been sent to kill him. Then he remembered the security cameras mounted on the outside of the warehouse. Someone must have been monitoring them remotely, saw him yesterday, and emptied the contents of the building.

Ryan left the warehouse and marched back to his SUV. As he did so he rubbed his forehead, trying to massage away his throbbing headache, a result of the blows he'd received.

# Chapter 18

*Midtown*
*Atlanta, Georgia*        .

J.T. Ryan unlocked the door to his apartment and went inside. He sensed movement behind him in the hallway and quickly pulled his gun. He whirled around and took aim.

"Don't shoot!" Erin said. "It's me."

Seeing the FBI woman in the doorway, Ryan holstered his pistol. "Sorry about that, Erin."

"You're awfully jumpy today," she replied, coming into his living room.

He closed the door behind her. "I had a tough day yesterday. Two thugs broke into my motel room in Darton and tried to kill me."

Her eyes grew wide and she pointed to the bandage on his temple. "Is that how you got that?"

He nodded.

"I tried calling you a couple of times but I got no answer," she said.

Ryan took out his cell phone and saw that its glass front was cracked. "I didn't notice this before. My phone was damaged during the attack."

She glanced around the sparsely furnished living room, obviously looking for somewhere to sit. She went over and perched on the worn sofa and he sat on the metal folding chair that fronted it. As usual Erin was wearing an expensive outfit: Today it was a navy blue Dolce and Gabbana business suit with a Ralph Lauren white blouse. She seemed a bit uncomfortable sitting on the well-worn couch.

"This place could use a woman's touch," she muttered under her breath.

Ignoring this, he said, "Why'd you come here?"

"Two reasons. First I couldn't get a hold of you. And second, I found some interesting information about the town you just went to."

"Darton, Georgia?"

"That's right, J.T. But first things first. Fill me in on what happened there."

He spent the next fifteen minutes detailing the events of his trip.

"Interesting," she said. "That may tie-in with what I learned. I did research on the town of Darton. There's not much to the place, as you found out. But twenty miles east of the town, close to the South Carolina border, is a large government facility."

"Really?"

"Yes. And you'll never guess which part of the government runs it."

"Ok," he said, "I give up. Which one?"

"The NSA."

"The National Security Agency?"

"One and the same, J.T."

Ryan shook his head. "The warehouse I went to out in the woods. That was no NSA operation. The NSA is super high-tech. The building I found didn't have cyclone fencing, 24/7 armed guards, or any other extensive security."

"I get your point," she said. "But remember what the president told us. That rogue elements within government are involved in the criminal syndicate. What if people who work at the NSA set up this warehouse and hacked into the driverless truck's software. They may be the same people who committed the other murders as well. Clearly rogue government agents couldn't initiate all that while inside an NSA facility. They would be caught and arrested. But I find it suspicious that a large NSA facility and this warehouse are so close to each other."

Ryan nodded. "I agree." He leaned back on the unpadded metal folding chair, trying to get comfortable.

"I learned something else," Erin added. "The warehouse you went to is owned by a foreign company. A company based in Denmark."

"That ties in with what Mike Corso told us. That there's an international connection."

"That's right, J.T."

"So what's our next step?"

"I call Corso and tell him what we learned."

"And then what, Erin?"

"Then you and I are going to pay a visit to this NSA facility and find out what's what."

Ryan grinned as he rubbed his still throbbing temple. "Sounds good to me. I want to kick some ass. I want payback for this."

# Chapter 19

*Copenhagen, Denmark*

Rachel West hadn't heard from her CIA contact in days, although she'd left numerous messages on his cell.

Rachel was getting worried. Pulling out her sat phone, she punched in a number. When her boss in Langley picked up, she said, "I can't get a hold of Hans Frederick. Can you find out where he lives, Alex?"

"Hold on," Miller replied. She heard the clicking of a keyboard and a minute later he came back on and gave her an address in Koge, a small town south of Copenhagen.

Hanging up, she left her hotel room and drove her rented Volvo along the coast until she reached the town. Koge, a quaint seaside village, appeared to be a suburb of the Danish capital of Copenhagen.

Finding his apartment building, she parked on the street and took the creaky elevator to the sixth floor. She knocked on the apartment door about a dozen times. There was no answer and she glanced around the corridor to make sure no one was about. Then she took out her lock-pick set and fiddled with the lock until she heard a metallic click. After putting away the lock-pick and pulling out her Glock, she turned the knob and slipped inside, closing the door behind her.

Rachel tensed, knowing something was wrong immediately. The distinctive odor of congealed blood hung in the air of the living room. Then she heard it, the buzzing of flies coming from the kitchen.

Holding her weapon with both hands, she trained it in front of her and advanced cautiously toward the stench. Frederick's bloody corpse was on the kitchen floor, flies swarming over it. A pool of blood spread out from underneath the body and she noticed ants covering the floor. The dead man faced up and she realized he'd been murdered the same way as the Danish informant. Multiple stab wounds were visible on his torso and neck. It was clear from the stench that he'd been dead at least a day, probably more.

Trying not to disturb the murder scene, she quickly searched his pockets for a cell phone, but didn't find one. Then she carefully searched the man's apartment for any type of electronics, but came up empty.

Not wanting to repeat the hassle with the Danish police, she carefully retraced her steps, wiped off her fingerprints from the rooms, and quickly left the building. Getting back in the Volvo, she drove back to Copenhagen.

When she arrived at her hotel room, she called Alex and filled him in on what had happened. Then she stripped off her clothes and jumped in the shower, wanting to wash off the stench from the decayed body, which had permeated her hair and clothing.

After toweling off from the long, hot shower, she threw on a terry cloth robe and poured herself a shot of Absolut. She gulped down the vodka and poured herself another. As she sipped the drink, she tried to erase the image of the bloody corpse from her thoughts. Although she was a trained covert agent who had witnessed and caused plenty of death, seeing Frederick's brutally carved-up body had burned into her psyche. She knew the image would haunt her dreams for days to come.

She sat in the couch of the hotel suite for the next hour, sipping vodka, mulling over the case. Then she reclined on the sofa and fell asleep. Sometime later she felt a buzzing sensation in her robe's pocket. Waking up fully, she sat up and pulled out her cell phone. She recognized the Atlanta area code and hoped it was him.

"Hey, beautiful," she heard Ryan say.

"J.T.," she replied. "It's been awhile. I'm really glad you called."

"I missed you, Rachel."

She visualized the rugged, good-looking man. By the tone in his voice she could tell he was grinning that boyish grin of his. "I've missed you too. A lot."

"Did I catch you at a bad time?"

She ran a hand through her long blonde hair, which was still damp from the shower. "Not at all. I've had a hell of a day. Your call is very welcome. Is this a personal or business call?"

"It's both." He paused a moment. "I understand we've both been assigned to the same case."

"That's right, J.T. By the way, although this call is encrypted, we need to be careful of what we say."

"Agreed. I've been working on my end and found an international lead. Figured you could run it down."

"I'd be glad to." She thought about the two cadavers she'd seen recently. "I've run into a few dead ends here."

"I located a warehouse in Darton, Georgia," he said, "that's pertinent to the investigation we're both working." He told her the address of the warehouse and said, "That building is owned by a Danish company. That firm is based in Skagen. Do you know where that is?"

"I do. Skagen is a city on the northern tip of Denmark."

"Okay, Rachel. That's all I've got. Hope it helps."

"I'll run it down."

"Good. I want to see you again, beautiful. Soon."

"I want that too," she replied. "I've missed you." She recalled the warning her boss had given her about Ryan and decided not to tell him about it. *I'll cross that bridge when I get to it*, she thought. She visualized his face again, then recalled their torrid lovemaking. Her cheeks flushed from the stimulating thoughts.

"Are you coming back to the U.S. anytime soon, Rachel?"

"I don't know. Alex assigned me to Europe – guess I'll be here awhile."

"Call me," he said with a chuckle, "when you do get back to the states. So we can get together for coffee, or dinner, or whatever ...."

She laughed, recognizing the line from their previous conversations. "I like the whatever best," she replied.

"Me too, Rachel. Me too."

"We should probably hang up now."

"I guess so."

They continued talking about nothing in particular for the next couple of minutes. It was clear to her neither one of them wanted to hang up. Finally she said, "I've got to go now, J.T."

"Okay, beautiful."

She clicked off the call and put the phone away in her robe pocket.

Then she went to the hotel suite's small kitchen. From a cabinet she pulled out an unopened bottle of Absolut. Pouring out a glassful of the vodka, she drank it down slowly, this time not to forget about the bloody murders, but to chase away the intense loneliness she felt.

# Chapter 20

*National Security Agency – Georgia*
*Fort Gordon, Georgia*

"What can you tell me about the NSA?" Ryan asked, as he slowed his Tahoe, getting in line to enter Fort Gordon, the military base that housed the NSA complex in Georgia. "I don't know that much about them."

There was a long line of vehicles ahead of them, all waiting to be allowed into the highly-fortified facility.

Erin Welch, who was in the passenger seat, turned to face him. "I did quite a bit of research on the NSA when I found out we were coming here. The National Security Agency was created in secret by President Harry Truman in 1952. Not even Congress knew about them back then. In fact, for a long time the NSA was referred to as No Such Agency by its own employees. The NSA's main headquarters is in Fort Meade, Maryland where it employs over 30,000 people."

She paused and pointed to the entrance gate. "The NSA has satellite facilities across the U.S. and around the world. The one here in Georgia employs about 2,000 people. The overall purpose of the Agency is to analyze all data transmission – including phone calls, emails, and social media data – to identify national security threats." Erin paused again. "After the terrorist attacks on September 11, 2001, the size of the Agency mushroomed. Now it's the largest, most costly, and most sophisticated spy organization in the world. It dwarfs the CIA in size and scope, although most people in the U.S. don't even know it exists."

Erin folded her arms over her chest. "When I called Mike Corso and told him you had found that warehouse in Darton, and told him it was located close to an NSA facility, he didn't seem surprised."

"He didn't?" Ryan said.

"No. I think he already suspected people within the National Security Agency could be involved in the conspiracy. Anyway, he arranged for us to meet the officer in charge of this Georgia facility."

"Okay." Ryan saw that they were next in line at the gate entrance. When the uniformed guard waved them forward, he drove his Tahoe up and stopped.

Erin gave Ryan her cred pack and he handed her ID as well as his own to the guard. The young corporal scanned the IDs with a hand scanner then made a phone call. A minute later they were waved through the heavily-fortified gate to a small parking lot nearby that was staffed by more armed soldiers. Ryan and Erin were frisked by the guards and his SUV was searched thoroughly. The soldiers took their cell phones and told them they would be returned on their departure. It was clear that the security precautions in the facility were extremely tight.

Eventually they were allowed to drive to a three-story, red-brick building at the center of the complex, and then shown into a small conference room.

They were joined a few minutes later by a tall, bald man wearing an officers dress blue Army uniform. "I'm Colonel Hesler," he said, as they shook hands and sat down around the conference table. "I manage this facility."

"Colonel," Erin said, "I believe Mike Corso, the Director of National Intelligence, talked to you about our visit."

"He did, although I'm mystified why you're here."

"You're familiar with the recent deaths of the Senate Majority Leader, the Supreme Court Justice, and the Cardinal?" she asked.

The colonel nodded. "Of course. Everyone knows about that. But what does that have to do with us?"

Erin recounted Ryan's experience at the warehouse in the nearby town of Darton.

Colonel Hesler shook his head. "I still don't see the connection."

"The FBI believes," Ryan said, "that there are rogue elements within government that are responsible for the murders."

Hesler scoffed. "The FBI is wrong to think the NSA is involved."

"We're not accusing your Agency of anything," Erin continued. "We're just conducting an investigation."

The colonel glared at her. "The FBI has no jurisdiction here. We're a military installation."

Erin tried to control her anger at the man's attitude. "We're on the same side here, Colonel. We all work for the U.S. government."

Hesler said nothing, his grimace defiant.

"I'm sure Mike Corso, the Director of National Intelligence," she said, "asked you to cooperate with us."

"What *exactly* is it you want, Ms Welch?"

"That's Assistant Director Welch," Erin snapped, getting tired of the man's attitude.

The colonel shrugged. "Whatever your title is."

"We want to question your employees," she pressed on. "Find out if any of them are involved with the criminals."

"We have over 2,000 people here," he said angrily. "That's out of the question!"

"I can get the DNI to order you to cooperate, Colonel."

The officer stood abruptly. "I don't work for the DNI. I work for the Director of the NSA. You'll have to take it up with him." He glared at Erin and then at Ryan. "This meeting is over."

The colonel stalked out of the room, slamming the door on his way out.

"That didn't go well," Ryan mused.

# Chapter 21

*Atlanta, Georgia*

J.T. Ryan stopped at his favorite Krispy Kreme store and bought a dozen chocolate doughnuts. Then he got back in his Tahoe and drove the rest of the way to the FBI offices in downtown.

After clearing security, he made his way to Erin Welch's office and knocked on her open door. She looked up from her laptop and waved him in. Ryan stepped inside, closed the door behind him, and took a chair fronting her desk.

With a flourish he opened the box of doughnuts and placed them in front of her. "A present," he said with a chuckle.

Erin inspected the contents of the box. "What's this for?"

The PI smiled. "I figured after yesterday's lousy meeting at the NSA, you could use a sugar high."

"Yeah. That went like a lead balloon." She picked up one of the doughnuts and a napkin from the box and placed them on her desk in front of her. Then she slid the box toward him.

"Chocolate," she said. "This looks yummy."

"You know what they say," he replied with a grin. "Chocolate is one of the three major food groups. The other two are beer and pizza."

"Smartass."

Ryan laughed as he dug into the box, took out a doughnut and happily munched on it. He watched as Erin daintily tore her doughnut into two, then tore it into even smaller pieces and carefully bit into one of them.

She swallowed the morsel and said, "You trying to make me fat?"

He glanced at her slender, attractive figure. "I don't think that's going to be a problem for a long time."

Erin nodded and looked pensive.

"Given any thought to how we're going to handle the NSA issue?" Ryan asked.

She grimaced. "That's *all* I've been thinking about."

"I could always go back there, pull my weapon, and at gunpoint force the colonel to let us interrogate his people."

Erin gave him a hard look. "There's a lot of armed soldiers at Fort Gordon. I don't think that's such a good idea."

Ryan laughed. "I was just kidding."

She appeared perplexed then realized he'd made another joke. She shook her head slowly. "Smartass."

"That's me," he replied as he finished his doughnut. Picking up another one, he began wolfing it down.

Erin daintily chewed on another tiny morsel of hers, then wiped her hands with a napkin, and threw the rest of the doughnut in a trash bin. "That was delicious, J.T. Thanks. Now let's get to work. I've decided how to proceed."

"Great. What?"

"I really don't want to do it," she said, "but I don't have a choice. We have to call Mike Corso and enlist his help."

Ryan nodded. "Makes sense. As DNI, he's the guy to take care of this."

Erin picked up the handset of her desk phone and tapped in a number. Then she said, "I'll put it on speaker, J.T., so you can hear."

A moment later the call was routed through the White House until they reached Corso's office.

As soon as Erin started talking, Corso said, "Is this call encrypted?"

"Yes, sir, it is. J.T. Ryan is also in the room with me."

"Okay, Erin," Corso said. "This must be important otherwise I know you wouldn't be calling me."

"It is, sir. As you know we found a lead regarding the investigation. That lead took Ryan to a location very close the NSA facility at Fort Gordon, Georgia. You'll recall that you arranged a meeting with that facility's manager."

"Of course, I remember that. Go ahead, Erin."

"We met with Colonel Hesler."

"And?"

"He refused to help us, sir. In fact, he told us the FBI has no jurisdiction at a NSA facility."

"Technically, Erin, that's true. However, in the spirit of agency-to-agency cooperation, I was hoping he would assist in your investigation."

"I had assumed that also. But the colonel refused to cooperate."

"How did you leave it with him, Erin?"

"He literally walked out of the meeting. He told us take it up with the director of the NSA."

"I see. The fact that the colonel is stonewalling you is troubling. Very troubling."

"I agree, Mr. Corso. Don't all of the seventeen intelligence agencies of the U.S., including the NSA, report to you as the DNI?"

"That's technically true. As Director of National Intelligence groups like the National Security Agency report to me ... but ... the federal government is a massive, nine-headed Hydra monster. And corralling all those people and getting them to cooperate is difficult. That's what makes this scheme so sinister. It could be composed of a dozen or a hundred rogue people."

"I understand, sir. How should we proceed from here?"

The line went quiet for a minute, then Corso said, "I'll call the director of the NSA and demand his assistance in the investigation. He can't disobey a direct order from me."

"Thank you, sir."

"And Erin. One other thing. The director of the NSA is located at their headquarters in Fort Meade, Maryland. I want you and Ryan ready to go there at a moments notice."

"Of course, sir."

# Chapter 22

*Copenhagen, Denmark*

Located on the northern tip of Denmark's largest island, the town of Skagen had a population of 12,000 people. Rachel West had never been to the place before, and knew their only claim to fame was the fact that Skagen watches were manufactured there.

Rachel boarded a ferry which took her from Copenhagen to Skagen. There she rented a car and drove through the city, looking for the address J.T. Ryan had given her.

She found it quickly, since it was located on Skagen's main street. But as soon as she pulled up to the building, she knew something was wrong. The CIA woman had expected to find a commercial establishment of some type, a lawyer's office or a stand-alone company building. But instead the address turned out to be one of those mailbox rental places that are so common in the U.S. and also in Europe. They're useful for small companies because with them a firm has a street address as opposed to a post office box, making the company appear well-established.

Rachel checked her notes again and confirmed that this was the correct address. So the owner of a warehouse in Georgia was a mail drop in Denmark? That made no sense.

She pulled the rental car to the curb and got out of the vehicle. Going inside the building, she saw the wall of mailboxes on the left side of the room. Approaching them, she scanned the area and located the correct mailbox immediately. Then she went to the counter and asked the clerk on duty the name of the box owner.

The young man consulted his computer and said, "That box is listed as private."

"But who owns it?" Rachel asked in Danish. "There must be a person or a business listed in your records."

"I'm sorry, Miss. This one just says 'private'. We have a few of those. The mailbox renters just have to pay a year in advance to get those."

"So I can't find out whose it is?"

The young man looked doubtful. "I'm sorry, Miss. Maybe, with a court order, you could find out. But ... as you probably know ... the privacy laws in Denmark are –"

She grimaced and finished the sentence for him, "I know, I know, the privacy laws in Denmark are very strict."

Rachel turned and stalked out of the building. *Looks like another dead end.* Just like her last two leads, the informant and the CIA contact.

"Damn," she muttered as she climbed back in the rental car.

# Chapter 23

*An undisclosed location*

Number 27 hung up the phone, disturbed by what he'd just learned.

He knew what he had to do now, but waited another hour as he debated with himself on the best way to handle it. Realizing bad news is bad news, no matter how it's presented, he picked up the handset on his encrypted desk phone and tapped in a number.

"Yes?" the woman answered.

"It's 27."

"You have information for me?"

"I do, number 3."

"Well, damn it, spit it out! I don't have all day."

"Yes, ma'am," he replied, steeling himself for her reaction. "I received a phone call from one of my sources. The FBI was at the southern facility ... it appears they're investigating the murders of the three key leaders ... and somehow they've traced a lead back to the warehouse."

"The FBI? You're sure of this, 27?"

"Yes. My source was positive about this."

"Damn it all to hell!" the woman screeched. "How could you let this happen!"

"I'm sorry, ma'am ... I had no control over it ... I'm just ..." he stammered a bit "... informing you ... of what's happened ...."

The phone went quiet for a long moment and he wondered if the woman had hung up. "Are you still there, number 3?"

"I am, you idiot. I'm thinking. I'm trying to figure out how to fix this fuck-up of yours."

"Please, ma'am, it's not my fault," he pleaded.

"I'm not a forgiving woman," she replied, acid in her tone. "You know *that* by now."

"I do."

"And you know that I deal with problems decisively. I *eliminate* problems that get in my way."

Number 27 swallowed hard, knowing this to be a fact.

"But," she continued in a calmer voice. "Since you've been a loyal member of my group, I'll let it slide this time."

"Thank you, number 3."

"Don't thank me yet. We still have a ways to go before the operation is complete."

"Yes, ma'am."

He heard a click on the line and knew the woman had hung up.

# Chapter 24

*Oslo, Norway*

The woman known as number 3 replaced the handset on her desk phone and stared out the windows at the half-frozen lake below. As usual it was snowing outside, the gale-force winds buffeting the two-story chalet with such strength that the three-pane glass rattled in their sturdy wooden frames.

Acid began to churn in her stomach, the by-now-familiar nauseous sensation pushing bile up her throat. It was a common occurrence with her whenever she received bad news. The ulcers had started years ago, when she'd been held as a prisoner at Guantanamo Bay, Cuba.

After she escaped from the prison and had been hired to run the operation, she figured she'd outgrow the gastric condition. But to her chagrin, even the best doctors and the most potent medicine couldn't cure it. She cursed silently at the people responsible for putting her in that hell-hole Guantanamo. Another surge of bile rose up her throat as her hatred intensified for the American system that had banished her to that vile place.

She reached into her desk drawer, took out a bottle of prescription-strength antacid, and chugged directly from the container. It would provide only momentary relief, she knew, but it was better than nothing.

As her stomach settled, a cold smile formed on her lips. Then she laughed out loud. "Soon," she murmured. "Soon I'll get my revenge."

There was no one else in the large, beautifully appointed office. In fact, there was no one else in the luxurious chalet. The only people on her property was her security detail, and the guards stayed in a guest house nearby.

The woman liked living alone. That was another result of her time in prison. There she had been kept in isolation for years and as a result had come to accept, and then enjoy solitude.

Number 3 stood and walked to the high-end sound system on the teak bookcase along the wall. She pressed a selection from her extensive music collection and Brahms Intermezzo in A symphony emanated from the expensive speakers. She had always found that particular piece of classical music soothing, something she needed now as she dealt with the bad news.

Number 3 went to the windows and stared out at the half-frozen lake. She was a beautiful, raven-haired woman who had just turned forty years old. Her long black hair cascaded past her shoulders and her exquisitely sculpted good-looks were marred by only a slim scar on her left cheek.

The scar had come as a result of a fight with another prisoner years ago. After she escaped she considered having it removed with plastic surgery. But since the scar fueled her determination for revenge, she decided to postpone the facial surgery until the operation was complete. As she stepped closer to the rattling windows, she felt the chill of the frigid air that battered the chalet. She wrapped her arms around her waist, brooding over what to do next. The last time she had received bad news, she had decided to handle it on her own.

This time though, she realized, she'd have to inform the others. After all, she was ultimately an employee of the operation. An extremely high-paid one.

But number 1 and number 2 needed to know.

Turning away from the windows, she picked up her phone. She needed to make the arrangements for her trip.

# Chapter 25

*Reykjavik, Iceland*

The private Lear jet touched down at Keflavik Airport, and after taxiing on the tarmac, rolled to a stop in front of an unmarked hangar. The hangar doors slid open and the jet advanced into the cavernous steel structure.

Number 3 unbuckled her seat belt and stood. After donning her parka and thick gloves, she said goodbye to the pilot and then made her way down the plane's airstairs to the waiting Mercedes SUV.

She nodded to the SUV driver as he opened the rear door of the vehicle and she stepped into the back seat. Normally the jet would have flown her directly to her final destination in Iceland, but the weather had turned even nastier than usual, the fierce, frigid wind buffeting the Lear so severely that they'd been forced to land in Reykjavik, Iceland's capital city. She'd have to take the four-wheel drive vehicle the rest of the way.

Number 3 took off her gloves, unbuttoned her coat, and leaned back on the butter-soft leather seats. The SUV exited the hangar and drove through the outskirts of the city and soon after merged onto the coastal highway, going east. It was a long drive to her destination and the woman fell asleep.

She awoke many hours later, and in the distance she spotted the white peaks of the Vatnajokull mountains, the massive icecap that covers 14% of Iceland's surface. The vast, unspoiled area was over 5,300 square miles.

The SUV left the highway and went north along a snow-covered road that ran alongside one of the immense glaciers. The Vatnajokull icecap was a vast, pristine national park, and was off-limits to all commercial and residential development. It had taken her employer years of lobbying and bribes to get his estate built on the edge of the national park.

The man's massive estate was situated among the snow-covered terrain, and it took the SUV another hour of traveling before reaching it. Finally, after going through the many layers of security checkpoints along the way, the Mercedes reached the four-story estate.

Number 3 had always thought the mansion, with its turrets and high walls, resembled a medieval castle. But it was ultra-modern in construction and built of bombproof white concrete. Its color blended with the snow and ice so that the estate appeared to be part of the frozen landscape.

One of the home's many garage doors opened and the SUV slid inside. The door whirred closed behind them. The driver quickly exited the vehicle and opened the rear door. Number 3 stepped out and was escorted into the home's massive study by one of the servants and asked to wait.

Taking off her parka, she approached the roaring stone fireplace to warm her hands.

Hearing a noise behind her, she turned and saw number 1 at the open door, a smile on his kindly face. He was tall and stooped, with a thick mane of white hair. The old man was in his mid-eighties.

"Number 1," she said, "it's so good to see you."

He grinned broadly. "We can dispense with the numbers for one day, don't you think?"

"I'd like that, papa," she replied, using the term of endearment she used for him. It had started years ago after she'd been hired to run the operation. She had become close to number 1 and his wife, number 2. The elderly couple had, in effect, become her family.

The old man approached her and embraced her with both arms. They hugged briefly and afterwards she said, "How's mama?"

The man's smile faded. "Not well, I'm afraid."

"I'm sorry to hear that, papa. What can I do to help?"

He nodded, his kindly face showing concern. "Mama has the best doctors. I flew in a new specialist from Switzerland last week." He shrugged. "But he has no answers."

"I'm sorry, papa."

"As am I." He got a far-away look in his eyes, then he focused on her and led her by the hand to one of the opulent, heavily-brocaded 17th century French sofas.

"Let's sit and talk," he said, his tone more business-like now. They sat on opposite couches and he leaned forward as his eyes gazed into hers.

"Tell me about the operation, Angel," he said, using her real name.

"Of course, papa." She stared down at her clasped hands, then back at the elderly man. "Everything is proceeding on schedule, but ...."

"But what?"

"We've had a few complications, papa."

"I see," he replied, a sharp edge in his voice. "I don't like disappointments. And neither does my wife."

"I know. I hate to bring you bad news." She glanced down at her clasped hands again, the familiar acid taste in her mouth returning.

"Get on with it, number 3," he snapped. "Tell me!"

She gazed up at him. "Of course." She hated to disappoint the man, but she had no choice. "The FBI has started an investigation into the three high-profile murders. It appears the people investigating are part of a small team created by President Harris. A secret team that doesn't report through regular government channels."

The old man's face turned a deep shade of crimson. "That's bad news. Very bad news."

"There's more, papa."

"More?"

"Yes. Apparently the FBI investigation has led them to the warehouse in Darton, Georgia. And could lead them to our source at the ... government facility nearby."

Number 1's bushy white eyebrows shot up and his fists clenched. "That's unacceptable, Angel."

"I agree. But don't worry, I'll handle it."

"How?" he demanded.

"I've gotten us to this stage, haven't I?"

The man nodded thoughtfully. "That's true, you have." He paused a moment. "What about the rest of the operation? Is it on schedule?"

"Yes, papa. Operation Fireball is on schedule, just like we planned. We now have 38 people embedded within the government organization. With that many eyes and ears on the inside, we can execute the operation without difficulty. And with our people outside the government covering the other aspects, our goals are within reach. It's been very expensive. But like you've always said, money buys influence."

"That's excellent news, number 3."

She smiled, rose from her sofa and sat down next to the elderly man. Looking eagerly into his kindly, wrinkled face, she placed a palm on his cheek. "Please, papa," she whispered. "Please call me by my name. You know how much I like that."

The man returned her smile. "Of course, Angel. You've been like a daughter to us, child."

# Chapter 26

*National Security Agency - Headquarters*
*Fort Meade, Maryland*

J.T. Ryan had never been to the NSA headquarters before and found the massive complex of buildings a staggering sight. After an hour of intensive security checks to gain access, he and Erin Welch had been cleared into the site.

Ryan drove his rented sedan through the complex, as Erin, who was knowledgeable about the place, pointed out the various landmark buildings. Nestled within the U.S. Army's highly-secure Fort Meade, the NSA headquarters was its own city, with over 30,000 employees and contractors. The area was so large that it had over 37 miles of roads. The parking lots covered 325 acres of land and 37,000 cars were registered at the place. The four dozen buildings at the complex contained over seven million square feet of floor space. The location had its own post office and also its own police force with seven hundred uniformed officers. It also had its own SWAT team and fire department. To those outside of the NSA complex, the place was virtually invisible, hidden from the world by tall walls and a labyrinth of barbed wire and electrified fences. Enormous security boulders, motion detectors, hydraulic anti-truck devices, cement barriers, and attack dogs provided additional layers of security. The NSA complex was also guarded by submachine-gun toting commandos in black uniforms nicknamed 'men in black' by the facility's employees.

Erin, who was sitting in the passenger seat, pointed to a massive building that towered over the rest of the facility. "That's the actual headquarters building, where the general's office is located."

Ryan nodded as he gazed at the impressive, but yet sinister-looking structure. Ultra-modern and boxy, it had a shiny black-glass exterior that made it look like a giant Rubik's cube. Erin had told him earlier that the building contained over three million square feet of office space, and was so large that you could fit the U.S. Capitol inside – four times over. The large expenditure it took to build the complex was justified because the NSA was the national-level intelligence agency for the U.S. Department of Defense. The NSA was responsible for global monitoring, collection, and processing of information of foreign intelligence and counter intelligence. It specialized in a discipline known as Signals Intelligence, with the acronym of SIGINT. It uses its own network of satellites to monitor voice transmissions, along with electronic data. The Agency scrutinizes all email, phone call, and social media transmissions. Its annual budget exceeds $11 billion per year.

The NSA maintains a physical presence in the U.S. and also has facilities in many countries around the world. The overseas locations eavesdrop on high-value targets such as presidential palaces and embassies of foreign governments.

Ryan drove into the parking lot of the massive headquarters building. After going through several more layers of tight security, he and Erin were shown into the office suite of Lieutenant General Thomas Kyle.

The general greeted them and ushered them into a sitting area adjacent to his office where they all sat down. A burly man with a tight crew-cut, Kyle appeared much more affable than Colonel Hesler had been during their visit of the NSA - Georgia facility. The general was wearing a dark blue uniform and by the ribbons on his chest Ryan could tell the man had served tours in Iraq, Kosovo, and Vietnam.

"Mike Corso called me," the three-star officer said, "and told me that you'd be coming to see me. I understand it has to do with an investigation the Bureau is conducting."

"That's correct, General," Erin replied. "The FBI is investigating the murders of the Supreme Court Justice, the Senate Majority Leader, and the Cardinal."

Kyle nodded. "Tragic, those deaths. I knew the senator personally. A fine man."

"It is tragic," Erin said. "We believe the murders were part of a conspiracy possibly involving government employees."

The officer's eyebrows raised. "Really? Since you're here, I assume you think someone at the NSA is involved?"

"It's possible, General."

The three-star rubbed his jaw. "I've run this agency for years and am proud of the work we do here and across the world. Our mission is to keep Americans safe from our enemies. And I believe we've done a good job at exactly that."

"I understand, sir," Erin continued. "I'm not accusing you of anything. But the NSA has over 50,000 employees worldwide. It's possible rogue agents within your ranks are involved."

The general rubbed his jaw again and looked deep in thought. He was quiet a long moment, then said, "We have become such a large government agency that keeping track of all of our people, 24/7, is not easy. I grant you that. We do extensive background checks on everyone employed here, but ...." He paused. "Things were simpler before the invention of the dark Net. Before that we could track all internet communication by a user's IP address. But now criminal elements use software like TOR, also known as an 'onion router', to hide IP addresses through multiple phony layers. Even we at the NSA have trouble deciphering these communications."

"Sir," Ryan said, "I've developed leads that took me to Darton, Georgia, a town close to the NSA facility at Fort Gordon. When Erin and I met with Colonel Hesler there, we received a very chilly reception from him. That reinforced our suspicion that he was covering up something."

General Kyle gave them a tight grin. "I wouldn't read too much into that, Ryan. The colonel is old school and a hard-ass. A good man, but a hard-ass nevertheless. He probably kicked you out of his office."

"Pretty much," Erin said.

The general nodded. "I'll take care of it. I'll call Hesler and tell him in no uncertain terms that you're to be given his full cooperation."

"Thank you, General," Ryan said.

"You're welcome," the officer replied. "Anything I can do to help, please let me know. By the way, Ms Welch, I had a question for you."

"Sir?"

"Since Mike Corso is involved," the general continued, "and since he's the president's DNI, I'm assuming this plot is somehow related to the White House?"

Erin glanced at Ryan, then back at the officer. "I'm sorry, General. But that's classified."

The three-star smiled. "I'm in charge of the National Security Agency, the country's premier intelligence agency. Surely I'm cleared for that information."

"As I said," Erin repeated, "that's classified."

The general's smile vanished. "I see."

After the meeting concluded, Ryan and Erin made their way out of the massive building. When they got back inside their parked car, Erin said, "What'd you think?"

"Well," Ryan replied, "we got a hell of a lot better reception than at Fort Gordon. On the surface at least, it appears General Kyle wants to cooperate."

Erin nodded. "What's your gut say, J.T.? Do you trust Kyle?"

Ryan glanced out the window of the car up at the sinister-looking building with its shiny black-glass exterior. "I think so. But we can't be sure, can we? Remember what President Harris told us: 'Suspect everyone. Trust no one.' I say we follow the evidence and see where it takes us."

"I agree," she said. "We follow the evidence."

"I had a thought, Erin. For when we get cleared to return to the NSA facility in Georgia."

"What's that?"

"The colonel is going to be pissed about cooperating with us. Especially after his boss the general calls him and reads him the riot act. I think I should go back by myself. I'm an Army guy. I think I can relate to him better on my own."

Erin thought about this a moment. "Okay, J.T. That's a good idea. Just one thing. If he still gives you a hard time, promise me you won't pull one of your Rambo stunts."

Ryan grinned. "Who me? I'm a choir boy. I always go by the book."

Erin rolled her eyes. "Spare me. I know you too well."

He laughed, started up the car, and drove out of the parking lot.

# Chapter 27

*An undisclosed location*

Number 12 went outside of his office building and walked to a nearby wooded park. Pulling out his satellite cell phone, he made a call.

"This is 12," the man said when the other side picked up. "I have information for you, number 3."

"Are you using an encrypted phone?"

"Yes, number 3."

"Go ahead then."

"Per your direction, we've accelerated the demonstrations. We've been able to infiltrate our people into the protest groups in over ten major cities."

"That's excellent. What about the other matter we discussed?"

"Yes, number 3. That part of the operation is also on track. We've been able to persuade several more congressmen to join our cause. We now have enough."

"Was it expensive?"

"Extremely," number 12 replied. He went on to describe the large amounts of cash involved.

"All right. I expected it would take an incredible amount of money. When do you think you'll see results?"

"Very soon, number 3. Keep an eye on the news. I expect it'll break within days."

"Excellent. One other thing. Make sure to keep number 27 apprised of your progress. We need to coordinate our efforts."

Number 12 heard a click on the line and knew the woman had hung up.

# Chapter 28

*Vatnajokull, Iceland*

Angel had intended to leave Iceland and return to Norway days ago, but bad weather had restricted air travel and she'd had to extend her stay at papa's estate. As she hung up the call from number 12, she was glad she'd stayed so she could relay the good news to the old man personally.

Going out of her guest bedroom, she took the elevator to the first floor and went into the large study. There she found number 1, sitting close to the stone fireplace, where a roaring fire was burning.

She approached him. "Papa, I have good news."

His wrinkled, kindly face broke into a smile. "I'm glad. Sit, get comfortable and tell me."

Angel perched on a nearby wingback chair and said, "I just spoke with one of my key people. He told me things are progressing extremely well. We've been able to obtain support for one of our main objectives."

"Which one, Angel?"

The woman grinned. "The one requiring congressional approval."

"Ha – that one! Tell me more!"

"As you know, papa, we needed a certain number of congressmen in order to begin impeachment proceedings. We now have that."

Number 1 nodded, his smile lighting up like a Christmas tree. "Yes. That is one of my major goals."

"My source told me we should see something on the news very soon."

"You've done well, Angel. Exceedingly well. I know it's a long process to impeach and then indict an American president, but this is an excellent start. Good work!"

"Thank you, papa."

"One day, hopefully soon," the old man said with venom, "I'll see that bastard, President Harris ejected from the White House. I'll finally get my revenge for what he did to me. I'd rather see him dead, but I'll accept his disgrace and fall from power as a good substitute."

Angel nodded. "Yes, number 1. I'm sure you'll see him impeached and convicted." She was elated at seeing the old man so euphoric. She wondered if now was a good time to bring up her own agenda and incorporate it into the operation. Angel had mulled this over for months, trying to decide on the timing. Realizing it could be now or never, she plunged ahead.

"Papa," she said sweetly. "I had an idea. An idea to enlarge and enhance Operation Fireball."

"Change Fireball?"

"That's right, papa. I think we should utilize all of the resources at our disposal. To make Fireball even bigger and better than it already is. Now that we have so many people within the NSA involved, we can tap any phone, listen to any conversation, look at any bank account, monitor every aspect of every American's life. With that much power, we can blackmail anyone that we can't bribe."

Number 1 stared at her, a perplexed look on his face. "The whole purpose of Fireball is to bring down President Harris and everyone else in the United States who supports him. Isn't that enough?"

"Of course, papa. That's my goal also. It has been for years. But what if we take it one step further."

"I don't know what you mean."

She leaned forward in the chair and began describing the enhanced operation. When she was done twenty minutes later, he looked at her in disbelief.

"You can't be serious," he said, a stunned expression on his face.

"But I am, papa. I am. You see, with this new, bigger operation you'll get your payback and so will I."

Number 1 sat there quietly for several minutes as he processed the enormity of what she proposed. Finally, after what seemed like an eternity to her, he spoke.

"I like it, Angel. I like it very much."

# Chapter 29

*Copenhagen, Denmark*

Rachel West had run into a brick wall.

She had been trying for days to get the Danish government to release the name of the person who rented the mailbox in Skagen, Denmark.

The authorities, citing the country's strict privacy laws, had insisted she obtain a court order. She knew that could take weeks, if not months, to obtain, and time was something she didn't have. Her boss at Langley had told her it was imperative they find the conspirators ASAP.

Realizing she'd have to use illegal means to learn the information, Rachel was in her hotel room now, doing research on her laptop. She needed to find where the mailbox records were kept, hack into that system, and learn the person's identity. But as she scanned through a variety of websites, a breaking news banner scrolled along the bottom of her computer screen. Rachel clicked on the link and was shocked at the news story.

A group of United States congressmen had introduced a bill on the House floor. The bill called for the impeachment of President Steve Harris. She read further in the *Washington Post* story, which stated that the Articles of Impeachment, as the bill was described, was already generating widespread support in Congress.

But before she could finish reading the article she felt her cell phone buzz. Pulling the phone out of her pocket, she saw the info screen, which said *Langley*.

"You've seen the news?" Alex Miller asked.

"About the impeachment proceedings?"

"That's right, Rachel."

"Just read about it."

"Okay," her boss replied. "I need you back here. Now. Mike Corso called an emergency meeting at the White House. Since you're on the task force you have to attend."

"Yes, sir."

"When's the next flight out of Copenhagen to D.C.?"

Rachel recalled the schedules for SAS Airlines. "There's one leaving in two hours."

"Be on it," he said and hung up.

# Chapter 30

*Atlanta, Georgia*

J.T. Ryan was driving east on I-20. He was on his way to the NSA-Georgia facility in Fort Gordon. Glancing at his rearview mirror, he spotted a semi approaching fast.

Traffic was light on the Interstate and the large truck was easily visible as it closed the distance between the vehicles. Ryan steered his Tahoe from the passing lane into the right hand lane of the highway so the semi could pass.

But instead of passing, the truck followed Ryan's SUV.

The PI tensed and gripped the wheel tightly as he stomped on the accelerator, trying to pull away from the speeding semi.

He noticed the twin-smokestacks of the truck spewing thick black smoke as it raced forward, inching closer and closer to the SUV's back bumper. His heart thudding in his chest, Ryan jerked the steering wheel left to get away from the huge vehicle.

But the truck mimicked his actions and a split-second later he felt the shuddering impact of the crash as the semi smashed into his Tahoe. The SUV's rear window imploded and shards of glass rained on him.

Ryan fought the wheel as the Tahoe began spinning out of control. He saw the guardrail rushing toward him and felt a blinding pain as his vehicle crashed into the railing.

Then everything went black.

# Chapter 31

*Washington, D.C.*

Hobbling painfully on crutches, J.T. Ryan reached the hotel room window and opened the drapes. In the distance he could see the White House, his destination for tomorrow's meeting.

He had checked into the Trump Hotel earlier, and after filling Erin in on the details of his recent car crash, had come up to his room to recuperate.

Opened in 2016, the hotel was built on the site of the historic Old Post Office Pavilion. It was built by Donald Trump, the businessman turned president, whose term in office had preceded the Harris administration.

Turning away from the window, he lowered himself onto a wingback chair and propped his aching left leg on the bed. He was asleep in minutes and awoke sometime later by a knock at his door.

Ryan stood and after positioning the crutches under his arms, he awkwardly pulled his revolver, and hobbled to the door. He glanced through the spyhole and was amazed at who he saw in the corridor.

He eagerly opened the door. "You're a sight for sore eyes!" he said with a grin. "Come in, beautiful!"

Rachel West, a radiant smile on her face, entered the room and he closed the door behind her.

Her smile turned into a frown and she pointed to the crutches. "What the hell happened, J.T.?"

Ryan shook his head slowly. "Car crash."

She placed a hand on his cheek and caressed it. "That black eye looks nasty. Are you okay?"

He nodded. "I will be in a couple of days. The doctor told me my leg is badly bruised – luckily no bones were broken."

"That's a relief."

He slipped his revolver back into his hip holster and said, "Got to sit down, though." Using the crutches he hobbled over to the bed and sat.

Rachel perched on the wingback chair nearby and leaned forward. "Tell me what happened, J.T."

"A semi crashed into my SUV. When I regained consciousness, the cops and EMTs were there, but the truck was long gone."

"You think it was an accident?"

"I doubt it, Rachel. The truck intentionally smashed my Tahoe. I'm sure it's connected to our investigation. You know what really pisses me off?"

"What?"

He shook his head sadly. "My SUV. It's totaled! I loved that Tahoe."

Rachel smiled. "Men and their cars." Then she turned serious. "You're lucky to be alive."

"I know I am." He shifted his leg to alleviate the pain. "God, I'm so glad to see you! I was hoping you'd be here for this meeting."

Ryan gazed at the stunningly beautiful blonde, who as usual was dressed in casual clothes. She was wearing a blue, long-sleeve denim shirt and black jeans, and her long hair was pulled back in a ponytail.

"You look gorgeous as always, Rachel. I've missed you."

Her vivid blue eyes sparkled. "I've missed you too. A lot." She got up from the chair and sat next to him on the bed.

Ryan put his arms around her and drew her close, then leaned down and kissed her tenderly on the lips. She kissed him back, hungrily.

They held the kiss and loving embrace for several minutes, their hands exploring each other's body over their clothes. Both of them were breathing heavy and by the look in her eyes he knew she was as aroused as he was.

Suddenly she pulled away from him. "I've got to tell you something, J.T. Something important."

"You're pregnant," he said with a grin. "From the last time we saw each other."

She cuffed his shoulder. "No smartass. I'm not pregnant." She stood and began pacing the room.

"Oh, oh," he said in a serious tone. "You're stalling. Okay, Rachel. You might as well give me the bad news."

She stopped pacing and faced him. "It's my boss."

He pointed an accusing finger at her and laughed. "You fell in love with your boss so you're dumping me."

Rachel glared at him. "God, don't be such a wiseass! Quit joking around!"

He held his palms in front of him. "Sorry. I get carried away sometimes."

"I know, J.T. But this is serious, okay?"

He nodded.

"My boss, Alex Miller," she continued, "told me in no uncertain terms that for the duration of this investigation, you and I ...."

"You and I what, Rachel?"

She grimaced. "You and I can't carry on a personal relationship."

Ryan's heart sank. "Why the hell not?"

"Remember when we were on that mission together in China?"

"Of course."

"I disobeyed a direct order, J.T., in order to help you out."

"I know you did. Without your help I probably would have been killed."

"What I never told you," she said, "was that disobeying Alex's order almost cost me my job." She paused and her eyes misted. "We can't be intimate until this mission is over." A tear rolled down her cheek and she dabbed it away with her hand. "You know how I feel about you, J.T."

He nodded sadly, his heart aching as much as his wounded leg. "I know you do, babe. I feel the same way about you. I have for a long time. But we're both professionals. We have a job to do."

"I'm glad ... you understand," she replied, her voice breaking a bit. It was clear by her morose look that she was as torn up over this as much as he was.

Rachel gazed around the room. "You got anything to drink around her? I could use some Absolut right about now."

"Check the mini-fridge," he said.

She strode to the small refrigerator, opened it and rummaged through the miniature bottles of liquor stored there. "No vodka, but there's bourbon in here." She pulled out four of the miniature bottles and two Heinekens, and placed them on a small table by the bed where Ryan was sitting.

"I'm taking medication for the pain," he said, "I shouldn't mix it with liquor."

She grinned. "Screw that, J.T. I'm not drinking alone."

Rachel sat on the chair, opened one of the miniature bottles of bourbon and gulped it down. Then she popped open a can of Heineken and drank from it.

Ryan reached over, opened the other can of beer, and took a sip.

They sat silently for a minute as they drank Heineken.

"What do you think this meeting tomorrow is all about?" he asked.

"Two things, from what I can figure," she said. "I think the DNI, Mike Corso, wants an update on our investigation."

"And the second thing?"

"You've heard about the impeachment proceedings against President Harris?"

"Yes," he said. "But I don't follow politics much. In fact, I don't follow politics at all. And since I was in that car crash, I'm kind of behind on what's going on. But I did see something on the news about it. You think the impeachment hearings are connected with the rest of the attacks against the president?"

She drank more of her beer. "I'd bet on it." She waved a hand around the room. "This city. Washington D.C. is a swamp. It's built on dirty politics."

Ryan nodded. "You're probably right."

The woman finished her beer, then picked up another mini-bottle of liquor and after opening it gulped it down. She repeated the action with the third and the fourth mini-bottles of bourbon.

She sat there for a long moment as if in deep thought. Then a small smile played on her lips. "You know, J.T., that I'm in the CIA. And one thing we do extremely well at the CIA is to keep secrets."

"What's your point?"

Her grin widened. "My point is Alex never has to find out. As long as you can keep a secret also."

Catching her meaning instantly, he returned the smile. "I can keep a secret."

Her vivid blue eyes sparkled. "I had a feeling you could." Then she slowly undid the top three buttons of her shirt.

"I'm an injured man," he said with a chuckle. "You'll have to be gentle with me."

"I don't think you'll be complaining at the end of the night."

Rachel got up from her chair and stood in front of him. He was still sitting on the bed and he gazed up at her, intoxicated by her drop-dead good-looks. Even though the blonde wore no makeup and was dressed in simple clothes, he'd always found her to be the most exciting woman he'd ever been with.

"God, you're beautiful, Rachel."

That small smile played on her lips again. "I bet you say that to all the girls."

"There are no other girls. You're the only woman I want."

"Right answer," she said with a grin. She placed both her palms on his cheeks, leaned down and kissed him softly on the lips. They held the sensual kiss for a long moment and his pulse quickened.

When she pulled away, she whispered, "I've missed you John Taylor Ryan. A lot. We need to make up for lost time."

She glanced at his crutches, which were leaning against the bed. Reaching over, she grabbed them and took them to a far corner of the room.

"What are you doing?" he asked.

Rachel gave him a wicked grin. "I want you staying on that bed. Now you won't be able to get away."

"You're a hussy," he said with a chuckle.

"And you're a man-slut."

They both laughed as she walked back and stood in front of him. Her expression turned serious. "You know how much I care about you. How deep my feelings are for you, J.T."

His heart soared, feeling more elated than he had in a long time. "I feel the same about you. I ..."

She placed a finger to his lips. "Don't say it. Please."

The two people had danced around the "L" word for a long time, not quite saying it out loud. Both had come out of bad relationships with other people, and now were reluctant to express how much they meant to each other, fearing it would change their affection.

"You're right, Rachel. I won't say it out loud. But you know how much I care for you. I have for some time."

"I know. A woman can always tell."

"Really? How?"

She grinned. "Because women are smarter than men."

They both laughed again.

Then he said, "Are you sure about this? If Alex finds out ... even suspects we're ...."

"I don't care."

"You'll get fired, Rachel."

"So be it. You're more important to me than my damn job."

He nodded. "As are you."

She gave him that wicked grin again, and reaching with her hand she pulled off the scrunchie that was holding her hair in a ponytail. Her long blonde tresses cascaded past her shoulders. Then she slowly undid the rest of the buttons of her denim shirt. When she was done he could clearly see her bra and the deep cleavage of her sensual curves.

His pulse quickened and he became aroused.

Rachel seductively took off her shirt and let it drop to the floor. She stepped closer to him so that she was standing only an inch from where he sat.

With her vivid blue eyes sparkling, she held his gaze as she reached back with a hand and undid the clasp of her bra. Flashing that wicked grin of hers again, she whispered, "Let the games begin."

Totally aroused and intoxicated by her raw sexuality, Ryan reached up with both hands and pulled her to him. They kissed hungrily and then they rolled on to the bed, as they tore each other's clothes off.

# Chapter 32

*The Situation Room*
*The White House*
*Washington, D.C.*

"Along with the Oval Office," Mike Corso said as he began the meeting, "this room is the most secure in the White House. There's a high probability we can't be spied on in here."

On the conference table was the device J.T. Ryan remembered from a previous meeting. He watched as the DNI reached over and turned on the device, and a green light flashed on the instrument. "But we can never be certain," Corso added, "and that's why we have this."

Ryan glanced around the room at the other attendees. Next to him was Erin Welch. On the other side of the long table was Alex Miller, the Director of Special Operations for the CIA, and Rachel West.

Earlier, when Rachel had first come into the room, she had spotted Ryan sitting at the table and her cheeks flushed, no doubt recalling the prior evening's torrid lovemaking. She had glanced nervously at Miller, but her boss seemed oblivious to her reaction.

Mike Corso, who was sitting at the head of the conference table, leaned forward in his executive chair. "The president will not be joining us today," the DNI said. "I'll brief him later on the progress of your investigation. Before I tell you the reason for this meeting, I'd like each of you to brief me on what you've learned so far. Erin, as team leader, has kept me informed of course, but I wanted to hear it first hand from all of you."

Erin began, recounting what she'd found out, and she was followed by Alex Miller and then by Rachel West. The CIA woman concluded her remarks by stating that she was at a dead-end, since the Danish authorities were stonewalling her on releasing the name of the mailbox renter.

"I'll take care of that," Corso replied. "I'll call their government right after this meeting and get that info for you. As DNI I have a lot of pull with foreign governments."

"Thank you, sir," Rachel said.

The DNI nodded and faced Ryan. "Okay, J.T. It's your turn. I see you're using crutches and have a black eye. What happened?"

The PI recounted the details of the car crash. "I'm pretty sure, sir, that it was no accident."

"I agree, it's too coincidental." Corso shook his head slowly. "Those bastards, whoever they are, will stop at nothing."

Ryan continued, briefing the man on the rest of his investigation. Then he said, "My next stop is to re-visit the NSA facility at Fort Gordon, Georgia."

"Okay," Corso said. "Erin told me that both of you suspect people within the NSA are involved?"

Ryan nodded. "Yes. That's right. The National Security Agency has all the high-tech tools to plan and execute a sophisticated conspiracy like this." He pointed to the device resting on the conference table, which was still glowing green. "I remember when we had the first meeting of this task force, the meeting that was held in the Oval Office. Right before that meeting ended, someone was able to breach all of your security measures. It would take a hell of a lot of sophistication to do that."

"That's true, J.T. By the way, you met with the head of the NSA, General Kyle. Do you suspect him?"

"He was very cooperative, sir. At this point I would say no."

"And Colonel Hesler, who runs the NSA operation in Georgia. You met with him also."

"We did, sir."

Corso rubbed his jaw. "What's your opinion of him? You think he's involved with the criminals?"

Ryan shook his head. "I honestly don't know. He gave us a hard time and literally walked out of our meeting. It's possible he's covering something up. But it's too early to make that determination. I have to follow the evidence – that's the only way we'll know for sure."

"Okay." Corso gazed around the room at the other attendees. "Good work, everyone. Keep at it. I know this investigation is a difficult one. A dangerous one, as Ryan has already found out first hand. But the president needs you. The country needs you. Don't let us down."

The DNI glanced nervously at the device on the table, which was still glowing green. Obviously satisfied the meeting wasn't being bugged, he appeared to relax.

"All right," Corso continued, "now let me tell you why you're all here. We've had recent developments which are serious. Very serious. As you've no doubt seen on the news lately, there's been widespread demonstrations and even rioting occurring in many of our cities across the country. From the investigations we've conducted, it's clear these acts are not random. In many cases we've learned that people are being paid to protest and riot. We don't know who's paying them but it's obviously an organization with deep pockets. Tragically, innocent bystanders have been killed and injured during the riots. People who just happened to be nearby when the riots erupted."

Corso paused a moment. "These riots are ostensibly in response to President Harris's policies, but I believe it's deeper than that. There is an anti-American, anti-government tone to the protests. And sadly, we've seen fake news stories which support the protesters. The stories are fueling the anger and hatred. And these fake news stories are popping up everywhere – on TV newscasts, radio, and on social media sites. This rash of fake news is so well coordinated that we suspect it is also funded by the cabal."

The DNI leaned forward in his chair. "And three days ago things got worse. As I'm sure you saw on the news, a group of congressmen introduced a bill in Congress. Articles of Impeachment against President Harris. The process takes time and requires a multitude of public hearings."

Corso rubbed his jaw. "As you probably know, it's difficult to impeach a sitting president. It's only happened twice in the history of the United States. President Andrew Johnson was impeached in 1868 and President Bill Clinton in 1998. In both those cases the Impeachment was carried out by the House of Representatives and the matter was referred to the Senate. In both the Johnson and Clinton cases, the Senate did not convict, so the presidents stayed in power."

Corso stopped talking and glanced at the device on the table. It still glowed green and he continued. "But what's happening now is different. Much different."

The DNI reached into his suit jacket and removed a flash drive. He placed the flash drive on the table in front of him. "The president received this drive from a senator who is a close friend. Ever since the three key leaders were murdered, senators and congressmen have been reluctant to publically support President Harris. Luckily, there are still a few courageous people like the senator who gave us this flash drive."

Corso picked up the drive and held it up. "On here is a video. The video shows a masked man dressed in all black who describes in detail a sexual encounter between this senator and a fifteen-year-old girl. This encounter happened over forty years ago and according to the senator, it is all true. The teenage girl went on to become the senator's wife, so the extent of the scandal that would ensue if the information were to become public would be limited. Also the senator is retiring next year so he's less concerned than someone in the middle of their political career."

The meeting's attendees exchanged glances and a moment later Corso continued talking.

"There's more on the flash drive," he said. "The masked man goes on to say that the contents of the video will be kept secret and that a sum of ten million dollars will be deposited in an offshore bank account. But both of those things will only happen if the senator agrees to vote for impeachment conviction."

Ryan leaned back in his chair, shocked at what they'd just been told. "Are other congressmen and senators being blackmailed also?"

Corso nodded. "Yes. We know of two others who have been approached in the same way. An envelope arrived at their offices with the flash drive inside. Sordid, but true details about each of the elected officials. Different scandalous situations that happened in their pasts. Things unknown to the public. Dark secrets that could ruin careers. And in those cases also, a sweetener of ten million dollars as a bribe to obtain their vote."

"Sir," Ryan asked, "do you think that other people besides these three are being blackmailed and bribed?"

Corso nodded. "We do. We've heard rumors. But most people are afraid to come forward."

"Any clues on who the masked man is?"

"None, J.T. The video is professionally made. We haven't been able to trace it back to the source."

"I see," Ryan said. "Since the scandalous information was kept secret for so long, it would take quite a bit of research. Information only available if you had very sophisticated, high-tech resources."

"That's right," Corso said. "Which reinforces our suspicion that rogue elements within the NSA are involved."

"Sir," Erin interjected, "can I get a copy of that flash drive? I'd like to have our FBI lab in Quantico take a closer look at it. Maybe they can trace it back to the source."

Corso nodded. "Good idea, Erin. I'll have a copy made." He picked up the handset on the desk phone that was on the table, spoke into it briefly, and hung up.

Moments later Samantha Lowry, the Deputy DNI, stepped into the Situation Room. Ryan remembered her from a previous meeting. She was a very thin, mousy woman with frizzy hair. A dour-looking person, whose frown seemed to be a permanent fixture on her face.

Corso handed her the flash drive. "Samantha, please make a copy of this and give the original to Erin before she leaves today."

The mousy-looking woman took the flash drive. "Yes, sir." Then she left the room and closed the door behind her.

"All right," the DNI said grimly. "You can see what we're up against here. The situation, which was bad before, just got a lot worse. This blackmail and bribery scheme will accelerate the impeachment process. The president's prospects of being ejected from the White House are now higher. Much higher."

Corso paused and his shoulders sagged. "And something even more disturbing is happening. Something that I just started to realize recently. This blackmail and bribery scheme sets a very dark precedent. Everyone has secrets of some type in their past. Things they want to hide. There are no perfect people. If this conspiracy succeeds it would be open season on anyone. Everyone in positions of power, inside and outside of government. Judges, businessmen, religious leaders, entertainers, you name it."

Ryan thought through the ominous implications of what the DNI had just said. A sinking feeling settled in the pit of his stomach.

# Chapter 33

*Vatnajokull, Iceland*

Angel entered the bedroom and approached the hospital-style bed.

Number 2, a frail, white-haired woman in her eighties, was lying on the bed. Her physician was nearby, writing on a chart. Number 2 was sleeping and Angel whispered to the doctor, "How is she today?"

"Fairly well, considering," the man replied.

Angel nodded. "That's good. You can leave us now, Doctor. I'd like to have a word with her in private."

"Of course," the doctor said. He turned and left the room, closing the door behind him.

Angel lightly tapped the old woman's frail arm.

Number 2 woke with a start, her sunken eyes blinking rapidly.

"How are you, mama?" Angel asked sweetly.

The elderly woman's eyes focused and she scowled. "Don't call me that! I'm not your mother!"

"I'm sorry," Angel said. "I meant no disrespect."

The old woman's eyes burned with malice. "You can't fool me with your charm, number 3. Unlike that stupid husband of mine. I see right through you, you bitch!"

Angel lowered her eyes and stared at the floor. "I'm sorry, number 2."

"What the hell do you want, anyway?" the elderly woman screeched.

"I just wanted to see how you were feeling today."

"Why the hell do you care!" number 2 said vehemently. "My husband – " She tried continuing to talk but instead began coughing.

The old woman's coughing fit lasted several minutes and Angel waited quietly for it to subside.

When number 2 regained her composure, she used the bed-sheet to wipe dark green phlegm from her mouth. "My husband told me ... how you talked him into that ... crazy new plan of yours ...." She pointed a threatening finger at Angel. "I don't like it! It's insane! You're going to get us ... all killed ... you stupid bitch!"

Angel lowered her eyes again. "I'm sorry you don't like my new plan," she said nervously.

The elderly woman scowled. "You are a sorry bitch ... you're young and pretty ... and you've got my fool of a husband wrapped around your little finger ...." She coughed again, bringing up more phlegm. She wiped it away and continued. "But I see right through you, number 3 ... you can't fool me ... you and your whoring ways!"

"You and your husband are like family to me," Angel replied contritely. "Being an orphan, the two of you are like the parents I never had."

Number 2's eyes were like daggers. "Get out of my sight, you lying whore!"

"Please, ma'am ...."

The old woman pointed to the door and raged, "Get out! Now! Go back home to Norway! I'm sick of your lies ... and I'm sick of looking at you!"

Angel, sensing there was nothing she could do to change the elderly woman's mind, simply nodded. "As you wish." She turned and left the room.

Soon after, Angel was back in the Mercedes SUV that had brought her to the couple's secluded mansion days ago. She settled into the back seat as the chauffer began the long drive to Reykjavik.

Once there, she would board the private jet which would take her to her final destination in Norway.

# Chapter 34

*National Security Agency – Georgia*
*Fort Gordon, Georgia*

J.T. Ryan was shown into the same conference room as last time and sat down to wait.

Moments later Colonel Hesler stepped into the room, closed the door behind him, and sat down across from Ryan. As before, the tall, bald man was wearing his officer's dress blue Army uniform.

Colonel Hesler glared. "Where is she?"

"Where's who?" Ryan said.

"That uppity FBI woman. The one you were with last time."

"Oh. You mean Erin Welch."

Hesler nodded, still scowling. "Yeah. Her."

"She's back in Atlanta."

The colonel sneered. "That's good."

Ryan had a dawning realization. Hesler was old school, a man who resented women in positions of authority. Knowing he could use that to his advantage, he said, "I agree, Colonel. She's a hard ass."

Hesler stared at him, a curious expression on his face. "You don't like working for her?"

"Hell, no," Ryan lied. "But you know in today's world, a lot of women are put in charge. Gender equality and all that crap."

The colonel nodded. "Tell me about it. The Army is getting the same way. Can you believe we have women generals now?"

"So I've heard," Ryan said. "I'm glad I'm not in the Army anymore."

Hesler shrugged, his antagonistic attitude gone now. He leaned forward in his chair. "I looked up your service record, Ryan. Impressive stuff. Medal of Honor recipient for valor in combat. You served in the Rangers, the Green Berets, and you made captain in Delta Force. Tier 1. Not many people achieve that elite status."

"Thank you, Colonel. I appreciate that."

Hesler leaned back in the chair. "I guess we got off on the wrong foot, last time we met."

"Not a problem, sir."

"The Director of the NSA called me and told me to expect your visit. He asked me to give you and Erin Welch my full cooperation. I told him I always follow orders, even if I don't agree with them." The colonel smiled. "And seeing how it's just you here and not that uppity woman ...." Hesler extended his hand and Ryan shook it. "Welcome to Fort Gordon, Captain Ryan."

"Thank you, sir."

The colonel's brows furrowed. "You think there's a connection between this warehouse in Darton and people who work at this NSA facility?"

"I believe so, sir. The criminals we're investigating are using state-of-the-art technology to carry out its agenda. Technology readily available to rogue agents within the National Security Agency. I'm not accusing you. or your senior people of treason. But you have a lot of employees who work here."

"2,536," Hesler said, "to be exact."

"Yes, sir. It's possible some of them have been turned into conspirators."

Colonel Hesler got a far away look in his eyes. "There've been a few cases of that happening, Ryan. There was a contractor at the NSA facility in Hawaii named Edward Snowden. He leaked the NSA's secret surveillance programs. He was charged with treason and fled to Russia to evade arrest."

Ryan had heard of Snowden's case. It had made headlines when it happened in 2013.

"All right, Ryan. The possibility exists that we have some bad apples here. How can I help you?"

"Sir, I'd like to talk to your key people first. Your senior staff. See if I can gather information from them."

"What if that doesn't yield results?" the colonel asked.

Ryan thought through the daunting task of interviewing over 2,500 people, hoping it wouldn't come to that. "Sir, I'll cross that bridge when I get to it."

# Chapter 35

*Midtown*
*Atlanta, Georgia*

Instead of flying directly back to Denmark, Rachel West had decided to stop in Atlanta first, hoping to spend more time with J.T. Ryan. She was still waiting for Mike Corso to track down the mailbox renter in Denmark, and figured she'd put the downtime to good use.

After landing at Atlanta's Hartsfield, she rented a car at the airport and drove to Ryan's office in midtown. Rachel parked in the building's underground lot and made her way up to the seventh floor of the high-rise. She had never been to Ryan's office before and noticed that the name *J.T. Ryan and Associates – Investigations* was stenciled on the door.

Stepping inside, Rachel found a young woman at one of the desks in the sparsely furnished office.

The young woman glanced up from her laptop and cheerfully said, "May I help you, ma'am?"

"I'm looking for J.T.," Rachel replied. "Is he here?" She studied the young woman, a pert, attractive girl who looked to be in her late teens.

"No, ma'am, I'm sorry. But I can help you. I'm his associate, Lisa Booth."

Rachel remembered Ryan mentioning he'd hired a new private investigator to help him with his case load. "Oh, so you're Lisa." Rachel smiled. "You look awfully young to be a PI. You look like you just got out of high school."

Lisa sighed. "I get that a lot. I'm actually 25." Then in an eager tone added, "I graduated at the top of my class at the University of Georgia and aced my PI license exam!"

Rachel chuckled, amused at the young woman's enthusiasm. "Well, good for you, Lisa." She extended her hand and the two women shook. "I'm Rachel West."

Suddenly Lisa's eagerness vanished and a suspicious expression crossed her face. "So *you're* the super-secret-agent woman J.T. talks about." Lisa frowned. "How can I be sure it's really you?"

Rachel pulled out her CIA cred pack, flipped it open, and showed it to her.

The young woman inspected it carefully. "This looks real enough."

"That's because it *is* real."

Lisa stared at the CIA agent for a full minute, then said, "Wow."

"Wow, what?" Rachel asked.

"J.T. said you were pretty. But you're ... gorgeous. No wonder he's infatuated with you."

Rachel put away her cred pack and sat in the visitor's chair fronting the desk. "Where's J.T.?"

"I don't know, Ms West."

"You said you were his associate. How come you don't know where he is?"

Lisa frowned. "Normally I would. But he's on a secret operation. Something really hush-hush. He told me he was sworn to keep it secret."

Rachel nodded. "I understand."

Lisa pointed at her. "You're CIA – are you on that case also?"

"If I told you," Rachel said with a grin, "I'd have to kill you afterwards."

"So you are on it! Is that why you're here – to go over the case?"

"Actually I wanted to see him for personal reasons."

Lisa's mistrust returned. "What are your intentions with my boss?"

"Intentions? What do you mean, Lisa?"

"J.T. told me you two were an item. Like a girlfriend – boyfriend thing." Lisa frowned. "What are your intentions with him?"

"I don't see how that's any of your business."

Lisa pointed an accusing finger at her. "The last girlfriend he had dumped him. He was in a dark place for a long time. He almost became an alcoholic."

"I know," Rachel said. "When Lauren broke up with him he got very depressed."

"So I ask you again, Ms West. Are you planning on using him and then dumping him? He doesn't deserve that."

"I care for J.T. very much."

Lisa folded her arms in front of her and stared hard at the other woman for a long moment. Eventually her frown dissipated. "All right. I think you're being honest with me."

Rachel tucked her long blonde hair behind her ears. "You seem awfully concerned about J.T.'s love life. Is there something I'm missing here? Are you and Ryan, you know ...."

Lisa's face turned bright crimson. "Oh, God, no! He's my boss, for Christ sakes! I just want to protect him."

Rachel nodded. "Okay. I believe you." She paused a moment. "That's too bad J.T.'s not here. I was hoping to spend some time with him before I flew back to Europe. I left a message for him on his cell, but he must be tied up because he hasn't called back."

Just then Rachel's phone vibrated. She took it out of her pocket and answered the call.

"This is Mike Corso," she heard the man say. "Is your phone encrypted?"

"Yes, sir."

"All right, Rachel. I've talked with the authorities in Denmark. They've agreed to give you the information you need." Corso gave her more details.

"Thank you, sir."

"Not a problem. I assume you'll be heading back there?"

"Yes, sir. I'll be on the next flight to Copenhagen."

"Good luck," he said and hung up.

The CIA agent stood and put away her phone. "I've got to go, Lisa."

"Of course."

Rachel sighed, sad she wouldn't get a chance to see Ryan again. "When you see J.T., please let him know I stopped by."

"I'll do that, Ms West."

Rachel extended her hand. "It's good to have met you."

The two women shook hands and Rachel turned and left the office. She glanced at her watch and realized she could make the 3 p.m. flight to Denmark.

# Chapter 36

*An undisclosed location*

Knowing the woman would be furious at the news, the man had dreaded making the call and had postponed it for days. Realizing he had no choice, he picked up the handset of his desk phone, and after turning on the encryption setting, tapped in a number he'd memorized long ago.

When the call was answered, he said nervously, "This is 27. There's been a development, number 3."

"By your tone," she shot back, "I sense it's bad news."

"It is, ma'am."

"Well?"

"As you know, I've had someone tailing the private investigator who's been digging into our operation. Unfortunately it didn't go as planned."

"What the hell happened, number 27?"

"The semi crashed into his SUV, but Ryan wasn't killed ... only injured."

"Damn you, 27! I told you to take care of that fucking bastard! This is the second time you've fucked up! Are you totally incompetent?"

The man didn't answer, not wanting to antagonize her further, so he kept quiet. He could almost hear her teeth grinding.

"Listen you," she raged, "I don't care how you do it, just get rid of that maggot."

"Yes, ma'am."

"And 27," she added, "don't call me again until you have good news."

He heard her slam down the phone and the call went dead.

# Chapter 37

*Oslo, Norway*

Angel slammed the phone down, nearly cracking the plastic. Once again acid began churning in her stomach, the nauseous sensation pushing bile up her throat.

She reached in a desk drawer, took out her bottle of prescription-strength antacid and chugged directly from the container. She closed her eyes and took a few deep breaths to try to clear the negative thoughts from her mind. Gradually the stomach pain eased.

Opening her eyes, she gazed out her windows at the half-frozen lake below. It was snowing again, which was common during this time of year, and strong winds buffeted her luxurious two-story chalet.

Angel briefly considered calling number 1 to tell him about this setback, but knew it would be better to keep the news to herself. Especially since she had recently talked the old man into expanding the operation.

*No,* Angel thought, *from now on I'm not going to tell him bad news.* If she did, she realized, the old man would relay the info to his wife, and Angel's relationship with the old shrew was already poisonous enough.

A cold, calculating grin settled on Angel's beautiful face. *From now on, I'll run the operation as I see fit.* Her grin widened, wondering why she hadn't thought of doing this before.

# Chapter 38

*National Security Agency – Georgia*
*Fort Gordon, Georgia*

J.T. Ryan got up from the table, stretched his muscles, and limped over to the coffee machine in a corner of the conference room. After pouring himself another cup he limped back to the chair and sat, thankful that his injury had healed enough so that he was able to ditch the crutches.

He wasn't happy about the lack of progress he was making on the case.

He'd questioned all of Colonel Hesler's top people, the key officers, civilians, and NCOs at the NSA facility over the last several days. He'd talked with over 100 people and was no closer to finding a suspect.

In fact, everyone he interviewed had been cooperative. Having interrogated prisoners during his Army years, he was proficient at identifying 'tells', visual and aural clues guilty people unconsciously give off. None of those he questioned had shown any deception.

The problem was, he still had 2,400 more people to question, a daunting and exhausting task. And it wasn't like he could rush through the meetings – he had to carefully evaluate each potential suspect. But at the rate he was conducting the interviews, the process would take him months.

Just then a female sergeant came into the room and sat down across from him. She was next in line to be questioned. Ryan nodded to her, put down his coffee cup, and picked up her file from the high stack on the table.

# Chapter 39

*Midtown*
*Atlanta, Georgia*

J.T. Ryan parked his rented SUV in the underground lot of his office building, got out, and made his way up to his office on the seventh floor.

Ryan went inside and found Lisa Booth at work on her computer.

She glanced up from her laptop and smiled. "J.T.! You're back!"

"That I am," he replied as he slumped onto the chair behind his desk.

"I missed you, boss," the young woman said. She pointed to a stack of case files on her own desk. "We've had a ton of new work come in." The pretty girl grinned. "But being the resourceful employee that I am, I've been able to handle them all by myself."

In spite of his fatigue, Ryan chuckled at her infectious enthusiasm. "Good work."

Lisa studied him a moment. "You look exhausted, J.T. Are you okay?"

He was about to reply with one of his usual humorous retorts, but instead blurted out the truth. "Actually, no. I'm not okay. I'm getting nowhere fast on my investigation. And I'm running out of time."

"The secret case you won't tell me anything about?"

Ryan nodded. "That's the one."

"Maybe I can help, J.T."

He mulled this over. "I told you before. I can't."

The young woman folded her arms across her chest. "I'm your partner, remember? You need to trust me."

"Actually you're not my partner. You're an associate."

Lisa grinned. "One day soon I'll be your partner."

He smiled back. "I'll probably have to make you partner so you'll stop asking about it."

They both laughed at this.

"J.T.," Lisa said, "a few days ago you had a visitor." A sly smile crossed her face. "Your girlfriend was here."

"My girlfriend?"

"Yes, J.T. The super-secret-agent woman, Rachel West."

"Rachel was here? Where is she now?"

"Gone to Europe from what I could tell."

"And I missed her," Ryan said glumly.

Lisa nodded. "She's quite a looker. No wonder you fell for her."

"It's not just her looks," he replied testily. "I really care for her."

"Yeah, I bet."

"What does *that* mean, Lisa?"

"It means that men, in general, are much more attracted by the size of a woman's boobs than by the size of their brains."

Ryan was about to object but realized Lisa was right. As a rule, most men were like that. "I can't argue with that. But just so you know, I care for Rachel very much."

"I know, J.T. I can tell. I just want you to be careful. Remember what happened when that other woman broke up with you."

"That's not going to happen this time. Rachel and I are very close."

Ryan's cell phone buzzed in his pocket. He took it out and answered the call. It was Erin Welch, who gave him a disturbing update on the case. He hung up and put away the phone.

"Who was that?" Lisa asked.

"Erin at the FBI. We're running out of time. We need to solve the case and do it quick. The clock is ticking."

"Let me help, J.T."

Ryan was torn over what to do. He'd been sworn to secrecy by the president and by Mike Corso. But without additional resources, he knew he was at a dead end. After mulling it over another minute, he said, "All right. I'm bringing you in."

Her face lit up with enthusiasm. "You are?"

"I am, young lady. But I'm swearing you to secrecy. Is that clear?"

"Yes, sir," she said earnestly. "You can count on me."

"Okay. Let me fill you in." Ryan spent the next half hour telling her the details of the case. When he was done, he said, "So, I spent several days at the NSA facility at Fort Gordon, Georgia. I interviewed over 100 people and came up empty. There's over 2,400 more employees that I need to talk with. But I don't have the time. That's the problem."

Lisa pondered this for a minute. "We could split up the list and I could question the employees also. But I don't have your interrogation skills. Someone could lie to me and I may not pick it up." She went quiet again for another minute, then said, "But, I am good with computers."

"I know," he said, rolling his eyes. "You tell me that all the time."

Lisa grinned. "Because it's true all the time."

"All right, smarty pants. So tell me how your vaunted computer skills are going to be useful in this case."

"Do you have a list of everyone who works at that NSA facility?" she asked.

Ryan reached in a pocket and pulled out a flash drive. "In here are all the 2,536 people who work at that location. Names, addresses, and all the other particulars."

He handed her the flash drive and she inserted it into her laptop.

"What are you going to do with the information, Lisa?"

"I'll write a software program and crosscheck each person's record against possible suspicious activity."

Ryan nodded. "Good idea. Corso told us there's also an international connection. Rachel West is looking into possible ties in Denmark."

"Okay, J.T. I'll be sure to write that into the software."

"How long will this take?"

Lisa glanced at her watch. "Hours. Maybe days."

"What can I do to help?"

The young woman laughed. "You're a cave man when it comes to computers. It's a miracle you know how to use a smartphone."

Ryan pointed a stern finger at her and was about to argue the point, then simply shrugged. "I do miss my old flip-phone."

Lisa laughed. "Go home, get some rest, J.T. Finish healing from your injury. I'll call you when I'm done."

# Chapter 40

*Midtown*
*Atlanta, Georgia*

Exactly twenty six hours later Ryan got a call from Lisa telling him she'd found something important. The PI quickly left his apartment, and after making a stop at his neighborhood Krispy Kreme, drove the short distance to his office in midtown.

"I brought you a proper breakfast," Ryan said as he came into the office. He set the box of a dozen doughnuts on her desk.

Lisa looked up from her laptop and squealed in delight. "Chocolate! My favorite!"

"Mine too," he replied. "The breakfast of champions."

She picked up one of the doughnuts and munched on it happily. "Yummy!"

"I'm having a cup of coffee," he said. "You want one?"

Lisa shook her head. "No, thanks. I've had a gallon of it already."

Ryan went to the coffee machine on the file cabinet, poured himself a cup, and perched on a corner of her desk. "On the phone you said you found something."

"I did," she said in between bites of her pastry. "But let me finish eating first. I'm famished." She quickly devoured a second and then a third doughnut and then wiped her mouth with a napkin.

He noticed her bloodshot eyes. "Did you pull an all-nighter working on this?"

"I did, boss."

"I admire your dedication."

Lisa grinned. "Does that mean I get a raise?"

"That depends on the results, young lady."

"Okay." She turned her laptop so he could read the screen. "I developed the software program and ran all the people's names and information through it. I used several databases, including NCIC," she said, referring to the National Crime Information Center list. This database contains 15 million active criminal records and is used by more than 80,000 law enforcement agencies across the U.S. The NCIC is operated by the FBI. "Almost all the hits I got were relatively benign – traffic accidents, a few domestic arguments where the cops were called, several disputes with neighbors that resulted in civil lawsuits, that sort of thing. But one name popped that looked interesting."

"Who was it?"

She pointed to a name on the screen. "That guy. Luis Vega. A civilian working at the NSA. Average guy, mid-level manager. Married, with two kids. Normal in most ways except a few."

"And what were those, Lisa?"

"Remember you asked me to look into international connections?"

"Yeah."

"Well, Vega traveled to Oslo, Norway three times in the last two years."

"Did he vacation there?"

"Unlikely, J.T. He went alone without his wife or kids."

"Maybe it's work related."

Lisa shook her head. "I checked his employment records at the NSA. He wasn't traveling to Norway on business."

Ryan rubbed his jaw. "Interesting. Good work."

She closed the lid on her laptop. "So what's next? Do we go interrogate Vega now?"

"Nope. Your part's done. I'll go and interrogate him."

Lisa frowned. "How come I can't do field work? I'm a PI also."

"You are. And a good one too." He pointed to the stack of pending case files on her desk. "But I need you here working on those."

She pouted. "Sometimes, J.T., you're no fun at all."

Ryan grinned. "Cheer up. One day, when you become a partner, I'll hire a third person to handle all the paperwork. And then you can spend more time doing field work."

Her pout dissolved. "Really?"

"Yes, really."

# Chapter 41

*Lewiston, Georgia*

Luis Vega lived in Lewiston, a town on the outskirts of the NSA facility at Fort Gordon. J.T. Ryan had been following Vega for the last two days as the man went to work and came home. The PI was waiting for the ideal opportunity to interrogate him.

Ryan had already interviewed Vega at the NSA offices and sensed right away that the man was evasive in his answers. But the PI hadn't pressed him hard, knowing he would flee if he thought he was a suspect.

It was 7 p.m. now and dusk had set in. Ryan was following Vega's car and knew the man was headed home. Traffic was light on the rural, desolate road. Up ahead and to the right was a wooded area, a place Ryan had scouted out yesterday.

The PI floored the accelerator and his SUV lunged forward. A moment later the vehicle came alongside Vega's Lincoln sedan. Ryan surged past it and he cut his wheel sharply to the right.

Ryan heard the squeal of brakes as Vega stopped his car before it slammed into the SUV.

The PI braked hard and screeched to a halt, jumped out of the SUV, pulled out his revolver, and sprinted to the sedan.

Vega, seeing Ryan charge toward him, grabbed his own gun from his glovebox and climbed out of his car.

Ryan raised his revolver, and using it like a club, struck the man on the head.

Vega went to his knees and sagged to the pavement, unconscious.

After glancing around to make sure there was no one on the deserted road, Ryan dragged the unconscious man into the sedan. Then he drove the car off the road and deep into the wooded area. That done, he sprinted back to the road and drove his SUV alongside the car.

Although there were no streetlights for miles around, there was a full moon out which provided adequate visibility. Ryan dragged Vega out of his car and propped him up against a tree trunk.

A minute later the man regained consciousness and his eyes focused on Ryan.

"Are you crazy?" Vega shouted as he gingerly touched the back of his head.

"Probably," Ryan said.

"You can't do this! It's illegal!"

Ryan nodded. "You're right about that. It is illegal. That's why I brought you out here in the middle of nowhere."

"I answered all of your questions the other day, Ryan."

The PI jabbed a finger on the man's chest. "You lied to me."

Vega's eyes narrowed. "Fuck you!"

"I don't like it when people lie to me."

The NSA employee glanced around the wooded area, obviously sensing he was in a bad situation, which was about to get a lot worse.

Ryan studied the tall, powerfully built man. He was about the PI's height and weight.

"What do you want, Ryan?"

"The truth."

"About what?"

"About everything," Ryan said. "Start explaining why you took trips to Norway. And tell me how you can afford a very expensive home and a Lincoln on your NSA salary."

The man's eyebrows furrowed. Suddenly Vega jumped to his feet and charged Ryan.

The PI had been expecting him to flee and he punched him solidly on the solar plexus, then followed that with a powerful left jab to his nose.

Vega staggered back, dropped to one knee, and howled with pain as blood spurted from his broken nose. But the NSA guy was big and tough and charged Ryan again, blindly swinging both his fists.

The PI ducked and side-stepped him, punching him in the kidney. He followed that with an uppercut to Vega's face and a kick to his groin.

The NSA guy screamed as he dropped to the ground and this time he stayed down.

He came to a minute later, groaning, his nose bleeding and his right eye puffed up. He sat up and rested his back against the tree.

"I can keep this up all night," Ryan said, "it's all up to you."

"What ... do you ... want ...." Vega gasped out as he gulped in lungfuls of air.

"The truth."

"The truth ... about what ...."

"The conspiracy. The one you're involved with. The one that murdered the senator and the chief justice and the cardinal."

Vega's eyes bulged. "I had ... nothing ... to do ... with those murders ... somebody else ... did that ...."

"But you're involved somehow."

The man shook his head forcefully. "I've said ... too much ... already ... arrest me ... if you want ... I'll hire a good lawyer ...."

Ryan glared. "That's not how this is going to work. I'm not going to arrest you."

Vega wiped his bleeding nose with a hand as he continued to suck in air . "You have to ... that's the ... legal process ... in this country .... you're FBI ... you know that ...."

The PI clenched his fist and punched the man in the nose again. Vega flinched and screamed as more blood poured out of his broken nose. His jacket and shirt were covered with the red gore.

"I do work for the FBI," Ryan said. "But I'm not an agent. I'm a contractor. So I make up my own rules. I learned a long time ago that my methods are a hell of a lot faster way to get information."

Vega pulled out a handkerchief and held it to his nose to stop the bleeding.

"Are you going to talk now?" Ryan demanded.

The other man said nothing, his face defiant.

"You leave me no choice, Vega." The PI pulled out his revolver, removed five of the rounds from the cylinder and clicked the cylinder shut. Then he pointed the pistol at the man's head.

"You know how this works, Vega? It's called Russian roulette. There's one bullet left in my gun. Are you going to talk or do I pull the trigger?"

Vega grimaced as he looked into the barrel of the .357 Magnum revolver.

Ryan squeezed the trigger and the empty chamber clicked. "You got lucky that time, Vega. What do your think the odds are when I pull the trigger again? Ready to talk?"

The man stared at the handgun, sweat dripping from his face. He closed his eyes and swallowed hard. The PI squeezed the trigger again and the gun didn't fire.

The man's eyes opened wide as Ryan pressed the muzzle of the gun to his forehead.

Ryan was about to pull the trigger a third time when he smelled a foul odor and knew Vega had lost control of his bowels.

"I'll talk!" the man yelled. "I'll talk now!"

"You're sure, damn it?"

"Yes ... yes!"

"Tell me everything you know about this plot."

"I only know my part in it."

"Why is that, Vega?"

"It's all compartmentalized ... I only know my role ..."

"What's your role?"

"Using NSA resources ... I listen in on conversations at the White House ... and a few other places ... and report back."

"Who runs the operation? What's his name?"

"It's ... a woman."

"What's her name?"

Vega wiped more blood from his nose. "I don't know ... her name ... she goes by a number ... number 3."

"Where is she?"

"She lives ... in Oslo, Norway."

"Is that why you traveled there?"

Vega nodded. "Yes."

"Are there other people at your NSA facility who are involved?"

"I think so ... but I don't know ... for sure."

"Why not?"

"I told you, Ryan ... it's all compartmentalized ... I'm number 27 ... in the organization ... so I assume there are others ...."

"You think they're all here at this location?'

Vegas shook his head. "From what I can tell ... they're spread out ... over several NSA facilities ... in the U.S. and in other countries ...."

"Did you set up that warehouse in Darton, Georgia?"

"Yes ... and I hired people ... to do jobs for me ...."

Ryan considered this. "Where do you get the money to do all this?"

"I get wire transfers ... to my offshore bank account ... I tell number 3 what I need ... and the money's there the next day ... the operation is very well funded ...."

"Tell me more about the woman who runs the operation. Where does she live, specifically?"

"I don't know ... I fly to Oslo ... a van with two men pick me up ... they blindfold me ... and take me to this house by a lake ... she lives there ...."

"Okay. Describe her, Vega."

More gore spurted from the man's nose and he pressed the bloody handkerchief to stanch the flow. Eventually he said, "She's ... a very attractive woman ... raven hair ... long hair, past her shoulders ... she has ... a small scar on her ... left cheek ...."

"Okay. That's a start. Why were you so reluctant to talk before? I almost killed you a moment ago."

The NSA man nodded. "I know ... I'm afraid ... for myself ... but more for my wife and kids ... number 3 warned me that ... if I told anyone ... about the operation ... she'd have someone kill me and them .... and she's ... a cold-hearted bitch ... beautiful ... but cold as ice ...."

"All right, Vega. I get that. But why did you become part of this criminal group in the first place?"

The man pressed the red-stained cloth tighter to his nose. "Money," he blurted out. "The money ... they offered me ... was too damn good ... to pass up ...."

Ryan nodded, knowing greed was at the core of most crimes. "What's the end game of the group? What do they want to accomplish?"

Vega shook his head. "I'm not sure ... I just did what I was told ...."

"You sold out your country for money? Without even knowing how it could affect the U.S.? Innocent people were murdered, you bastard. You disgust me, Vega!"

The NSA man stared at the ground. "I'm not proud of it."

"I should beat the hell out of you and leave you out here to die. It's what you deserve."

Vega glanced up at Ryan. The NSA guy's face blanched and he blinked rapidly. "Please no, Ryan. I've got a family."

Ryan mulled over what to do with the traitorous government employee. After a moment he said, "Lucky for you, Vega, you may still have more information. So I'll take you in for further interrogation by the FBI."

The other man's face flooded with relief. "Thank you ...."

Ryan closed his fist and punched Vega solidly on the nose. The man's head snapped back and hit the tree trunk. His body sagged, unconscious again.

The PI pulled out his encrypted cell phone and tapped in a number. When Erin Welch answered, he explained what had taken place and what he'd learned from Vega. Then he told her his location.

"I need you to send some of your FBI guys out here, Erin. To pick this guy up, take him to Atlanta and lock him up."

"Okay, J.T. I've got a few agents I can trust. Wait there until they show up."

"You got it. We need to squeeze Vega hard. Get every ounce of information he has."

# Chapter 42

*Copenhagen, Denmark*

Rachel West had been fighting the Danish government bureaucracy for days, trying to find the identity of the mailbox renter in Skagen. Even with Mike Corso interceding on her behalf, the authorities in Denmark were still reluctant to disclose the information.

Finally, after several more delays, Rachel had been granted a meeting with the country's Interior Minister. She had just been shown into his office, which was located in the historic Christiansborg Palace, home of the Danish Parliament.

Anderson Helsingor stood, walked around his desk and extended his hand. "Pleased to meet you, Ms West," he said in flawless English.

They shook hands and Helsingor pointed to the wingback chairs in the sumptuous office, outfitted with 18th century cherry-wood furniture, cut-glass chandeliers, and historic paintings.

Rachel sat across from the man, who was impeccably dressed in a gray, three-piece suit and brocade red silk tie.

"I have talked with Mr. Corso from the White House," Helsingor said. "I understand you are looking for information regarding a mailbox in Skagen."

Rachel nodded. "That's right. It's a pretty straightforward request. Unfortunately I've been stonewalled by your people."

The Interior Minister flashed an enigmatic smile. "They are only doing their jobs. You see, in Denmark, we take our privacy laws —"

"Very seriously," Rachel interjected. "So I keep hearing." She leaned forward in the deeply upholstered chair. "I'm trying to solve a triple homicide. It's a case involving U.S. national security. As an ally of our country, I'm sure you can make an exception in this case."

The man held his palms in front of him. "I wish I could help you. I really do. But I would be violating our Constitution if I were to release that information."

Rachel saw red, her jaw clenched, and she briefly considered slugging the imperious man. Instead she took a deep breath and let it out slowly. The last thing she needed was to get arrested in a foreign country.

"Surely you can tell me *something*, sir. Otherwise I'd think you were involved in a plot to commit murder."

The man's eyebrows arched. "Well ... I can tell you this. The person you are looking for is not Danish. They are from another country."

"That's a start. What else?"

"I have cooperated as much as I can, Ms West."

"I doubt that," she muttered under her breath.

Helsingor stood, walked over to his desk and pressed a button. Instantly two uniformed security guards came into the office. "These men will escort you out," the Interior Minister said curtly.

Once Rachel left the building, she strode to the parking lot and got in her rented Volvo. She started up the car and was about to drive off when she felt her phone vibrate. Reaching in her heavy coat, she pulled it out and answered the call.

"Hey, beautiful," she heard Ryan say.

"Hi, J.T. I missed you in Atlanta. I came by your office."

"So I heard. I wish we could have gotten together."

"Me too," she replied sadly. "Me too." She visualized the rugged-looking man with the boyish, easy-going grin.

"Don't worry. We'll see each other soon."

"I hope so, J.T. Is this a social call or business?"

"Both. I've got some information for you. Are you on a secure phone?"

"Yes."

"Okay, Rachel. I interrogated a guy who was involved."

"That's great. That's a big break."

"It is," he said. "The man is an employee of the NSA. His name is Luis Vega. He told me he secretly works for a woman who runs the criminal operation."

"What's her name?"

"No name, according to him. Apparently the scheme is highly compartmentalized. They refer to each other by numbers, not names. He's number 27 and the woman goes by number 3."

"Okay, J.T. What else did you learn?"

"This woman lives in a lakefront home somewhere in Oslo, Norway. Vega was there several times."

"Did Vega tell you anything else?"

"This number 3 is a striking-looking woman – very attractive, according to him. She has long black hair and a small scar on her left cheek."

"That's good. That's a hell of a lot more than I've been able to learn on my own. The bureaucrats in Denmark have been uncooperative."

"You think they're involved in a cover-up?"

"Hard to tell, J.T. Anything's possible. One thing's for sure: this criminal operation is big. Really big."

"I agree. And very well funded. Vega told me he received huge amounts of money whenever he needed it. No questions asked. This mysterious number 3 woman didn't hesitate to wire it to Vega's offshore bank account."

"I see. Did he tell you anything else?"

Ryan filled her in on more details, then said, "Vega is in FBI custody now. Erin Welch is continuing to question him. If I learn anything else I'll call you."

"Good. And when I find the raven-haired woman I'll let you know."

"Be careful, hon. These criminals are deadly."

Rachel laughed. "I'm a super-secret CIA agent. Bullets bounce off my chest and I can leap over tall buildings in a single bounce."

"That's only true in the movies," he replied, no humor in his voice. "I'm serious. I don't want to lose you."

"All right, J.T. You've made your point. I'll be careful."

They talked for several more minutes about nothing in particular, neither one wanting to hang up.

Eventually she ended the call, her heart heavy and her eyes misting.

She wiped her eyes as she put away her cell phone. Then she gritted her teeth, angry at herself for getting so emotional about Ryan. The CIA operative was a highly-trained agent. A lethal killer when the situation called for it. She wasn't used to having someone who really cared for her and caring about that person in return.

As she drove the Volvo out of the parking lot, she pushed away the thoughts of Ryan and focused on the task ahead.

She needed to get back to her hotel, check out, and catch the next flight to Oslo, Norway.

# Chapter 43

*Oslo, Norway*

Angel drummed her fingers on the desk as she waited anxiously for the call. Her stomach churned, the acid taste rising up her throat. Reaching in a drawer, she took out the prescription-strength medicine and chugged from the bottle.

That done, she continued drumming her fingers as she gazed out her office window to the half-frozen lake below.

Angel's desk phone rang and she snatched the receiver and held it to her ear.

"It's number 15," the man said.

"Talk to me," she demanded.

"It's done."

"You're sure?"

"Yes, number 3," he replied.

A cold smile formed on her lips. "Excellent."

"When can I expect payment?"

"I'll wire you the money today, number 15."

She hung up, a sense of relief washing over her. Booting up her encrypted computer, she set up the wire transfer to the man's offshore account.

Then she stood, pleased with herself for being able to contain what would have been a catastrophic situation. In fact, she was so pleased with herself she decided to get some much needed R & R. *Nothing like a day of drinking, drugs, and sex*, she thought, *to help me kick back and relax.*

# Chapter 44

*FBI Field Office*
*Atlanta, Georgia*

Erin Welch concluded her morning staff meeting, and after giving specific assignments to several of her agents, left the conference room. Her next task, interrogating Luis Vega a second time, was something she was handling on her own. Her first interrogation of the man yesterday had gone well, yielding pertinent facts. Today she planned on pushing him harder still.

After striding down the hallway of the field office, she took the elevator down to the detention center in the basement. Composed of ten high-security jail cells, the small prison was used for initial questioning during pre-trial proceedings.

Erin reached the end of the corridor where Vega was incarcerated.

As she had done yesterday, she went to the control panel by the jail cell door and was about to turn off the room's security camera, but was surprised to find the CCTV device was already off. She frowned, clearly recalling she had turned on the camera after her previous interrogation.

Pulling out her Glock and holding it at her side, she inserted her ID card on the reader, tapped in a code, and pulled open the heavy steel door.

Erin cautiously stepped inside the jail cell and was stunned at what she found.

Hanging from the ceiling was Luis Vega's inert body. His open, lifeless eyes bulged in their sockets and his tongue hung out of his mouth.

Vega's neck, black and blue and swollen, was constricted by an electrical cord connected to the ceiling.

# Chapter 45

*Midtown*
*Atlanta, Georgia*

J.T. Ryan was doing paperwork in his office, half-listening to the news on the small flat-screen TV mounted on the wall.

A breaking news banner scrolled along the bottom of the TV screen and he picked up the remote from his desk and turned up the volume. The CNN anchor began talking about the riots breaking out in several American cities. One riot had turned deadly in Baltimore, killing two innocent bystanders. According to the CNN newsman, the riots were apparently being incited by an anarchist group known simply as *Overthrow*. The group, the reporter added, had taken credit for the dozens of riots across the U.S. in the last six months.

Ryan watched for several more minutes, then changed the channel to Fox News. That news channel was covering the impeachment proceedings currently in progress in the House of Representatives. Ryan watched as several congressmen gave impassioned speeches calling for President Harris to be removed from office. From what Ryan could surmise, a vote on the president's impeachment could come within weeks.

The PI shut off the TV, disgusted with what he saw. He hated politics and felt the ugly partisan divide was tearing the country apart.

He picked up his pen and was about to go back to his paperwork when his cell phone vibrated. Removing it from his blazer, he took the call.

"It's Erin," he heard the FBI woman say.

"How's it going?"

"Not well," she said, her voice strained. "Terrible, in fact."

"What's the matter?"

"He's dead, J.T."

"Who's dead?"

"Vega."

"What?"

"I found his body this morning," she said. "Dead in his cell. He apparently hung himself."

"How's that possible, Erin? Don't your people monitor those cells 24/7?"

"Of course they do. We have cameras in all the jails. Somehow the CCTV feed from his was turned off."

"We needed him alive, Erin. Vega was our best lead."

"Don't you think I know that, damn it?" she replied angrily.

Ryan said nothing, giving the woman a moment to calm down. Then he said, "Was it suicide?"

"I don't know. It's possible."

"But not probable, Erin."

"I agree. The timing's too damn convenient."

Ryan gripped the phone tightly. "So what now?"

"We keep going. We keep pushing for answers." She went quiet a minute. "And above all else, J.T., we remember what President Harris told us at the beginning of this case: Trust no one. Suspect everyone."

# Chapter 46

*Oslo, Norway*

The armor-plated Mercedes SUV drove into the underground parking lot of the private club and stopped in front of the elevator banks.

Two hulking bodyguards climbed out of the vehicle, and after scanning the area for potential threats, stood by the rear passenger door.

Angel buttoned up her heavy coat and stepped out of the SUV. Then she was escorted into the elevator by her bodyguards, while her driver parked the vehicle. Moments later Angel entered the exclusive party club, which was a frenzy of activity.

Well-dressed couples danced on the crowded dance floor while ear-splitting music blasted from the speakers. Attractive strippers, men and women, gyrated naked on the stage, which was bathed in a riot of multi-color lights. The scent of opium, hashish, and marijuana hung in the air. Perched on stools along the long bar were beautiful, exquisitely dressed boys, girls, men, and women, sipping drinks, their faces eager.

Angel watched as a matronly, middle-aged woman walked up to a young boy at the bar and said something to him. The boy, who looked no older than fourteen, grinned widely. The matronly woman took the boy's hand and led him into one of the 'private rooms' at the far end of the large, high-ceiling space.

Just then the maitre-d' of the club, who was wearing a tuxedo, walked up to Angel. The man smiled. "Welcome back. Your usual?"

"Yes," Angel replied. "You know what I like and who I like."

"Of course, madam. I'll arrange it immediately." The maitre-d' clapped his hands and a young female waitress walked over and said, "If you'll follow me, I'll take you to your room."

The waitress led Angel up the stairs to the private rooms designated for the high-rollers, customers with unlimited funds. Angel's bodyguards went into the sumptuously furnished bedroom suite, searched it, and satisfied there were no threats, exited the room and stood outside the door, their expressions stony. One of the men nodded to Angel and she went inside, closing the door behind her.

Angel unbuttoned her bulky coat and took it off, then went to the suite's kitchen area. On the granite counter top was a bottle of Dom Perignon and a bowl of caviar. She poured the champagne into a cut-glass goblet and took a sip. Then she spread caviar on some crackers and bit into the savory snack. That done, she turned to the bowl of white powder that also rested on the granite counter top. Using one of the tiny spoons by the bowl, she scooped up some of the white powder and putting it up to her nostril, inhaled deeply.

She repeated that one more time and seconds later the familiar, drug-induced rush of excitement and pleasure overwhelmed her senses.

Closing her eyes, the cocaine rush reached every square inch of her body. She grinned, finished off the goblet of champagne, refilled it, and drank that down.

Just then she heard a knock at the door. She smiled in anticipation of what was to come. "Come in," she said.

A tall, muscular man entered the room and closed the door.

"I'm glad it's you," she said licking her lips. She gazed at the handsome man in the business suit. "You're my favorite." *The maitre-d' did well,* she thought. The man standing in front of Angel was indeed her favorite prostitute. She liked women too, but preferred male escorts.

"You can strip now," Angel ordered.

The man slowly and sensually took off his jacket, shirt and pants. When he was completely nude, she stared for a full minute, admiring his very fit physique.

The beautiful, raven-haired woman was wearing an exclusive, black cocktail dress. Using both hands she took hold of her dress and slid it up to her waist. Her eyes boring into his, she said, "Take it off."

The man approached her and lowered her panties to her ankles and removed them.

Then Angel strolled to the king size bed and sat on the edge of it, dangling her legs over the side. Once again she pulled her dress above her waist and opened her legs wide.

"You know what to do," she ordered. "Get on your knees and do what you do best."

The naked man approached her and without saying a word, kneeled in front of her. He leaned in and did as he was told, pressing his open mouth into her pink folds.

Angel grabbed the hair on the back of his head and pulled him tight against her, savoring the intense pleasure of the liquor, the cocaine, and the hired help.

# Chapter 47

*Oslo, Norway*

Rachel West had taken an SAS flight into Gardermoen, the main airport in Oslo, and had spent the next day getting acquainted with the layout of the city.

Ryan had told her the mysterious raven-haired woman lived in a lakefront home near Oslo. But as Rachel quickly discovered, the Norwegian countryside surrounding the city was dotted with hundreds of lakes.

After two days of fruitless driving through the mostly rural, heavily-forested countryside, Rachel went back to her hotel room and called her boss at Langley.

"It's me," she said cryptically. "I've been here awhile and I'm not even close to finding the target."

"All right," Alex Miller replied. "I understand the situation."

"I haven't contacted the local Norwegian authorities."

"Keep it that way," the man said. "The less people involved the better. As you know we had a serious breach of security at the FBI office in Atlanta. And since the NSA has been compromised, who the hell knows how many people are involved in this conspiracy."

"That's true. I know for a fact the Danish government wasn't very cooperative." She paused a moment. "This is my first time in Norway. I haven't worked with the CIA people stationed here. I need a contact."

"Where are you staying?"

"The Hotel Bristol in central Oslo."

"Okay. Hold on while I make some calls."

While she waited for Miller to come back on the line, Rachel gazed out the window of her hotel room. It was snowing heavily outside, the sky laden with dark storm clouds. Beyond the city's 19th century Neoclassical buildings she could make out the ice-capped mountains to the north of Oslo.

"Okay," Miller said, coming back on the line a few minutes later. "I've set it up. He knows the hotel where you're staying. He'll meet you in the Library Bar by the lobby at 6 p.m., your local time. His name is Henrik Johan."

"Can I trust him?"

"Johan is the CIA Station Chief in Oslo."

"That's not what I asked," she said.

"I've worked with him in the past. He's got a great track record and he graduated third in his class at Langley. And we're under the gun here. We've got to make progress on this case. We don't have a hell of a lot of choice but to trust him."

"All right, Alex. Tell me what he looks like."

"Tall, blond, Nordic-looking."

She laughed. "That describes every man in Norway."

"Don't worry. He'll find you. Call me when you learn anything about the target."

"You got it, boss."

Rachel hung up the phone and put it away. She checked her watch, realized she had an hour before Johan arrived. As usual she was wearing jeans, a long-sleeve polo shirt, and flats, clothes that would make her stand out in the classy, upscale hotel bar. She quickly changed into a stylish blue dress, heels, and loosened her long blonde hair from its usual ponytail.

Retrieving her compact purse from her suitcase, she placed her small Glock 43 semi-automatic and her carbon knife inside the purse. That done, she left her room and took the elevator to the first floor.

The Library Bar was located adjacent to the large, opulently furnished lobby. But instead of going inside the bar, she sat at a wingback chair in the lobby, with good visibility to the hotel entrance and the bar itself. She wanted to scout out the area well before 6 p.m. to make sure Johan wasn't being followed.

It was a quiet evening at the hotel with few guests arriving or leaving. At precisely six, a tall, blond, Nordic-looking man entered the lobby and went into the bar. Rachel remained where she was for the next fifteen minutes.

Sensing nothing suspicious, she stood and went into the high-end bistro.

The CIA Station Chief, who was seated at a small table toward the rear of the mostly vacant bar, rose to his feet and motioned her over.

"I am Henrik Johan," the man said in heavily-accented English. "You are late, Ms West."

Rachel smiled as she sat opposite him. "Actually I've been waiting for you for an hour. Just so you know, nobody's tailing you."

The Nordic man frowned. "I see you are the suspicious type."

"Keeps me alive. May I see your ID?"

Johan seemed slightly offended, but nevertheless handed her his CIA cred pack and she gave him hers.

Satisfied with his ID, Rachel said, "Okay. Everything looks good. And Alex told me I could trust you."

His blond eyebrows furrowed. "Of course you can trust me. I am the station chief here."

"Sorry. I don't mean to offend you. But the case I'm working is very sensitive."

Johan scowled. "We are Central Intelligence. Every case we work is sensitive."

Rachel nodded. "I know. But the matter I'm investigating has to do with the high-profile triple murders back in the States. The Supreme Court Justice. The Senate Majority Leader. And the Cardinal."

The man blinked rapidly several times. "Oh. That case."

"Yes," she replied, lowering her voice to a whisper. "We know for a fact that people inside the NSA are part of a deadly group responsible for those murders."

Johan's eyes got wide. "You are certain of that?"

"Absolutely."

"I see. Now I understand why you are so suspicious, Ms West. Tell me what you need. I will put my whole team at your disposal."

Rachel shook her head. "I need information. But only you can be involved. I can't trust anyone else."

He nodded. "Of course. I will help in any way I can."

"Good. I'm looking for a woman. She has long raven hair and she's described as beautiful. She has a small scar on her left cheek. Lives in a lakefront home near Oslo."

"All right. I assume you do not have her name?"

"Correct. She goes by a number. Number 3. We think she directs the operation."

"Is she Norwegian?" he asked.

"We don't know. We do know the organization is very well funded. She probably lives in an estate or a mansion that overlooks a lake."

Johan nodded. "We have many lakes in the area."

"I know. I already did a preliminary search. It's like looking for a needle in a haystack."

The man leaned back in the chair and looked deep in thought, obviously processing what she'd told him. Eventually he said, "I will need a few days. I have many contacts here. I should be able to help you."

"Good."

"How do I contact you?"

Rachel told him her cell phone number and said, "Only use secure phones. Since the NSA is involved, we suspect every call may be monitored."

"Of course, Ms West."

"I should tell you something else. We captured one of the conspirators recently. That's how we learned about the woman in Norway. The captive, Luis Vega, was found dead in his jail cell. It looked like he committed suicide. But we suspect it was staged."

"I see," he said.

Rachel stood. "Remember one thing most of all. Trust no one. Suspect everyone."

# Chapter 48

*Oklahoma City, Oklahoma*

The man turned the dial on the scope and adjusted the crosshairs. Then he slid his finger to the trigger guard of the high-powered Barrett M107 snipers rifle.

He was on the roof of a fifteen-story building and from this vantage point had an unobstructed view of the scene below. Exactly half a mile away was the entrance to the Federal Building, a location he had been scouting for the last several days. The sniper's target had a meeting scheduled in the building. It was 9:45 a.m. now, so the target would be arriving soon.

Just then a large black SUV with heavily-tinted windows pulled to the curb at the entrance of the Federal Building. Two brawny men wearing suits and earwigs climbed out of the SUV, carefully scanned the area, and one of them opened the rear door of the vehicle.

The sniper slid his finger past the trigger guard and rested it on the trigger itself. He slowed his breathing and watched tensely as a thin man wearing an expensive suit stepped out of the SUV.

As the target walked toward the entrance he was clearly visible through the custom-made Schmidt & Bender scope, its crosshairs aimed at the man's head.

The sniper gently pulled the trigger, the suppressed Barrett rifle coughed, and a split-second later the armor-piercing .50 caliber round found the target. The man's head exploded, sending bloody fragments of skull, and skin, and brain matter flying in all directions. The man's body dropped to the pavement, twitched several times, then was deadly still.

# Chapter 49

*FBI Field Office*
*Atlanta, Georgia*

Erin Welch was watching the president's impeachment proceedings on her office TV, listening as the CBS reporter narrated the tense scene in the House of Representatives.

Since many of the congressmen had already concluded their speeches on the House floor, the reporter felt a vote would be coming soon, possibly today.

"It will be a historic and somber occasion in our country's history," the CBS man said grimly. "Only two other presidents have been impeached. President Andrew Johnson in 1868 and President Bill Clinton in 1998. President Steve Harris would be third." The reporter paused a moment, then said, "And as you probably know, in the case of both President Johnson and Clinton, their impeachments were forwarded to the Senate for conviction and expulsion from the presidency. But in both those cases the Senate did not convict and the presidents remained in office."

The reporter's brow furrowed. "But if President Harris is impeached, many people feel he would be removed from office by the Senate. The mood of the U.S is very dark now, as manifested by the countless riots breaking out on a daily basis across the country. The *Overthrow* movement is growing exponentially and the government seems powerless to stop it. Just yesterday riots turned deadly in three American cities, Detroit, Seattle, and Los Angeles, taking the lives of over 30 innocent people —"

Erin watched as the CBS reporter abruptly stopped talking and pressed a hand to his ear, as if listening to some new information. The man's face turned ashen and in a somber voice said, "We have breaking news coming to us from our local news station in Oklahoma City. The police there are confirming that the American Secretary of State, Blake Donovan, has been murdered. Donovan, who is originally from Oklahoma, was killed by a sniper's bullet. An area-wide manhunt is underway for the killer, but so far no one has been apprehended for this shocking and senseless murder."

# Chapter 50

*Oslo, Norway*

Angel's encrypted desk phone rang and she snatched up the receiver and held it to her ear. "Yes?"

"This is number 4," the caller on the line said. Angel already knew who it was, since the caller ID on her phone's screen showed the six digit numeric code that represented number 4's identity. Angel had put in place an extra layer of security when conversing with number 4, since that person was the highest level employee who had infiltrated the ranks of the U.S. government. In fact, that government employee was the fourth ranking person in Angel's organization. The only people higher were Angel herself, and Papa and Mama in Iceland.

"You have information for me?" Angel asked.

"I do. The Secretary of State has been dealt with."

"Excellent news."

"And something else," number 4 said, "the House of Representatives is nearing a vote on impeachment. I expect the vote today."

Angel gripped the handset tightly. "And the outcome? Will it go our way?"

"Yes. It's been very expensive, as you know. I've been coordinating with number 12 on this part of it. But yes, I believe a yes vote is nearly guaranteed."

Angel breathed a sigh of relief. "Good work, number 4. But it's all for naught if the Senate doesn't convict President Harris. We have to make sure that happens."

"I understand, number 3."

"Spare no expense. I'll wire you whatever amount of money you need. Just get it done."

# Chapter 51

*The Situation Room*
*The White House*
*Washington, D.C.*

"In light of the recent tragic events," Mike Corso said, beginning the meeting, "I thought it best we talk in person."

Erin Welch, who was sitting across from the Director of National Intelligence, nodded. They were the only two people in the large, super-secure conference room.

"Of course, sir," she replied.

"You've been watching the news?"

"I have," Erin said. "It's horrible what happened to Secretary Donovan. I'm sure his murder in Oklahoma is connected to the other assassinations."

"I agree. As are the riots by the anarchist group *Overthrow*. It's all linked together." Corso leaned forward in his executive chair and shook his head slowly. "You've heard about the impeachment of President Harris?"

"I did, sir. When my flight landed at Reagan this morning, all the news channels at the airport were covering it."

The DNI let out a long breath. "Now that the president has been impeached by the House of Representatives, the matter has been sent to the Senate. The Senate will debate and then vote on conviction and eviction from office."

"How's the president taking the impeachment, sir?"

"Not well, as you can imagine. We know large amounts of money exchanged hands to buy votes in the House. And when that didn't work, members of Congress were blackmailed. The cabal threatened to expose incriminating situations from their past. But we can't prove any of this, nor do we have a way to stop it." The DNI paused, took a deep breath and let it out slowly. "We suspect the same thing may happen in the Senate. But Steve Harris is a strong man. A strong president. If anyone can survive this damn storm, it's him."

"Yes, sir."

Mike Corso glanced at the device resting on the conference table. The light on the device was still glowing green, the same color it had been throughout the meeting. Erin remembered the green light meant the room wasn't being bugged.

Corso seemed to relax a bit and turned back to Erin. "I need a status report on your team's progress."

"Yes, sir. We received a good lead regarding the international connection of the criminals. We've traced it to a woman who lives in Norway. CIA operative agent Rachel West is there now working that lead."

"Good," he replied.

"As you know, the NSA employee we had in custody, Luis Vega, allegedly hanged himself in jail."

"A staged suicide?"

"I'm almost certain, sir."

Corso shook his head. "That's an extremely disturbing development. That would mean that some people in both the NSA and FBI are compromised."

Erin grit her teeth, furious over the potential corruption in her own agency. She had come to the same conclusion as the DNI. "That's correct."

Corso shook his head again and his shoulders sagged. By his haggard appearance, the man seemed to have aged ten years in the last few months. "What else can you tell me about your team's investigation. Hopefully something positive."

"Yes, sir. We've been trying to find other NSA employees besides Vega who have gone rogue. We just got a break on that end. J.T. Ryan called me this morning. He now has a second suspect who works at the NSA facility in Georgia. We think this man and Luis Vega were working together."

"That's good work, Erin."

"Thank you."

"What now?"

"I instructed Ryan to go back to the NSA facility and arrest this man."

"All right, Erin. Anything else I should know?"

"No, sir. That's everything. I'll contact you the minute we find anything else."

Corso nodded. "We're running out of time. The president is counting on us. The country is counting on us. We've had four top-level people already assassinated. And we have no idea who could be next. The president has been impeached. And riots are breaking out everywhere."

He paused and leaned forward in his chair. "I repeat, Erin, we're running out of time. Find the bastards responsible. And do it fast, before it's too damn late."

# Chapter 52

*Midtown*
*Atlanta, Georgia*

J.T. Ryan finished packing up his gear in the Ford Explorer and closed the back hatch. After his own Tahoe SUV had been totaled during the attempt on his life, Erin Welch had lent him the Ford from the FBI's fleet of vehicles.

He pulled out his cell phone and pressed one of the preset numbers. When Lisa Booth picked up on the other end, he said, "I'm taking off now. I should be back in the office in a few days." He paused and chuckled. "If you don't hear from me after a week, call the Mounties."

"This is no joking matter, J.T.," the young woman replied, no humor in her voice. "People have already tried to kill you."

"I know, I know. I get carried away sometimes." He turned serious. "I'm trusting you to hold down the office all by yourself. If you need help, call Erin."

"Got it, J.T."

"Erin's in D.C. right now, but she'll be back soon."

"Okay."

"One other thing, Lisa. Good work on finding the second suspect at the NSA. Your computer skills are coming in handy."

"I told you I was good. So good in fact, that I think you should make me a partner."

"I gave you a raise. That'll have to do."

"Okay, Chief."

"Call me Chief again," he said, "and I'll start calling you Nancy Drew, Junior Detective."

They both laughed at this, said their goodbyes, and he disconnected the call. Putting away the phone, he climbed in the Explorer and fired up the vehicle. Soon after he was driving on I-75 and then I-20, headed toward the NSA facility.

*** 

The man's name was Ted Wallace, who it turned out had been an NSA employee for over ten years. Like Luis Vega, Wallace had traveled to Oslo, Norway several times. Also like Vega, he owned a very expensive home and several cars, more expensive than he could have afforded on a government salary.

J.T. Ryan was tailing Wallace now and had been following his Cadillac sedan since the man left work at the NSA facility at Fort Gordon. Ryan had decided not to question the man in his office, but rather shadow his movements and check out his routine. For the last two days Wallace had left work and gone home, then returned to the NSA the next morning.

But today was different. Instead of driving to his residence, the man headed north, exited the highway and was now on a rural back road. Traffic was light here and Ryan stayed well back of the Cadillac sedan.

Ten minutes later the Cadillac slowed and took a left onto a rutted gravel path that led into a heavily-wooded area. Ryan slowed his Explorer and passed by the gravel path. Then he doubled back and carefully entered the unmarked, bumpy road. There were no streetlights anywhere and the whole desolate area was dim.

It was nighttime now and Ryan knew he'd be spotted easily as he followed Wallace. So he turned off his headlights and continued driving slowly along the rutted track using moonlight for illumination.

Ryan was about an eighth of a mile behind the Cadillac, but could still make out the vehicle by its taillights. After another mile Wallace's car stopped and parked in front of an unmarked warehouse. Three other vehicles were already parked there, all of them pickup trucks.

The PI slowed the Explorer and pulled off the path into a copse of trees. Taking out his night-vision binoculars, he watched as Wallace got out of the vehicle and went into the warehouse, which was about a hundred yards from where Ryan had parked. The building had several windows and he could see lights on inside. There was no outdoor illumination. *Interesting,* he thought. *It looks like the criminals have a second secret warehouse fairly close to the NSA facility. A place Vega didn't know about.* This confirmed something Ryan already knew: the group was highly compartmentalized, its members not knowing what roles other members played.

Ryan climbed out of the Explorer and opened the back hatch. Rummaging through his rucksack, he took out two items. One was a bullet-proof vest, which he donned. The second was a Remington 870 Blackhawk Special Ops shotgun, which he slung over his shoulder. That done he closed the hatch, checked the load on his .357 Magnum revolver, and holding the handgun at his side, slowly made his way toward the warehouse.

When he was fifty feet away he stopped, and using the vegetation for cover, crouched and waited. He could hear voices coming from the building along with the hum of machinery. He was still too far away to peer into the windows, so he advanced further.

When he was five feet away from the building he heard the creak of a metal door. Suddenly outdoor floodlights blazed on, bathing the area with illumination. Blinded by the intense light, he threw away the night-vision binoculars.

Ryan instantly dropped to one knee, heard the crack of a shot, and felt a sharp pain in his chest. The bullet knocked him to the ground, sending his handgun flying.

He gasped for breath, knowing the bullet-proof vest had saved his life. Ignoring the pain in his chest, he pumped the slide on his shotgun and fired in the direction of the gunfire.

Ryan heard a scream and he quickly fired again, the tactical shotgun spitting out 12 gauge shells into the front entrance. He saw a second man go down as a third fired his way, the rounds whistling over his head.

The PI heard the groans of pain, and shouting, and more gunfire targeted his way. Ryan pulled the trigger on the Remington again, then got up and sprinted to the side of the building. As he hugged the wall, he listened as the front door opened and quickly closed. He heard two voices from the interior of the warehouse. A moment later the lights inside the building dimmed and the outside floodlights went dark.

Ryan's mind raced as he worked out his next steps. Clearly there were two armed men inside, one of them being Wallace. The fact that the men had opened fire without asking questions meant only one thing: whatever was going on inside the warehouse was illegal. He briefly considered calling Erin to get FBI backup, but dismissed that immediately, knowing someone inside her organization had already been turned.

The PI was close to one of the windows. Standing off to one side of it, he fired two shotgun shells into the dim interior. The glass imploded and he sprayed two more rounds inside. Grabbing hold of the window sill, he pulled himself inside the building and dropped to the concrete floor.

Shots rang out and a round slammed into the metal wall, an inch above his head. He pumped two more shotgun shells toward the direction of the muzzle flash, heard a scream, a thud, and then nothing.

The PI crouched behind a large piece of machinery and waited in the dim interior, letting his eyes adjust to the darkness. A moment later he could make out a slight movement close to his location and heard a groan.

Carefully he advanced, the shotgun leading the way.

"Help me," he heard. "I'm shot ...."

Instantly Ryan stopped and crouched by a stack of pallets. Glancing around the pallets, he could make out two men. One was inert, lying in a pool of blood – the second man was sitting up on the floor, holding his bleeding stomach, groaning.

Ryan again scanned the dim interior of the warehouse. It appeared no one else was alive.

"Help ... me ...," he heard the wounded man gasp. "I'm ... dying ...."

The PI approached him carefully, still expecting a trap. There was a handgun next to the wounded man and Ryan kicked it away. Then he knelt by the guy, pointing the shotgun at his head.

"Who are you?" Ryan demanded.

"Wallace ... Ted ... Wallace ... please ... I'm bleeding ... to death ... I need ... a doctor ...."

By the copious amount of blood gushing from Wallace's midsection, he knew the man probably wouldn't make it. He'd taken a direct hit from the 12 gauge shotgun shell. Very few people survive that. "Okay, Wallace. I'll call an ambulance. But first you answer some questions."

The man's eyes lost focus as he clutched his stomach with both hands trying to staunch the flow of bright red blood. Then his eyes focused again. "Yes ... ask me ... I just ... don't want ... to die ...."

"You're part of a conspiracy. Correct? To overthrow the government. You and Luis Vega."

"Yes ... I'm part of it ... but ... I didn't work ... with Vega ... but I knew other ... NSA people ... were involved ... I don't know who .... I'm number 19 ... please, mister ... call an ambulance ... I'm dying ...."

"Sure, Wallace, I'll call them. Just a couple of more questions."

The man groaned and blood seeped from his mouth. "Please ... call ...."

"Were you paid?"

"Yeah ...."

"By the woman in Norway?"

The man nodded.

"What's her name?"

"Number ... 3 ...." he gasped.

"Who else in the NSA is involved?"

Wallace shook his head. "Don't ... know ... we're all ... numbers ...."

"What's this building used for?"

The man's eyes lost focus again and more blood seeped from his mouth. When his eyes focused, Ryan said, "What's this building used for?"

"We plan ... produce stuff ... for *Overthrow* ...."

"For the anarchist group behind the riots?"

"That's ... right ...."

Ryan glanced around the warehouse and saw that the man was telling the truth. The building was filled with printing presses. Stacked on pallets were printed signs made to look like they were hand written. The words *Overthrow the government* and *Government kills* were written on the signs. He also saw printed T-shirts and other items with the same messages.

"And the other men here," Ryan said, "are they the ones who commit the murders during the riots?"

"Yes ... I hire them ... that's my job ... to hire people ... to riot ...."

"Who are these guys? NSA employees?"

Wallace shook his head. "No ... they're thugs ... criminals ... I pay ... to work ... for Overthrow ... please, mister ... call ... a doctor ...."

Ryan took out his cell phone. "I'll call now. But before I do, what else can you tell me about this criminal gang of yours?"

"The woman ... in Norway," the man said as more blood seeped from his mouth. "She called it ... something ... one time ... I overheard her ... talking to one ... of her bodyguards ... she called it ... Operation Fireball ...."

"Fireball?"

"That's ... right ...."

"What does it mean, Wallace?"

The man was about to say something else, but his eyes rolled white, blood gushed out of his mouth, and his body sagged.

Ryan touched Wallace's neck and felt for a pulse.

There was none.

# Chapter 53

*Oslo, Norway*

Angel was gazing out her window, sipping chardonnay, and humming along to the Brahms symphony playing on her sound system.

The raven-haired woman was relishing her recent victories: the impeachment of President Harris and the murder of one of his cronies, Secretary of State Donovan. *The dominoes are falling*, she mused, as a smile formed on her lips. *Yes, the dominoes are falling.* It was only a matter of time before Harris was convicted by the Senate and thrown out of the White House. Papa's dream of taking down President Steve Harris will be a reality. Fireball will be a success.

*A partial success*, she reminded herself. *Now that I've convinced Papa to take Fireball to the next level.* Angel grinned, knowing that when the new enhanced Fireball operation was successful, she would get the ultimate revenge.

Angel idly rubbed the small scar on her cheek, the scar a permanent reminder of her detestable treatment by the U.S. government and the long years in prison at Guantanamo she had endured. She savored the satisfaction she would gain when she obtained her revenge. *It will be sweet*, she thought, as she finished her glass of wine.

Just then a dark thought crept in. When she had visited Iceland last time, she'd had a testy exchange with Mama regarding the enhanced Fireball operation. As usual, Mama hadn't succumbed to Angel's charm as easily as her husband. *No matter*, Angel thought. *I'll convince the old hag soon enough – I just need more time and more sweet talk to change Mama's mind.*

Angel poured herself another glass of wine and downed it in one gulp, pushing away the thoughts of the irksome old woman, focusing instead on Papa, a man she deeply admired. Not just admired, but even lusted for. Which was odd for her since she craved sex with virile, handsome, young men, the type she hired. Not old men like Papa, who was over twice her age. *It must be the power*, she mused. *That's why he makes me wet. I'm attracted to the power that comes from having so much money.* Papa was a multi-billionaire. In fact he was one of the world's richest men. And he wasn't afraid to spend his fortune. When he wanted something badly enough, like Fireball, he turned on the taps and let money flow like rain water.

Suddenly there was a knock at her office door. Turning away from the windows, she said, "Come in."

A tall, muscular, Nordic-looking man with a crew-cut and a square jaw opened the door and entered. As usual he was wearing a blue, button-down shirt and black slacks. He was Angel's head of security; he and his team of bodyguards were quartered in the guest house, adjacent to her luxurious chalet.

"What is it, Gustav?" she said.

The man shook his head. "Bad news."

She rested her wineglass on the desk. "What?"

"Our sources are picking up chatter. Right here in Oslo. The CIA is asking questions about a woman who lives by a lake. A wealthy woman who is known as number 3."

Angel's beautiful face drained of color. "How the hell is that possible? The CIA? Here in Oslo?"

"Yes, Angel."

The woman's jaw clenched and her hands formed into fists. "I pay you very well Gustav, to make sure I'm always protected."

"Yes, of course."

"You've failed me, you miserable son-of-a-bitch."

The man took this stoically and said nothing in reply.

Angel slapped him hard across his face, leaving a bright red mark on his cheek. A trickle of blood seeped from his lip.

He didn't react and didn't flinch, simply stood there ramrod straight. He was used to the woman's frequent bouts of anger. And since he towered over her by a foot, was heavily muscled and much stronger than his boss, his reaction to being struck by her was always the same. To do nothing.

"Do they know my name?" she demanded.

"No, Angel. Just that you go by a number. Number 3."

"Have they found out where I live?"

"No, I do not believe so, Angel. But they will investigate, and in time, find us here."

Angel nodded, knowing the man was right. She had always feared something like this could happen. Luckily she was a strategic thinker, a chess-playing tactician, always planning two or three steps ahead.

"Let's put the backup plan in place, Gustav."

"Now?" he asked.

"Of course now, you idiot!"

# Chapter 54

*Oslo, Norway*

Rachel West was at the Library Bar of the Hotel Bristol nursing a vodka tonic, waiting for a callback from Henrik Johan.

She glanced at her watch for the thousandth time, impatient for the CIA station chief to get her the info. It had been three days since she'd met with him and was anxious to track down the mysterious raven-haired woman. But being a well-trained CIA operative, Rachel knew that getting information from confidential informants wasn't easy. It was usually a laborious and uneven process, full of dead ends.

Just then her cell phone buzzed and she removed it from her jacket. "Yes?"

"It is Johan," she heard the man say.

"You have what I need?"

"I believe so," he replied. "My CIs have a location. A large, lake-front home. A mansion really, with an adjacent guest house on the property. A wealthy woman lives there. Very beautiful, from what I am told. She has a small scar on her cheek, on an otherwise flawless face."

"Do you have an exact address?"

"I do," he said. He read it off and she wrote it down.

"What's her name?" Rachel asked.

"We do not know. She is apparently very reclusive."

"All right. She lives alone?"

"No. She's often seen with a group of muscular men, most likely bodyguards."

"Okay. How were you able to track her down?"

"I have good CIs. It just takes time. And money to pay them."

"Good work, Johan."

"I assume you want to meet with me so we can go together to her location? I have a special ops team at my disposal."

Rachel thought about this briefly, recalling the treachery happening at the NSA and at the FBI. "No. I'll handle this myself."

"Are you sure? That would be very dangerous."

"I like to work alone."

The CIA station chief didn't reply for a moment, then said, "Suit yourself."

"I will need some tools, though. Gun laws in Norway are strict – I could only bring my handgun on the flight over."

"I understand, Rachel. Just let me know what you need."

She described the equipment and they arranged to meet later in the day for the pickup. After saying goodbye, she hung up.

***

Rachel drove the rented, all-terrain Land Rover over the uneven snow, making slow progress toward her destination. It had been snowing all day, the drifts collecting on the rural road she was traversing.

Although it was only 3 p.m. it was pitch black outside. This was normal for Norway in January, where the sun was out for only a few hours a day. There were no streetlights in the mostly uninhabited area, so she was navigating strictly with her vehicle's headlamps, the lights casting a ghostly image over the heavily-wooded area.

Rachel crossed over a deep drift of white powder, then glanced at the GPS Nav screen. The lakeside mansion was about a mile away, assuming Henrik Johan's CI was correct. She drove along the road for another 100 yards, then spotted a smaller track up ahead, leading into a dark forest.

Knowing her vehicle's headlights would be easily spotted if she drove much further, she pulled the Land Rover into a copse of trees and shut it off. She removed her Glock 43 handgun from her holster and slid it into the outside pocket of her heavy coat. After zipping up the parka, she climbed out, only to be hit by an icy blast of frigid snow. The howling wind sliced her exposed skin and she quickly donned her gloves and zipped the parka to her neck.

Then she stomped over the snowy drifts to the back of the SUV and opened the rear hatch. The first tool she removed from her duffel was the night-vision goggles she'd obtained from the CIA station chief. She put on the goggles and the area around her went from pitch black to a green glow. That done, she pulled the coat's hood over her head and fastened it securely. Then she removed the Heckler & Koch MP-5 submachine gun from the duffel, and after racking the slide, turned on the safety. She then screwed on the gun's suppressor and slung the weapon over her shoulder. The MP-5 was the type of assault rifle used by most special ops operators, including the CIA and the Army's Delta Force and Navy SEALS. It was one of Rachel's favorite tools.

After turning on her hand-held GPS device, she closed the vehicle's back hatch. Then she slowly made her way over the snowy mounds to the rural path in the heavily-forested area. She noticed tire tracks on the snow-covered path, indicating someone had recently traveled in or out of the area.

Her boots sank into the deep powder as she strode closer to her destination. Minutes later she spotted lights up ahead and she dropped to one knee to get a better look. Adjusting the night-vision goggles, she zoomed in and saw a large, two-story chalet, a mansion actually, with a smaller home nearby on the property. Floodlights lit up the grounds and lights were on inside the main house. The property overlooked a frozen lake and she realized this was the correct location. After confirming the address on her GPS device, she got off the rural road and continued toward the main structure through the forest.

She reached a clearing soon after and stopped, once again going to one knee. The mansion had been built on the cleared area of the property with the lake facing the rear of the home.

Zooming in with her goggles, she noticed two men patrolling the snow-covered grounds, both carrying assault rifles. The icy road led to a circular driveway in front of the mansion, which had a four car garage attached to one side.

Realizing she'd be spotted by the guards if she approached any closer using the clearing, she stepped deeper into the woods. Using the vegetation for cover, she began making her way to the back of the home, an area she hoped would be less well patrolled.

When she reached the edge of the lake's icy banks, she studied the mansion. There were no guards visible in the back yard. Lights shone out of several of the windows, although she was still too far away to see inside.

Un-slinging the MP-5, she took off the safety and trained the submachine gun forward. Then she advanced cautiously over the uneven drifts of white powder. A howling wind was blowing, blasting icy snow in all directions. The bitter cold gusts sliced into the exposed parts of her face and she shivered from the frigid air.

Suddenly she heard the crack of gunfire and saw chunks of frozen snow and ice fly up all around her, as rounds slammed into the drifts.

Firing blindly, she squeezed the trigger and the MP-5 spit out a three-round burst.

More incoming shots rang out and she threw herself flat on the snow-covered ground. She burrowed into the soft powder for concealment, the snow and bone-chilling cold burning the exposed parts of her face.

Rounds whizzed over her head and she knew the guards would figure out her exact location quickly. With her heart thudding in her chest, she pulled out an RPG grenade from her coat pocket and attached it to the front of her assault rifle.

Then she waited for the next round of incoming fire, which took place a second later.

Zeroing in on the muzzle blast, she fired the MP-5 and the rocket-propelled grenade flew toward its target, an area at the rear of the home. The grenade exploded, she heard a scream, and she quickly got on her feet and clumsily ran through the deep drifts of snow toward the mansion.

More gunfire erupted, the incoming rounds kicking up mounds of ice all around her. She dropped to the ground and once again burrowed her body into the drifts of snow, shivering from the arctic cold.

Rachel reloaded with another RPG and pulled the trigger.

The grenade struck the mansion's back entrance and detonated, creating a large hole in the structure. She heard more screams and saw a man limp inside the house. Expecting more gunfire she stayed burrowed in the snow. When no more shots rang out, she peered over the mound of powder. She saw no movement on the grounds.

Rachel cautiously advanced over the irregular drifts, her boots sinking into the soft snow. Training the MP-5 forward, she kept her finger on the trigger. Reaching the back entrance, she saw two inert, bloody bodies lying on the icy ground. Their jackets and faces were ripped by the RPG's shrapnel.

After checking to make sure the men were dead, she hugged the home's back wall. Then she peered inside the interior through the jagged hole created by the grenade. There was a third bloody body inside and she noticed a trail of bright red blood leading deeper into the home. It was evident that at least one of the guards had survived.

With her assault rifle leading the way, she slowly advanced inside the mansion. The smell of gunpowder was strong here and she stepped over the debris as she entered a large den. Firmly gripping the weapon, she followed the trail of blood as it led deeper into the home.

She held her breath, half-expecting gunfire to erupt at any moment. None came and she followed the blood trail until she reached a lavishly-appointed living room. The area was well-lit so she took off her night-vision goggles.

Just then she saw movement out of the corner of her eye and felt rounds tear a hole in her coat sleeve. Rachel squeezed the trigger and fired off a three round burst in that direction. Dropping to one knee, she put the MP-5 on full auto and sprayed that side of the room with automatic fire, the rounds shredding the furniture and pock-marking the walls.

She heard a scream, then a thud, and then nothing.

Ducking behind a wooden cabinet, she listened for sounds as her heart pounded in her chest. The CIA woman waited a full two minutes without advancing. She glanced at her coat sleeve, which was torn from the gunfire. She felt no pain and saw no blood – luckily the shots had missed her.

Hearing a groan nearby, she cautiously peered around the cabinet. A man, bleeding heavily, was sprawled on the floor. She approached him warily and when she was next to him, she kicked away his rifle. Although from the looks of it, the man appeared close to death.

Kneeling by him, she searched him for other weapons. Finding a revolver, she pocketed it, then took out zip ties from her coat and cuffed his hands and feet. The man had lost a lot of blood and his face was drained of color. She was about to ask him questions when she realized he'd slipped into unconsciousness.

Then she methodically searched both levels of the large, two-story home. Leaving the main house, she strode to the smaller home nearby and searched that structure, then went back to the mansion. She found no other guards, nor anyone else in the houses. But she did see evidence, specially in the bedrooms, that people had fled in a hurry. The closets in most of the bedrooms were empty and she found clothing strewn on the floor and on the beds. It appeared that the mysterious raven-haired woman and some of her guards had fled the mansion earlier in the day. That would explain the fresh tire tracks Rachel had noticed on the road leading to the property.

Rachel continued searching the mansion, this time looking for electronics – personal computers, tablets, or cell phones, but found none. Obviously they were taken when the people fled. Although Rachel didn't find any files or paperwork, she did locate one item of interest. Inside a desk drawer she found a color 5"x7" photograph. Shown on the photo were three people – one was a beautiful woman who looked to be in her late thirties. She had long, black hair and a small scar on her left cheek. Most likely she was number 3. Standing next to the woman was an elderly couple, probably in their 80's. The man looked vibrant and distinguished, while the old woman appeared gaunt and frail.

Rachel pocketed the photo and continued searching the house. She found a fireplace in one of the rooms. Embers were still burning in the hearth and she noticed charred scraps of paper among the embers. Rachel assumed number 3 had burned files before leaving.

After inspecting the rest of the mansion and finding no other clues, she returned to the wounded man she had hand-cuffed earlier. He was still bleeding profusely but was now conscious.

She knelt by his side. "Are you one of the bodyguards?" she asked, holding her Glock to his head.

The man nodded.

She took out the photo she'd found and showed it to him. "Who are these people?"

The guard pointed to the younger woman in the picture. "Angel ...," he managed to say as he gulped in air. "... that is Angel."

"Is she number 3?"

"That ... is right ...."

"And the two other people? Who are they?"

"Don't ... know ...."

She pressed the muzzle of her handgun to the man's temple. "Are you sure?"

"Yes ... I do not know ... who they are ...."

"Okay. Did Angel flee?"

The man nodded.

"By herself?" she asked.

"No. She and ... most of her ... guards ... left ...."

"Why did she leave?"

"Don't ... know ...."

"Where did Angel go?"

The man shook his head. "I don't ... know ...."

Rachel was about to ask him more questions, but his body sagged and his eyes rolled white. She felt for a pulse and found none.

Rachel stood, unzipped her heavy parka, and put away her handgun. Then she took out her cell phone and snapped a picture of the photo of the three people. Hitting one of the preset numbers on her phone, she waited for the other side to pick up.

When Alex Miller answered the call, she said, "It's me. I'm at the location. Unfortunately the target had already left."

"That's not good news."

"I found something of value, though."

"What is it?" he asked.

"A photo of three people – one of them is a woman who fits the description of number 3. Her bodyguard identified her – her first name is Angel. I don't know the identity of the other two in the picture."

"Send me the photo," he said. "I'll run it through facial recognition software."

Rachel pressed a button on her phone and transmitted the picture to Miller.

"Got it," he said. "I'll call you when I learn something. By the way, I'm assuming you arrested the bodyguard? We can interrogate him."

"Can't. He's dead."

# Chapter 55

*Special Operations Division*
*CIA Annex Building*
*Langley, Virginia*

Alex Miller printed out the color photo Rachel had sent him and studied it carefully. The woman with long black hair looked oddly familiar. He didn't recognize the elderly couple.

He pressed a button on his intercom and a minute later one of his technicians came to his office. The tech took the photo and went back to the lab.

Two hours later the technician was back. He gave Miller the photo and a handwritten report. When the man left, Miller read the report, shocked at what it contained.

*No wonder the woman in the photo looked familiar*, he thought. *She was one of us*. The raven-haired, stunningly beautiful woman was Angel Stone, a former CIA agent who had gone rogue years ago. She was the perpetrator of a ransom plot to bomb Washington D.C. She threatened to blow up the city if she was not paid one billion dollars. Luckily the plot had been foiled and she was arrested. After her arrest she was sent to Guantanamo, Cuba, where she was imprisoned. But she managed to escape the maximum security prison and had never been found.

Miller read further. The facial recognition had also been able to identify the elderly couple in the photo. They were Viktor Papadopoulos and his wife. Papadopoulos was a billionaire who had made his vast wealth in commodities trading. After proof surfaced that he used illegal means to make his billions, he was charged with multiple counts of fraud. Papadopoulos was prosecuted and convicted for money-laundering by Steve Harris when he was the Texas Attorney General years ago. Harris had gone on to become President of the United States. Papadopoulos, who was sentenced to twenty years in jail, never spent a day in prison, and instead fled the country. A large-scale manhunt ensued but neither Papadopoulos nor his wife was ever found.

# Chapter 56

*FBI Field Office*
*Atlanta, Georgia*

After going through the FBI security checkpoints, J.T. Ryan took the elevator and reached Erin Welch's office soon after.

Ryan tapped on her glass door, which today was closed. Erin glanced up from her laptop, stood, unlocked her office door and let Ryan inside, closing the door behind him.

"What's with the locked door, Erin? You've never done that before."

She gazed out through the glass walls of her office to the large bullpen. Over twenty agents were at their desks, clicking on computers or on the phone.

"After our prisoner Vega 'hanged' himself in our building," she replied, "I'm not sure who to trust."

Ryan nodded and sat down on one of the visitor's chairs as she went back to her desk.

She leaned forward in her executive chair. "You learned something important from Wallace, the NSA employee?"

"I did. I didn't want to tell you over the phone." Ryan looked around her office. "Is it okay to talk in here?"

Erin nodded. "I just swept the place for bugs. We're okay for now."

"The NSA employee, Wallace, told me the criminal operation is named 'Fireball'."

"Fireball? What does it mean, J.T.?"

Ryan shook his head. "Don't know. Wallace died before he could tell me more. But whatever it is, it involves the *Overthrow* movement. I found pallets full of printed signs in that warehouse. The signs read 'Overthrow the government' and 'Government kills'. Wallace told me his job was to hire protesters and rioters. So 'Fireball' is connected to the anarchy groups that have been rioting all over the country. The guy said the organization is very well-funded. He would ask his boss, the elusive number 3, for large amounts of money and she would wire it to him."

"Good work on finding all this out, J.T."

Ryan grinned and gave her a half salute. "It's all part of the job." He chuckled. "I throw in my charm and wit at no extra charge."

Erin frowned, then said, "Your attempts at humor are going to land you in hot water one day."

Ryan laughed.

Erin reached into one of her desk drawers and took out a file folder. "Alex Miller from the CIA called me this morning. They got a good lead on the mysterious woman, number 3. We now know who she is."

Ryan leaned forward in his chair. "Who?"

Erin opened the file folder, took out a printout of a color photo and handed it to the PI.

He stared at the picture, which showed three people. He didn't recognize the elderly couple, but the beautiful, raven-haired woman seemed very familiar. He tapped on the photo. "This woman ... I think I've seen her before."

Erin nodded. "You have. In fact you arrested her years ago. She was involved in the plot to blow up Washington, D.C. Her name is Angel Stone."

"Angel Stone? How's that possible? She's locked up at Guantanamo."

"She *was* a prisoner there," Erin replied. "But she escaped. Was never found."

"How the hell did she manage to escape? I thought Gitmo is a Supermax type of prison – impossible to break out."

"Apparently she had inside help, J.T. She seduced several of the prison guards and fled."

Ryan nodded. "She's a looker – I can see her using sex to get what she wants."

"From what the CIA found out, Angel Stone is one of the ringleaders. She runs the operation from Oslo, Norway. Agent Rachel West from the CIA found Stone's location, but the woman was gone by the time she got there."

Ryan smiled when he heard Rachel's name mentioned.

"What's with the grin?" Erin asked.

"Nothing. Just thinking."

Erin frowned. "Do you and agent West have a thing going on?"

"A thing?"

"A personal relationship."

"What makes you say that, Erin?"

"Because I'm a trained FBI agent. I interrogate people for a living. I can sense things without being told."

Ryan smiled, but said nothing.

"Don't let this relationship," Erin said tersely, "get in the way of solving our case."

The PI gave her another half salute. "Yes, ma'am."

"Okay. Enough about that," she said. "The CIA was also able to identify the elderly couple in the photo. The man is Viktor Papadopoulos, a billionaire, and the woman is his wife. Papadopoulos was tried and convicted of a whole host of crimes but never served time. He and his wife fled the U.S. and were never found. Guess who prosecuted him?"

Ryan shook his head. "No idea."

"None other than Steve Harris, President of the United States. Harris was the Attorney General of Texas at the time."

"That would explain a motive for the plot, Erin. To get back at Harris."

She nodded. "Yes, that makes sense."

"Since Papadopoulos is a billionaire," Ryan said, "he would have plenty of money to fund the *Overthrow* movement, and to fund the impeachment of President Harris."

"I agree, J.T. This 'Fireball' operation requires lots of cash – millions and millions of dollars. It would take a billionaire to bankroll it."

"So what's Angel Stone's connection with Papadopoulos?"

"It's unclear," she said. "Also unclear is the current whereabouts of this billionaire and Stone. Rachel West is still in Norway. She suspects these three people are there somewhere."

"Okay, Erin."

"So, what's your next move?"

Ryan leaned back in the chair. "So far I've found two NSA employees who have gone rogue – Vega and Wallace. Their identification in the criminal organization were number 27 and number 19. It's a safe bet that more corrupt NSA people are out there. I'm going to focus on finding them."

"All right. That's a good strategy."

"What about you, Erin? What are your plans?"

"I'm scheduled to go back to D.C. and meet with Mike Corso again. He wants another status report on our progress."

Ryan nodded and stood. "I'll get going then."

"Okay. And remember one thing. The clock is ticking. We need to solve this case and solve it fast."

# Chapter 57

*Bethesda, Maryland*

The target was clearly visible through the Schmidt & Bender high-powered scope. The target was three-quarters of a mile away, playing with his children in the back yard of his home.

The sniper slowed his breathing and made a final adjustment to the scope's crosshairs. Then he slid his finger off the trigger guard and moved it to the trigger itself.

He waited tensely, wishing the target's children would move safely away. Although he was a highly-trained assassin with over 25 kills to his name, he detested eliminating young children. He hated collateral damage and knew it was bad karma to murder the innocent.

Just then the children moved away from the target and began playing with the family's cocker spaniel. The target strolled to one the back yard's chaise lounges and sat down.

The sniper moved the Barrett M107 rifle an inch to the left to account for the target's new position. Then he slowed his breathing again as his finger caressed the trigger.

The sniper pulled the trigger and the suppressed, high-powered rifle coughed. A split-second later the armor-piercing, .50 caliber round slammed into the target. The bullet tore a large hole in the man's chest, cracked his ribcage, pierced his heart and lungs, and came out his back. The bullet's bloody fragments lodged in the chaise lounge.

The target's body twitched for several moments, then was deadly still.

The Secretary of Defense was dead.

She considered this. Johan probably hadn't set her up. Or warned Angel Stone ahead of time. Still, she'd almost been killed the firefight.

"Thanks, Johan. But no thanks. I'll keep looking on my own."

"As you wish."

The CIA station chief stood. "If you change your mind, you now how to reach me."

"I do."

The man turned and walked out of the bar.

Rachel took a sip of her vodka and pondered her next move. After a long moment, she set her drink down, paid the tab, and made her way to her hotel room. Once there she pulled out her encrypted cell phone and made a call.

"It's me," she said when Alex Miller answered. "I need your help."

"Of course. By the way, did you meet with Johan?"

"I did. Just now."

"Can you trust him?"

"I don't know, boss."

"All right. What do you need?"

"I need to find a connection between Angel Stone and the NSA. How did she hook up with them? There's got to be a link somewhere. Find that and I may be able to locate her."

Alex Miller went quiet a minute and she thought he'd hung up. "Are you still there, boss?"

"I am. I'm thinking."

Rachel had worked for Miller for years. She felt he was the smartest man at the CIA. If anybody could help her, it would be him.

"I'll start working on this immediately," he said. "I'll call you when I have something."

"Thanks, boss."

"In the meantime, lay low. Try not to get killed. I need you on this case."

Rachel laughed. "I'll try to stay out of trouble. But you know me. Trouble follows me around."

# Chapter 58

*Bergen, Norway*

Angel, acid churning in her stomach, felt a nauseous sensation pushing bile up her throat. She reached into a desk drawer, took out the bottle of prescription-strength antacid and opened it. She gulped the medicine straight from the bottle.

That done, she turned up the volume of her sound system. As usual she was listening to Brahms's Intermezzo in A symphony, the classical music she always turned to in times of stress.

And Angel was stressed. Damned furious, actually. She glanced around her modest office in her second home. The home, located in Bergen, a coastal city in Norway, wasn't nearly as plush as her mansion in Oslo.

Still, she had no choice.

Somehow the CIA had located her home in Oslo – although she couldn't fathom how they'd managed to do that. Her only option had been to run. She drummed her fingers on the desk as she waited for the medicine to take affect.

Then Angel's encrypted desk phone buzzed and she snatched up the receiver and held it to her ear. "Yes?"

"This is number 4," the caller said.

"You have information for me?"

"I do, number 3. My associate has completed his latest task. The Secretary of Defense has been terminated."

Angel smiled in satisfaction. "That's excellent news. You've done well, number 4. I won't forget your loyalty to the cause."

"I was hoping for more than just praise."

Suddenly irked by the caller's greed, Angel gripped the phone tightly. She took a deep breath and let it out slowly. *Calm yourself*, she thought. *I need number 4 to finish the job*. Number 4 was a key player in Fireball.

"Of course," Angel replied. "I'll wire you a large bonus after this phone call."

"Thank you."

"Is everything else moving along according to schedule, number 4?"

"It is."

"Excellent," Angel said and hung up the phone.

Elated by the good news from number 4, Angel forgot about her disappointment of losing her mansion in Oslo.

She sat at her desk for several minutes as she mulled over what to do next. She idly rubbed the small scar on her left cheek, a nervous habit she'd acquired during her years as a prisoner in Guantanamo. Coming to a decision, she pressed the intercom device on her desk. "I need you," she said.

A moment later Gustav, her head of security, stepped into her office. The tall, muscular, Nordic-looking man approached and stood ramrod straight in front of her desk. As usual he was wearing a blue buttoned-down shirt and black slacks.

"How may I serve you, Angel?"

"Get my jet fueled and ready to go."

"Of course. What destination should I give the pilot?"

"Iceland," she said.

# Chapter 59

*Oslo, Norway*

"Did you set me up?" Rachel West said, clenching her

"Of course not," Henrik Johan replied, holding his p front of him. "Why would I do that? We are on the same si

Rachel's piercing blue eyes bore into his, trying to deter the CIA station chief was lying. "Angel Stone fled before there, Johan. No one knew I was going to her house excep Explain that!"

He grimaced. "Keep your voice down. Someone's goir hear you."

Rachel glanced around the Library Bar of the Hotel Bri She noticed some of the customers were looking her way.

"All right," she said in a lower tone. "But answer my dat question."

"I do not know how Stone found out. Possibly one of n informants double-crossed me."

The CIA woman thought about that a moment. Some of he own CIs had been treacherous, playing both sides for money "Okay. I'll buy that for now. The real problem is Angel Stone is gone and I have no idea where she is."

Johan nodded. "I understand. I assume you do not want me to look for her further?"

"That's correct."

"What will you do now, Rachel?"

"I keep looking."

Johan leaned forward in his chair. "I would like to help. We are both CIA after all."

# Chapter 60

*Oslo, Norway*

Rachel was having dinner by herself at the Theatercafeen Restaurant when her cell phone vibrated.

She put down her fork, took out the phone and looked at the info screen. By the alphanumeric code she knew it was Alex Miller calling. It had been two days since she'd last talked to him.

"Hey, boss."

"Sorry it took so long to get back to you, but it hasn't been easy finding what you were looking for."

"Okay. I'm in a restaurant. I can leave and go somewhere more private."

"Not necessary. Don't talk. Just listen."

"You got it, boss."

"I think I found a possible Norway connection between Angel Stone and the NSA. It was difficult to find, since the National Security Agency is so secretive. Even for me, with my top security clearance at the CIA."

"The U.S. intelligence operations are so big," she replied, "that the left hand doesn't know what the right hand is doing."

"That's the truth. It turns out the NSA has a facility in Norway. Ultra-secret, only a few people even know it exists. It's a surveillance post with a couple of big satellite dishes. It was set up originally to spy on the Russians. Anyway, this NSA facility in Norway is not like the massive operation at Fort Meade. This Norwegian operation employs only twelve people."

"Where is it located, boss?"

"A small town by the name of Voss."

"Never heard of it."

"Me neither," he said, "before I started doing this research. Anyway, Voss may be where Angel Stone originally got involved with NSA employees."

Rachel realized that what Miller had just told her could either be a huge break or it could be a dead-end. Either way the NSA facility in Voss was the only lead she had. "Thanks, boss. I appreciate this."

"What are you going to do now?"

Rachel stared at her half-eaten meal, which consisted of *raspeballer*, a Norwegian dish of potato dumplings and *boknafisk*, salted cod. "I'm going to finish my dinner, then do what I do best. Kick ass and take names."

# Chapter 61

*Vatnajokull, Iceland*

Angel's trip to Iceland had taken her much longer than expected. Instead of hours the journey had taken days. The January weather had brought with it a massive snowstorm, its fierce, arctic winds forcing her Lear jet to land in Iceland's capital, Reykjavik. She then continued the trip via a four-wheel-drive vehicle to Papa's mansion.

Angel was in one of the guest bedrooms now, unpacking her clothes. The elegantly appointed room looked out toward the scenic frozen tundra, which was a blanket of white. In the distance she could make out the icy mountain peaks of Vatnajokull, the massive icecap that constituted 14% of the country's surface. The beautiful but desolate arctic landscape covered a vast and unspoiled area of over 5,400 square miles. The sun was out now, its light reflecting off the pristine white snow to the point that it was almost blinding.

Angel finished unpacking quickly, eager to meet Papa and share the good news with him. Exiting the guest bedroom, she took the elevator to the first floor of the mansion and went into the large study.

Number 1 was already there, sitting close to the stone fireplace, where a roaring fire was burning. The 85 year-old man with the mane of white hair was reading a book.

"Papa!" she said excitedly, "it's so good to see you!"

He glanced up from his book and his kindly, wrinkled face broke into a smile. "It's great to see you too, child. Come, sit with me so we can talk."

She sat on a wingback chair across from him. "I have good news. Excellent news, actually."

Number 1 nodded. "I love good news. Tell me."

"The operation is going as planned. Everything is falling into place. We've been able to eliminate several obstacles recently."

The old man smiled. "Yes. I heard about the U.S. Secretary of State and Secretary of Defense."

"And the riots are spreading like wildfire across the country. Our people have been successful in inciting demonstrations in most major cities of the United States."

"Very good, Angel."

"And the best news is that President Harris has been impeached by the House of Representatives. The Senate has taken up the proceedings now. It's only a matter of time before Harris is convicted and thrown out of office."

Number 1's bushy, white eyebrows knitted together. "How long do you think that will take?"

"Not long, papa. The Senate has to hold hearings. But rest assured it will happen."

The elderly man leaned back in his wingback chair, a smile on his lips. "You have done well. Very well. I'll finally get my revenge on that bastard Harris and the evil government he represents."

"You will get your revenge. I promise you."

The man frowned. "Have there been any problems?"

Angel had been prepared for this question and had decided not to tell the old man about the recent complications. She hated to bring him any bad news. The less he knew of the operational details the better. All he needed to know was that Fireball was on track and would be successful.

"Everything is going exactly as scheduled," she said. "There have been no problems."

"That's excellent, Angel."

Then he rubbed his wrinkled face with a hand and gazed away from her and toward the floor-to-ceiling windows of the den. Like her guest bedroom, the study looked out toward the frozen landscape of the property and beyond to the white mountain peaks of the massive ice cap.

She sensed he was concerned about something, something he was reluctant to tell her.

"What's wrong, papa?"

He gazed at her again, a worried look on his face. "It's mama."

"What about mama?"

"She's concerned ...." his words drifted off without finishing the sentence.

"About what?"

"The operation, Angel. She's concerned about your plan to expand it. She's actually more than concerned. She's totally opposed to your idea."

Angel grit her teeth and swallowed hard, trying to control her anger at the stupid old bitch.

"But, papa," Angel said, keeping her voice calm, so her rage wouldn't show, "when you and I talked about this last time, we agreed to go ahead with the enhancement to Operation Fireball."

"I know, child. I know." He threw up his hands and shrugged. "But you know mama – when she disagrees with something, she's like a dog with a bone."

Angel clenched her fists. "So what are you saying?"

"I'm saying ... that we have to listen to her. She is number 2. Her opinion matters."

Angel's stomach began to churn, the acidic taste of bile rising up her throat. "Please, papa, let me talk to her. I know I can convince her. I know I can explain the incredible benefits of my plan."

Number 1 appeared doubtful, but after a moment he nodded his head. "All right. Maybe you'll be more successful than I."

"Thank you! Thank you, papa. I'm certain I'll be able to convince her."

"I hope you can. I like your enhanced Fireball plan very much."

"By the way," Angel said, "how's mama's health?"

"Not good, child. Every day she appears more frail and weak. She has the best doctors, but ...." He got a faraway look in his eyes. "I hope she can bounce back. We've been married for sixty years. I love her ... very much ...."

"I know you do, papa. And I do too. She's like a mother to me. I love her very much."

He nodded. "I'm sure you do, child. I realize mama's a difficult person sometimes, but I treasure our sixty years of marriage."

***

Angel entered the large bedroom and approached the hospital-style bed. The room was full of electronic monitors and medical equipment of all types.

Number 2, a frail looking 83 year-old woman, was lying on the bed, a sheet covering her torso. She was sleeping, her snores coming in fitful stops and starts.

"How is she today?" Angel murmured to the physician who was hovering by the bed.

"Not well, I'm afraid."

Angel nodded. "You can leave us now, Doctor. I need to speak with her in private."

"Yes, of course." The doctor hung the clipboard he was holding on the wall and left the room, closing the door behind him.

Angel rubbed the old woman's feeble arm. Number 2 woke with a start and her sunken eyes snapped open.

"How are you feeling today, mama?" Angel said in a soothing tone.

"Don't call me that! You know I don't like it!" the sickly woman spat out, venom in her voice. "I'm number 2 to you, you whore!"

Stung by the insult, Angel nevertheless responded in a sweet voice. "I apologize, number 2. I meant no disrespect."

The old woman's eyes blazed with hatred. "What the hell do you want?"

"I came to see how you were feeling."

"You lie, you bitch!" mama screeched, then began coughing uncontrollably. Dark green phlegm came out of her mouth, staining the sheet. When her bout of coughing subsided, she jabbed her index finger toward Angel. "I bet you came to talk me into that insane plan of yours. Well, it won't work, you bitch. I've already decided. It's a fucking crazy plan. It's going to get us all killed."

"But, number 2 –"

"No! How many times do I have to say it! No!"

"But papa likes my plan."

"Don't call him that, you lying slut! Call him number 1."

Angel lowered her gaze to the floor. "I meant no disrespect."

The old woman started coughing again, phlegm spitting out of her mouth. After a minute, she regained her composure.

"I don't care if my husband likes your plan!" the elderly woman screeched. "He's weak. His judgment is clouded because you're young and pretty. You've got him wrapped around your finger with your sweet talk. Calling him papa, batting your eyelashes, making sure you wear tight clothes to show off your tits and ass. Well, you can't fool me, you whore." She stabbed her finger in Angel's direction again. "You're a lying piece of garbage. I'll never agree to your enhanced Fireball plan. Never! Do you hear me? Never!"

Angel needed every ounce of self-control to stop herself from slapping the old bitch. She gulped in a lungful of air and let it out slowly. "Please consider the plan, number 2."

"Get out!" mama screamed. "Get out now, you whore!"

Angel nodded, feeling utterly defeated. She turned and left the room. Going back to her guest bedroom, she spent the next hour mulling over what to do next. After considering all her options, she selected a course of action.

**\*\*\***

Viktor Papadopoulos and Angel Stone had just begun eating in the mansion's enormous dining room. The elegant teak-wood dining table could seat forty people, but they were the only two having dinner. A roaring fireplace blazed in a corner of the room, and four servants hovered nearby, catering to their every need.

Number 1 picked up his flute of champagne and took a sip. "I assume you talked with mama?"

"Yes, papa," Angel replied brightly. "I convinced her!"

The man's bushy white eyebrows shot up. "You did?"

"I did! I told you I would."

The elderly man nodded. "Yes, you did. I should never doubt you, child." A wide smile settled on his face. "You're a miracle worker." He patted her hand. "I'm glad it worked out this way. This new plan of yours is perfect."

"I agree, papa."

"After we have dinner," he said, "I'll go see mama. I'd like to commend her for seeing things your way."

"I don't think that's a good idea," Angel replied. "She's exhausted. In fact, by the time I left her room she was already fast asleep. And her doctor told me she needed to get as much rest as possible."

"You're right, child. Mama needs her rest. I'll see her tomorrow."

Angel nodded. "That's best."

They continued with their seven-course meal, sipping champagne and talking about Operation Fireball. The servants hovered nearby, catering to their every wish.

After the lavish dinner Angel went back to her guest bedroom, excited by papa's companionship and by their future plans. Still wearing her stylish, curve-hugging dress, she stretched out on the king-size bed and took a nap. When she awoke hours later, she glanced at her Rolex watch. It was well past midnight.

Rising from the bed, she smoothed down her dress, put on her heels, ran a hand through her raven hair, and left the room. Bypassing the elevator, she took the stairs to the fourth floor, where's mama's bedroom was located. Slowly opening the door, she glanced around the dim room. As she had expected the physician had already retired for the night and the nurse had apparently retired as well.

Angel approached the hospital-style bed and found number 2 fast asleep, her jerky snoring sounds filling the room.

Then Angel quietly went to the closet and removed a pillow from the shelf. Going back to the sleeping old woman, she placed the pillow over her face. She pressed down hard, leaning in to get the most leverage.

To Angel's surprise, the elderly woman struggled vigorously, pushing back against the suffocating pillow for a long time, with her bony arms. But Angel was much stronger and after a few minutes mama's body sagged. She kept pressing down on the pillow for another minute to make sure the old hag was dead. Then she lifted the pillow and found mama's eyes wide open, her wrinkled mouth full of green phlegm.

Angel closed the dead woman's eyes. Then she removed the soiled pillowcase and deposited it in the laundry basket. That done, she put the pillow back in the closet and headed toward the door of the room. But before she left, she looked back toward the corpse.

"Poor mama," Angel spat out. "You will be missed." She laughed. "But not by me, you wretched old bitch."

Then Angel left the room, closed the door behind her, and went back to her guest bedroom. After removing her clothes, she took a long, hot shower and went to bed. She slept for the next eight hours straight. It was the most satisfying sleep she'd had in months.

# Chapter 62

*National Security Agency - Headquarters*
*Fort Meade, Maryland*

J.T. Ryan had spent several more days trying to ferret out other rogue employees at the NSA facility in Georgia. But neither his sleuthing, nor Lisa Booth's computer program, had been able to come up with more suspects. The two PIs came to the conclusion that there were no other conspirators at that location. That was why Ryan was at the NSA's headquarters now, waiting to speak with its director.

The door to the conference room opened and General Thomas Kyle stepped inside and closed the door behind him.

Ryan stood, the men shook hands, and sat across from each other at the conference table.

"Thank you for seeing me on such short notice," Ryan said.

"No problem," Kyle replied. "I want to get to the bottom of this as much as you do." As during their previous meeting, the general was wearing his blue uniform. He was a burly man with a tight crewcut and an affable manner.

"I'm sure you're familiar with what's been happening, General?"

"I am. My staff's been keeping me informed." He shook his head slowly. "I still can't believe two of my people at the Georgia location were involved. Do you think there are others as well?"

"From what we can figure out, sir, they were the only two at that facility. And that's why I'm here. I need to broaden my net and investigate others throughout the NSA."

"You suspect employees here at headquarters?"

"It's certainly a possibility, General."

Kyle looked deep in thought as he rubbed his jaw. "A month ago I would have said you were crazy to make a statement like that. But with all that's happened at the Georgia facility ... and the high-profile murders, including the Secretary of State and Defense ... well ... anything seems possible now."

"Then you'll help, sir?"

"I will. Mike Corso, the DNI of the U.S. vouches for you, and he's the most trustworthy man I know. So yes, I'll help you. What do you need, Ryan?"

"A list of names, addresses, and job descriptions of every person here at this location."

Kyle let out a low whistle. "That's a big list. We employ over 33,000 people here at NSA headquarters. What are you going to do with this list?"

"The same thing I did before," Ryan said. "One of my associates developed a software program that correlates the names with parameters in our search. That's how we came up with Vega and Wallace."

"All right. I'll have my staff get you this ASAP. But you won't be able to remove the list from this location. The information is top secret. You'll have to work with it here."

"Not a problem, General. I brought my laptop with me – it already has the software installed."

"Good."

"One more thing, sir."

"What's that?"

"Please select someone you trust implicitly to compile this list. We've had several instances where information about our investigation was leaked. People have been murdered as a result."

The general nodded, a grave expression on his face. "I will."

**\*\*\***

A day later Ryan was back in the same conference room, this time holding a flash drive he'd received from General Kyle. Posted outside the room were two armed MPs. They were stationed there to insure two things: That Ryan didn't leave with the information and that no one else came inside.

The PI placed his laptop on the table and booted up. After opening the software program, he inserted the drive into his computer. Then he began running the program and sat back to wait. Lisa had told him it could take hours, if not days, to get a hit.

After staring at the computer screen for an hour, Ryan began pacing the room, impatient with the process.

It was a long, tedious process, the hours stretching into the evening. At midnight one of the MPs opened the door and brought in a boxed dinner and a cot, a pillow, and a blanket.

Ryan thanked the sergeant, and after eating the meal, he used the adjoining bathroom to wash up. After checking the software program to make sure it was still running, he took off his blazer and stretched out on the cot. He was asleep in minutes.

The PI woke with a start the next morning. Jumping off the uncomfortable cot, he stretched his stiff muscles.

Going to his laptop, he stared at the computer screen. To his amazement he noticed the program had completed its task.

A name was highlighted in yellow.

Ryan rubbed his jaw, now stubbly from a day's growth of hair, and wondered who the man could be. He didn't recognize the name, but he hadn't expected to since the list included over 33,000 people.

Ryan quickly turned off his laptop and took out the flash drive, eager to get out there and find the suspect.

# Chapter 63

*Columbia, Maryland*

The man's name was George McNab and he was a GS-15 federal government employee. The GS-15 designation, J.T. Ryan knew, meant the man was a high-level manager at the NSA. Unlike the other National Security Agency employees who were involved in the criminal plot, McNab was a top-tier asset, a person who had access to the NSA's most sensitive and classified secrets.

Ryan had considered telling General Kyle about McNab's connection, but considered it only briefly. Although the general had been cooperative and was not a suspect himself, Ryan knew the military officer would have to treat McNab like any other criminal. The suspect's rights would be read and an attorney would be called. In other words, McNab would clam up and it would take weeks, if not months, to pry information from him.

*That's not what they pay me to do*, Ryan mused. *No, I get paid to get answers fast. How I get the answers is my business.*

McNab lived on the 15th floor of a luxury condo in an exclusive area of Columbia, a bedroom community for Fort Meade. The PI was in the condo building now, on the elevator going up to the 15th floor. Since he wanted to remain anonymous in case things turned sour during the interrogation, he had changed out of his customary blazer and slacks and donned a brown uniform and brown cap. It was the type of clothing worn by employees of the largest parcel company in the U.S. – making him instantly recognizable but also forgettable. The building's security cameras would spot him and see him as no threat. Under his arm he carried an empty cardboard box and on his lapel he had a fake ID badge with an assumed name.

The elevator chime sounded, the doors slid open, and Ryan stepped out. He quickly scanned the corridor both ways, saw no one, then strode on the lushly carpeted hallway to apartment 1518.

Ryan pressed the buzzer and waited. He knew the man was not married and lived alone. He'd also been tailing the man for two days and knew the guy was home now. The PI heard muffled footfalls from inside the apartment and sensed being observed through the spy hole.

The apartment door opened partway. "Can I help you?" the man asked.

"I have a package delivery for Mr. George McNab," Ryan said cheerfully.

"That's me."

"Okay. You just need to sign for it." Ryan fumbled in his uniform pockets for a pen he knew he didn't have. "Darn. I forgot my pen again."

"That's all right. I'll just take the box."

Ryan frowned. "Company policy, sir. I have to get a signature. Especially on this package. It's showing as a high-value item."

"All right. I'll go get one. Wait here."

"Of course, sir."

The man turned and disappeared inside and Ryan slipped into the apartment a second later. He closed and locked the door behind him.

McNab came back to the foyer and was surprised to find Ryan there. His eyes grew wide when he spotted the handgun the PI was holding.

"What the hell is this?" the man demanded. "Is this a robbery?"

Ryan leveled the weapon at his face. "No."

"Crap," McNab said, shaking his head slowly. "You're here for the money I owe."

Ryan had done research and learned the guy owed money to a bunch of bookies. McNab was an avid gambler in Vegas and was in deep. Probably the reason he'd been easy to bribe and blackmail.

"I'm not here to collect," the PI said. "I'm here for another reason."

"What then?"

"This isn't 20 questions, buddy. Now shut up and get on the floor."

"Hell, no! Fuck you, whoever the hell you are!"

"Wrong answer, McNab."

Ryan punched him with a solid blow to his solar plexus and as the guy staggered back he struck him again in the gut. McNab grunted and folded, sagging to his knees. Although the man was fit and strong, the PI was 6'4" and built like a weightlifter. Two blows from him put most men down.

Quickly re-holstering his gun, Ryan pulled out plasticuffs and bound the man's hands behind him. Taking out a small roll of duck tape, he tore off a piece, and slapped it across the guy's mouth. That done he dragged him and lifted him onto the living room sofa.

When the NSA man recovered moments later he stared at Ryan defiantly.

"I know all about you, McNab. I know you're a bottom-feeding gambler who's way behind on your vig payments to the mob. You're dead broke, even though you make good money from your NSA job. I suspect you've been blackmailed by the Fireball conspiracy to give them NSA secrets. You've even traveled to Oslo, Norway to meet with one of the ringleaders."

The guy's defiant look melted when he heard the name Fireball mentioned.

Ryan took out his gun and leveled it at McNab's head. "This is how this is going to work. I ask questions. You answer them. It's that simple. If I like your answers I won't beat you to a pulp. And I won't kill you." He grinned. "That's fair, don't you think?"

Ryan removed the duct tape from the man's mouth. "Are you going to talk?"

"Hell, no. I'd be incriminating myself. If I talk I'll go to jail. I figure you for a Fed and I'll end up doing 20 to life for treason."

"That's true." Ryan smiled again. "Life sucks sometimes."

"I won't talk. Since you know so much about me, you know this isn't the first time I've gotten behind on what I owe my bookies. I've gotten beat up before. Plenty of times. Look at my nose and the scar over my eye."

Ryan noticed the man's bent nose and the ugly gash on his forehead – it was obvious he was telling the truth. Still, it wouldn't hurt to find out for sure.

He punched McNab with an uppercut and followed it with a right hook. The blows snapped the guy's head back and drew blood from his nose and lips.

After a moment McNab recovered and showed a crooked grin. "I'm not talking, you asshole."

"Think you're a tough customer, huh?" Ryan spat out, pressing the muzzle of his .357 Magnum to the man's forehead.

"Go ahead, shoot," McNab replied defiantly. "Put me out of my misery. My life sucks. I'm in so deep to the mob they'll probably kill me anyway. But I know one thing for sure. I'm not going to talk and go to prison."

The PI lowered the handgun and let out a long breath. *This guy is tough*, Ryan thought. *He has nothing to lose. Shit. Now what?* Still, he wasn't about to give up. The NSA man was the best lead he had – the only lead.

Ryan slapped the piece of tape across the guy's mouth and stood.

Then he scanned the living room, looking for clues to the man's inner feelings. He knew a lot about him from his online trail, but he didn't know what he needed most – the man's fears. Something that could be used as leverage to get him to talk. McNab wasn't afraid of being roughed up or killed. But everyone has fears. A fear of being locked up in a tight space or a fear of drowning.

Seeing nothing indicative in the living room, he searched the luxurious kitchen and plushly-appointed bedroom. Unfortunately he found no clues there either. Going back to the living room, he noticed the glass sliders which overlooked an expansive balcony and a panoramic view of the city. It was nighttime and he gazed out at the beautifully lit skyline. Opening one of the sliders, he stepped out on the large balcony. Looking around the terrace, he noticed something odd right away. There were no chaise lounges or tables out here. Also absent was a barbecue grill, or even potted plants. *What kind of person doesn't take advantage of this kind of scenic view?* he thought. Ryan smiled, realizing the answer.

Going back inside, he went to the bedroom and took off one of the bed-sheets. After rolling up the sheet, he took it back to the living room and tied one end of the makeshift rope to McNab's feet.

Then he tore the tape off the man's mouth. "Ready to talk? I'm giving you one last chance."

McNab shook his head. "Hell, no!"

"It's your call, friend. Don't say I didn't give you a chance."

"Why'd you tie that bed-sheet to my feet? What are you going to do?"

Ryan laughed. "You're going to find out." He slapped the duct tape across the guy's mouth again.

Using the rolled up sheet like a rope, Ryan pulled on the free end and dragged the man off the sofa and across the floor to the open glass doors. After turning off the outdoor terrace lights, he continued dragging him across the balcony to the retaining wall at the far end of terrace.

By this time McNab seemed to sense what was going to happen because he was thrashing around, trying to free his bound hands and feet. It was a losing battle and his eyes grew big.

"I'm going to slowly lower you over the side, McNab."

The man's eyes got wide as saucers and Ryan knew he'd hit pay-dirt. McNab was terrified of heights.

"So," the PI said, chuckling, "I'll lower you down – your head will be facing the ground 15 stories below. And when I let go you'll have a great view of what to expect." Ryan laughed. "But don't worry too much. Gravity is your friend. I estimate it'll only take seconds before your skull smashes on the concrete below."

The man's eyes bulged, his face flushed bright red, and he tried moving away from Ryan without success.

The PI grabbed the man roughly by the shoulders and propped him up against the balcony's retaining wall. Then he said, "I'll lower you over the other side of the wall, a foot at a time until I run out of sheet. Then I'll let go. If you change your mind and decide to talk, give me a thumb's up with your hand. I'll pull you back up."

By the terrified expression on his face, it was clear the guy would talk now. But Ryan didn't have time to play games, getting half-truths and lies. He needed to show the man he was deadly serious.

"Okay McNab, here we go. Remember, thumbs up when you're ready to talk."

McNab struggled to get loose and Ryan slugged him hard across the jaw, making his head snap sideways and hit the wall. His head sagged as he lost consciousness.

The PI hauled him to the top of the balcony wall ledge, and after grabbing the loose end of the rolled up bed-sheet, began to slowly lower him to the other side.

Although the skyline was well-lit, Ryan had turned off the balcony lights and the immediate area was dim. It would be difficult for someone to see the body dangling from the side of the building.

Ryan's heavily-muscled shoulders and arms tightened as he felt the full weight of the guy suspended on the makeshift rope. He realized the man was still unconscious because his body was unmoving.

Suddenly McNab began thrashing around. Ryan could only see the guy's bound legs and bound hands, but not his face but knew it must have shown terror. The PI slowly let out more of the makeshift rope and the guy's body lowered another foot. His bound hands were jerking violently with both thumbs pointed up. It was clear McNab was scared shitless, more than ready to talk. Just to make sure, the PI let out another foot of the rolled up bed-sheet.

Just then Ryan smelled the foul stench of excrement and realized the guy's bowels had loosened. He also noticed that McNab's thumbs were jerking up wildly.

"Okay, McNab. I know you'll talk now. I'll bring you up." He began to pull up on the makeshift rope, relieved he didn't need to hurt the man further. The PI didn't like using extreme interrogation techniques, but knew they were often the only way to get the truth.

Several minutes later Ryan pulled the man over the wall ledge, then dragged him across the balcony and inside the apartment. After closing the sliders and the window drapes, he hauled the man up to a sitting position on the sofa.

McNab looked nauseous and disoriented, his face blotchy red and his eyes glassy. Ryan tore the duct tape off his mouth and quickly moved aside to avoid the foul-smelling vomit that spewed out.

After a few minutes the NSA man's eyes focused and Ryan pulled up a chair and sat across from him. "Start talking. Now."

"What ... do you ... want ... to know ...."

"Everything, McNab. All of your involvement in the plot."

The man nodded. "I get paid ..." he replied, his breathing labored, "... large amounts of money ... to give them information .... NSA info ... we have ... sophisticated eavesdropping technology ... we can tap any phone ... any computer ... all of it ... with wiretapping gear ... and NSA satellites ... and other tech tools ...."

"You give this to the Fireball people?"

His eyes lost focus again. He was obviously still disoriented. Eventually his eyes refocused. "Yes ... that's what ... I do ...."

"Who do you report to, McNab?"

"Number ... 3."

Ryan nodded. "You went to see her in Norway?"

"Yeah."

"She runs the operation?"

"Yes ...."

"What's her name?" Ryan already knew this but wanted to make sure he wasn't lying.

"I always referred to her," McNab said, " ... as number 3 ... but I heard one of her bodyguards call her Angel once ...."

Ryan nodded, satisfied with his answers. "What's your code name in the organization?"

"I'm ... number ... 9."

"So you're pretty high up."

The NSA man nodded. "I think so ... but I'm not sure ... everything ... is compartmentalized ...."

"Who else from the NSA is involved?"

McNab shook his head. "Don't ... know."

Ryan pointed toward the balcony. "Bullshit. Tell me or I'll dangle you again. And this time I'll let you go."

The man got bug-eyed again and his face turned red. "Please! Please ... not that!"

"Tell me more, damn it!"

"I know there's ... someone else ... involved ... who's high up ... in government ...."

"Higher than you?"

"Yes ...."

"Who is it, McNab? What's his name?" Ryan slapped the man hard to jar his memory. "Who is it, damn it?"

"Don't know ... his name ... goes by a number ... number 4."

"Did you meet him?"

McNab shook his head. "No ... I had a phone ... conversation ... his voice was altered ... distorted ... I didn't recognize it ...."

"Tell me more, damn you! Or I'm going to fucking drop you off that balcony!"

"Washington ... Washington D.C. ... I know number 4 ... lives there ...."

# Chapter 64

*Columbia, Maryland*

J.T. Ryan spent another half-hour trying to learn more about number 4 without success. It appeared McNab didn't have any additional information. The PI spent another hour interrogating him, questioning him about the Fireball operation in general. The NSA guy confirmed much of what he already knew, though he did learn a few new details about the organization.

Leaving the man tied up in the living room, Ryan thoroughly searched the rest of the apartment, looking for any clues, paperwork, or electronic devices that could aid in the investigation. Locating a laptop, he tried booting up but it was encrypted and he couldn't access the files.

Taking out his cell phone, he tapped in a number. When Erin Welch answered, he said, "It's me. I located a high-value target. Just got through interrogating him."

"Did you find out anything new?" she asked.

"I did." He spent a few minutes giving her some of the details. "But I don't want to say more over the phone. Better when I see you in person."

"Good idea, J.T."

"I found his computer. It's encrypted. I hope one of your tech guys can break the code."

"My tech guys are top-notch. They should be able to. What are going to do with the target?"

Ryan thought about this. He recalled the man who had allegedly 'hung himself' in an apparent suicide. "Last time we put a suspect in an FBI jail cell, it didn't end well for him."

"I remember, J.T. All too well."

"Here's what I'm thinking. I'll call General Kyle at the NSA and have him take custody."

"Can you trust the general?"

Ryan rubbed his jaw. "I think so."

"That's not a ringing endorsement."

"I just remember what President Harris told us that first day, Erin. Trust no one. Suspect everyone."

"I have that hard-wired into my brain. The problem is we're rapidly running out of people we *can* trust."

"I know, Erin."

They were silent a moment, then he said, "All right. I'll call the general now. I'll have him send a team of MPs to my location to take custody of this guy. I'll stay at Fort Meade for another day or so, trying to get more out of McNab. What are you doing?"

"I'm leaving Atlanta today, J.T. I've got another meeting with Mike Corso tomorrow."

"Okay. I'll keep in touch." Ryan hung up and began tapping in General Kyle's phone number.

# Chapter 65

*The Situation Room*
*The White House*
*Washington, D.C.*

Erin Welch stared at Mike Corso, noting his haggard appearance. The DNI seemed to have aged years since their last meeting, which had only taken place a week ago. As usual, the two people were the only ones in the highly-secure room. They were sitting across each other at the large conference table.

"I hope you have good news for me," Corso said. "We could use it."

Erin nodded. "Yes, sir, I do. My team has made several key findings in our investigation."

Corso rubbed his bloodshot eyes with a hand. "Okay. Let's have it."

"Yes, sir. Rachel West has learned the identity of number 3, who is the person that runs the criminal operation. Her name is Angel Stone."

"Has this Stone woman been arrested?"

"Unfortunately not, sir. West found out where she lives and went there to do just that, but Stone escaped."

"I see."

"Agent West is in Norway now," Erin continued, "searching for her. We're hoping she's successful, since we think Angel Stone is the key to the operation."

Corso drummed his fingers on the table, his impatience evident. "What else do you have?"

"Sir, we now know who's bankrolling the Fireball operation. His name is Viktor Papadopoulos, a billionaire who was convicted of money-laundering years ago."

The DNI snapped his fingers. "Papadopoulos? I remember him. When President Harris was Attorney General of Texas, he prosecuted Papadopoulos."

"That's right. Which explains his motivation and hatred of Harris. It also explains why he wants to bring down the president's administration and the rest of the U.S. government."

Corso nodded. "I agree. I know Papadopoulos fled before he was locked up in prison and was never found. Do you know where he is now?"

"Since Angel Stone lives in Norway," Erin said, "we think he's there also."

"All right. What other leads have you developed?"

"As you know, sir, Ryan tracked down two NSA employees who had gone rogue. He's now found a third person. His name is George McNab, a high-level manager at the National Security Agency. His code name is number 9 and he appears to be a key player. He had access to the NSA's top secrets. And he worked for Angel Stone."

"Where is McNab now?"

"We have him in custody. Ryan is continuing to question him. Ryan also found the man's encrypted computer. We hope to access more information from that."

"Good work, Erin."

"Thank you. But the credit goes to John Ryan and Rachel West. They're the two people most responsible for what we've learned so far. By the way, Ryan also found another important lead."

Corso rubbed his bloodshot eyes again. "What is it?"

"This NSA guy, McNab, communicated with another person high-up in U.S. government who is also involved in the plot."

The DNI's eyebrows shot up. "Who is it?"

"We don't have a name yet, sir. McNab talked to the man on the phone, but the voice was altered electronically. He's known in the group as number 4, which would make him a key asset."

"Any guesses on who it could be, Erin?"

"Someone really high up in the food chain. It's possible it could be General Kyle, who runs the NSA."

"But hasn't the general been cooperative in your investigation?"

"He has, sir. Very cooperative."

"Jesus," Corso said with a long sigh, his shoulders sagging. "This damn plot has more layers than those Russian nesting dolls ... we have traitors everywhere."

"Yes, sir," Erin replied.

*Everybody is a suspect*, she thought. *Could Mike Corso himself be part of the criminal organization?* She pushed that ominous thought away.

"Do you have anything else to report, Erin?"

"No. That's about it."

"All right."

"Sir, how's the president holding up?"

Corso shook his head slowly. "As well as can be expected. The impeachment hearings continue in the Senate. Luckily that process can take time, which gives us a small window of opportunity to find and arrest the Fireball criminals. Unfortunately the *Overthrow* riots are increasing across the country. And more innocent people have been killed because of them. The country is in a mess. Everything seems to be falling apart. And we expect a new shoe to drop every day."

"What do you mean by that , sir?"

"We could have another assassination of a highly-placed government official. After the murders of the Secretary of State and Defense, in addition to the Supreme Court Justice, the Senate Majority Leader, and the Cardinal, anything's possible."

"I understand, sir."

Corso loosened his paisley red necktie and undid the top button of his shirt. "God, it's hot in here."

Erin knew the Situation Room was kept at a cool 70 degrees – the conference room didn't feel hot to her at all. She noticed Corso's forehead bead up with perspiration and his face turned pink. "Are you okay, sir?"

Corso stood abruptly. He took out a handkerchief and mopped up his wet brow. "I don't feel well ... I feel sick ...."

Suddenly his face flushed bright red and he clutched his chest with his hands.

Then he collapsed forward, crashing down on top of the conference table.

Erin bolted from her chair and raced around the table to the DNI. She managed to ease his body off the table and onto the floor, where she began to administer CPR.

Mike Corso was totally unresponsive and after a moment she checked his pulse.

The DNI was dead.

# Chapter 66

*Vatnajokull, Iceland*

Angel Stone zipped her parka up to her neck, trying to keep out the frigid air. She, along with a small group of people, were in the mansion's snow-covered back yard for mama's memorial service.

Angel listened as the priest droned on, citing the many accomplishments of mama's life. According to the priest, mama had been a paragon of virtue and a substantial contributor to many charitable causes. *No matter*, Angel thought. *Mama was an evil bitch who deserved her miserable ending.*

Standing next to Angel was Viktor Papadopoulos. He was sobbing quietly, a hand covering his face.

Just then a fierce gust of arctic wind swirled around them and Angel reached out and clutched papa's arm to steady herself. The old man nodded to her, then drew back into himself again, the tears flowing freely.

Angel turned her attention back to the priest, who mercifully appeared to be coming to a conclusion. Angel couldn't wait to get back inside the luxurious mansion, away from the bone-chilling temperatures. Snow began to fall and she shivered, looking forward to going to her room and soaking in the immense hot tub.

The priest finished his prayers, made a final sign of the cross, and sprinkled holy water on the gold-trimmed teak casket. On the far side of the massive back yard was an ornate marble mausoleum. The casket would be placed inside that structure later today.

Angel approached the priest and thanked him for his eulogy, then she returned to papa's side. The old man was still weeping silently, staring despondently at his dead wife's casket.

Angel took his arm and whispered, "Let's go back inside, papa. You'll catch pneumonia if you stay out here." He seemed reluctant but after a long moment he let her lead him back into the mansion.

***

After a long soak in the hot tub, Angel felt a thousand per cent better. Toweling herself off, she picked out her clothes carefully, dressed, and began combing her long raven hair, which cascaded past her shoulders.

She studied herself in the full-length mirror, pleased with what she saw. The tight-fitting black turtleneck and black skirt showed off her curves nicely, she thought. Leaving her guest bedroom, she took the elevator down to the mansion's first floor and went into the large study.

Viktor Papadopoulos was there, sitting close to the stone fireplace, where a roaring fire was burning. He was staring at the flames, his red-rimmed eyes still wet from tears.

She approached him, pulled up a chair and sat next to him. "How are you feeling, papa?" she asked soothingly.

The old man shook his head and said nothing, trying to hold back the tears. Then he covered his face with a hand, lowered his head and wept uncontrollably.

Angel lightly rubbed his back, trying to console him.

Eventually the crying stopped and he raised his head. Giving her a dejected look, he said, "Will it get better?"

"It will," she replied quietly. "The grief will lessen. It just takes time."

"I loved her so much, Angel."

"I know you did. As did I ... she was like a mother to me." Angel marshaled her emotions and forced herself to shed several tears.

Papadopoulos caressed her face gently. "I'm sorry, Angel. I've been so focused on my own loss that I forgot you're grieving also."

She brushed her tears away with a hand, gave him a sad smile, then hugged the old man. "Don't worry, papa. We'll get through this together."

He held her embrace and stroked her long hair gently with a hand.

When they parted a moment later, she said, "I guess we should talk about the future."

His bushy white eyebrows knitted. "The future? What do you mean?"

"The operation. The next steps."

"Oh, that. I haven't ... given that any more thought."

She patted his knee. "Don't worry, papa. I'll take care of everything."

The old man seemed relieved. "You will?"

"Of course."

"You're such a treasure, Angel. I don't know what I'd do without you."

She smiled, then caressed his cheek with her palm. "I'm always going to be here for you, papa."

# Chapter 67

*FBI Field Office*
*Atlanta, Georgia*

"I still can't believe he's dead," Erin Welch said.

"Me neither," J.T. Ryan replied. The two people were in Erin's office. "What was the cause of death?"

"The M.E.'s initial finding was heart attack."

Ryan frowned. "Mike Corso was in his fifties. Seems young for a heart attack."

"I thought the same thing. But being DNI is a high-stress job. Anyway, the medical examiner is conducting a thorough autopsy. If there's foul play involved, it'll show up."

Ryan nodded. "So what happens now?"

"I don't know, J.T. I'm sure President Harris will appoint a new Director of National Intelligence soon. But I haven't heard anything from the White House yet."

"And in the meantime?"

Erin leaned forward in her executive chair. "In the meantime we continue with our investigation. We still have our marching orders from the president."

"Good." Ryan had brought a laptop with him and he placed it on her desk. "This is McNab's encrypted computer. Hopefully your tech guys can access the files."

Erin tapped the lid of the computer. "I'll get this to them right away. Where's George McNab now?"

"He's in General Kyle's custody – locked up in a cell at NSA headquarters in Fort Meade."

"All right," she said. "By the way, good work on getting the information from McNab."

Ryan gave her a half-salute and smiled. "Is that a compliment I'm hearing?"

"Don't let it go to your head, J.T. It's already too big."

Ryan chuckled.

Turning serious, he said, "Where are we on the rest of the investigation?"

"I got a call this morning from Alex Miller at the CIA. They found out that there's a small NSA facility in Norway. Since Angel Stone lived in that country, the CIA suspects there's a connection between her and people who work at that facility."

"Makes sense, Erin. Where's this NSA operation located?"

"In a small town in the western part of Norway." Erin opened a folder and read from it. "Voss, Norway."

"Okay. Is Rachel West there now?"

Erin nodded. "She is."

# Chapter 68

*Voss, Norway*

It turned out that finding the NSA facility had been more difficult than Rachel West anticipated. Although Voss was a small town with few residents, none seemed to know about the secretive American base.

It had taken Rachel several days to find the facility, which it turned out, was nestled deep inside a heavily-forested area. The desolate, snow-covered mountainous region was twenty miles from the center of town. She had spotted it by accident, while driving long a deserted rural road. Peeking over the treeline she saw the telltale shape of two huge satellite dishes and a geodesic dome. Since the dishes and dome were white in color they blended in well with the ice-capped mountains and the snow-covered treeline.

After debating with herself on how to approach the facility, she decided a direct approach was best. After all she and the NSA were on the same side – at least on the surface, she mused.

Rachel was headed there now, driving the all-terrain Land Rover on the desolate rural road. She spotted an unmarked gravel path up ahead leading into the forest. It appeared to be the only way into the NSA facility, so she slowed her vehicle and turned onto the path. Like the road, the gravel path was covered with uneven drifts of snow and the Land Rover climbed and bounced over the icy clumps.

Five minutes later she came to a large area cleared of trees. There were four structures on the snow-covered clearing – the white geodesic dome, the two massive satellite dishes, and a long, rectangular one-story building. There were no signs or markings on any of the structures. Chain link fencing topped with razor-wire surrounded the grounds, which were well-lit by numerous floodlights.

Rachel drove the Land Rover to the manned sentry gate and stopped.

An armed security guard stepped out of the booth at the entrance and approached her vehicle.

"This is a restricted facility," the guard said in Norwegian.

Rachel opened her cred pack and handed it to the man. "I'm Rachel West, with the American CIA," she replied in Norwegian. "I need to speak with the person in charge."

The guard took the creds and studied them while his other hand rested on the butt of his holstered pistol. He glanced up and said, "Wait here."

Going back into the guard booth, he picked up a phone. He came back a few minutes later and said, "I will open the gate. Drive to the single-story building." He handed back her cred pack.

Once the entrance gate creaked open, she drove onto the facility grounds and parked in front of the all-white building. There was a second security guard by the entrance who escorted her inside and into a small conference room.

Soon after a thin, Nordic-looking blond man stepped into the room. "I am Karl Vaasa," he said in Norwegian. "I manage this location."

Rachel extended her hand and they shook. "Rachel West, CIA. Do you speak English?" Although she was somewhat fluent in Norwegian, it was a difficult language to master.

The man nodded. "Of course. Please have a seat."

They sat across from each other.

"As I said, I'm with the Central Intelligence Agency," she began. "I'm investigating several murders."

"I called your people at Langley," Vaasa replied. "They confirmed who you are and what you are investigating."

"Good."

The man adjusted his tie with a hand. "The part I am not clear about is why you are here."

"Let me explain. The murders are connected to people within the NSA. Rogue employees who have been complicit in the crimes. Specifically, employees who work at the NSA-Georgia facility and at your headquarters in Fort Meade."

Vaasa didn't reply, simply stared at her with no reaction. She thought her statements would have shocked him.

"You don't seem surprised, Mr. Vaasa."

He shrugged. "What you are telling me seems far-fetched." He smirked. "But then the CIA has been known to be wrong before."

She leaned forward in her chair. "This is no laughing matter. We have rock-solid proof of rogue NSA agents being part of this murder plot. We've already arrested three National Security Agency employees who are involved."

For the first time his face registered concern. "I see. But I still do not understand why you are here. We are a very small facility with few employees. Our location is far from America."

Rachel nodded. "True enough. But we've been able to track down the ringleader of this criminal group. She lives in Norway."

His eyes narrowed but he said nothing.

"Her name is Angel Stone," Rachel continued. "She's known as number 3 in the organization."

For a micro-second Vaasa's eyes widened.

"Have you ever heard of this woman, Mr. Vaasa?"

The man shook his head forcefully. "I know of no such person."

She decided to let that go for a moment. "I see. By the way, what do you do here at this location?"

He seemed pleased to move on to another topic. "We are a monitoring station. We do surveillance, mostly of Russian transmissions. Russia is not far from Norway."

"What kind of surveillance do you do?"

"That is classified information, Ms West. I am sure you understand."

"I do," she replied pleasantly, "since I'm in the spy business myself." She smiled, trying to put the man at ease.

Vaasa returned the smile. "I have been a terrible host. May I offer you some coffee?"

"That would be nice – it was a long drive to get here."

"Of course. I will go and get it. And some Norwegian pastries also. We make delightful cakes in our country."

"So I've heard. Thank you, Mr. Vaasa."

He left the conference room and came back moments later, carrying a tray laden with pastries and two steaming mugs of coffee.

After she nibbled on the cake and sipped the savory coffee, she leaned back in her chair. Smiling, she said, "I just had one more question before I go."

"Of course," he replied, his expression genial.

"Mr. Vaasa, have you ever heard of a man named Viktor Papadopoulos? We believe he's the money man behind the conspiracy. A conspiracy known as Fireball."

The man's face drained of color.

His eyes narrowed and he took in a deep breath. Recovering quickly, he said, "I have not heard those names before."

"All right. Just thought I'd ask. Well, I've taken enough of your time today." She smiled and extended her hand. "Thank you, sir. You've been very cooperative. I'll be on my way."

They shook hands.

"It was a pleasure meeting you, Ms West."

# Chapter 69

*Bergen, Norway*

Angel Stone was in her home's office, humming along to her favorite Brahms symphony playing over the sound system. She was ecstatic, buoyed by her recent successful trip to Iceland.

She smiled as she recalled how she'd dealt with the mama problem. The evil bitch was gone.

Her grin widened as she mused over the last discussion she'd had with papa. The old man, deep in grief over his wife's death, had practically ceded total control of the operation to Angel. And Angel had wasted no time in putting the new-found authority to use. While still in Iceland she'd been able to access some of Papadopoulos's financial records.

And now would come the payoff.

She lifted the lid of her encrypted laptop and booted up. Accessing her Swiss bank account, she transferred 500 million dollars from one of Papadopoulos's accounts into it.

The wire transfer was instantaneous.

She grinned, seeing all that cash in her name.

To a multi-billionaire like Viktor Papadopoulos, that amount of money only represented a small portion of his vast wealth. But to her it meant freedom. Freedom to do whatever she wanted after Operation Fireball was complete. And it was more than that, she mused. It was also an insurance policy in case the operation turned sour. There was a low probability of that happening, she thought. But it was better to be prepared for every contingency.

As she stared at the financial figures on the screen, she felt a sexual thrill course through her body. Her cheeks flushed and she became wet.

Then she had a disturbing thought and her grin vanished. *What if papa finds out I took the money without asking? What if the grief from his wife's death fades and he reasserts control back from me?*

She rubbed the small scar on her cheek, thinking furiously.

After a moment she let out a long breath, seeing a solution as clear as day. Men were weak when it came to sex. Very weak. Even an 85-year-old man still has carnal desires. Desires, Angel suspected, that hadn't been satisfied for long time by his frail, sickly wife.

Yes, she thought. I just need to ingratiate myself to him in a new way. Years ago their relationship had changed from employer and employee to more of a father and daughter one. It's time we became more. More like husband and wife. And it wasn't like this would be the first time Angel had used sex to get her way. Her past was littered with men she'd used and then thrown away or eliminated.

Papadopoulos would be a challenge, she knew. At his advanced age, it would take some doing on her part to bring him to climax.

She grinned, knowing she was up to the task. In fact, she relished the notion of sex with the elderly billionaire. Once again her cheeks flushed and she felt herself becoming wet.

Just then her encrypted desk phone rang. She snatched up the receiver and held it to her ear. "Yes?"

"This is number 5," the man said. "We have a problem."

She tensed and gripped the phone tightly, the thoughts of sex gone. "What kind of problem?"

"We had a visit today from a woman CIA agent. She was asking questions about the operation."

"What the hell!" Angel screamed into the phone. "This agent came to your location in Voss?"

"That's right, number 3."

"Who was she, damn it?"

"Her credentials identified her as Rachel West."

"What did she want?"

"She was investigating the murders tied to our project. She seemed to know quite a bit."

"Like what?"

"She was looking for the ringleader of the operation. She knew your name."

"My name?"

"That is right, number 3. She said Angel Stone was the ringleader."

Angel's stomach churned, the acid taste of bile reaching her throat. "How is that possible?"

"I do not know."

"What did you tell her, number 5?"

"Nothing. I told her nothing of value. But there is more. This CIA woman mentioned two other names. She said the operation was being funded by Viktor Papadopoulos. And she even knew that the code name for our operation was Fireball."

A throbbing headache pounded in Angel's skull. She massaged her temple with a hand. "Fuck!" she screeched. "Things were going so well. And now this. Fuck!"

Angel gulped in air and let it out slowly. "What did you do, number 5?"

"I finessed the situation. I told her I knew nothing about any of this."

"Did she believe you?"

"Yes. She seemed satisfied. We even had coffee and pastries. And then she left."

Angel rubbed her temple again, somewhat relieved by what the man had just said. Still, this new threat was a dangerous development.

"What do you want me to do now, number 3?"

"Be proactive. If she visits again, deal with her."

"Should I ...."

"Yes, number 5."

# Chapter 70

*Voss, Norway*

Rachel West stepped into her hotel room, closed and locked the door behind her, and went to the window. Her room was on the second floor of the quaint inn, giving her a good view of the snow-covered parking area below. Peeking past the curtains, she observed her rented Land Rover, which was parked alongside several other vehicles. There was no activity outside and it appeared no one had followed her from the NSA facility.

After closing the drapes fully, she removed her heavy parka and took out her cell phone. Pressing one of the preset numbers, she waited for the other side to pick up. It was 3 p.m. now in Norway which meant it was morning in Langley. She knew Alex Miller would already be at work.

"It's me," Rachel said when he answered.

"Where are you?"

"A hotel in Voss."

"Did you go to the facility?"

"Just got back, boss."

"And?"

"I met with the man in charge."

"What did he say?"

"Nothing. And everything."

"What do you mean?"

"He said he knew nothing about the murders," she replied, "or Angel Stone, or Viktor Papadopoulos, or Fireball. But."

"But what?"

"He was lying through his teeth, boss."

# Chapter 71

*Voss, Norway*

As she had done the previous day, Rachel West drove to the NSA facility, went through their security checkpoint, and was once again shown into the small conference room where she had met Karl Vaasa yesterday.

As Rachel waited for the man to come in, she nibbled on one of the flavorful pastries that were on a platter on the table. *How thoughtful of Vaasa*, she mused, *to provide a snack for me. Too bad for him this meeting isn't going to be pleasant like the one yesterday.* This time she had come prepared to get real answers. Her Glock, locked and loaded, was nestled in the pocket of her heavy parka, which she was still wearing.

Just then the conference room door opened and Karl Vaasa stepped inside, a wide smile on his face. "Ms West, how good to see you again."

They shook hands and sat down across from each other.

"I see you are already eating one of the pastries," he said pleasantly. "I hope you find them as delicious as we do."

"They're very good. It was very thoughtful of you."

Vaasa grinned. "We want to make your visit with us as pleasant as possible. Since you came back, you must need to ask me more questions. Which I am more than happy to answer." He smiled again. "Since we are on the same side, are we not?"

Rachel nodded. "Yes, we are."

The Norwegian man placed his hands flat on the table in front of him. "So. How may I assist you? I realize that your experiences with some of our other NSA facilities have been negative, but rest assured, we in Voss are an open book. We are more than willing to assist the CIA in any way we can."

"Let's start with something I asked about yesterday," she said, stifling a yawn. "The ringleader of the criminal group we're seeking is a woman named Angel Stone. Have you ever heard of her?"

Vaasa shook his head. "I know of no such person."

Rachel suddenly felt drowsy. "Are you sure, Mr. Vaasa?"

"I am."

"What about Operation Fireball?" she asked, stifling another yawn.

The man smiled. "As I told you yesterday," he said amiably, "I have never heard of that."

Rachel's eyelids felt heavy and her vision blurred. Sensing danger, she slipped her hand into the pocket of her coat. She gripped the butt of her pistol and pulled out the weapon. The Glock felt very heavy. Too heavy to hold and it dropped out of her hand and clattered to the floor.

Rachel tried reaching for it as a wave of dizziness hit her and she slumped over in her chair and passed out.

Her eyes snapped open hours later. Now fully awake, she realized she was in trouble. A hell of a lot of trouble.

She was still in the same conference room.

But now there were five other people in the room. Vaasa and four other men. And they were all pointing guns at her.

"I hope you had a nice nap," Vaasa said pleasantly.

"You bastard!" Rachel spat out. "You drugged me. You put something in those damned pastries of yours."

Vaasa nodded. "Guilty as charged."

Rachel thought furiously as she weighed her options. She glanced at the floor – her pistol was long gone. And they had also taken her coat, where she'd placed a backup gun in a hidden pocket.

She glared at Vaasa and said, "I'm assuming you've heard of Angel Stone."

Vaasa laughed and so did the other four men.

"Of course I know who she is," Vaasa said. "She is my boss. And you were right. She runs our operation."

"What happens now?" Rachel asked.

"Now we wait, Ms West. Angel will be here soon. She wants to interrogate you herself."

"And after that?"

Vaasa grinned. "You are a smart woman. I think you already know the answer to that question."

Rachel did know the answer. She'd be murdered as soon as they had pried whatever information they could out of her. Her thoughts raced, trying to figure out a way out of this mess.

Staring at the five armed men, she pondered her options. Angel Stone would arrive soon, most likely accompanied by more armed men. Rachel's odds of escape, which were already low now, would disappear entirely. *I have to make my move now.*

After mulling over her limited options, she selected one. It was a long shot, she knew. But her profession was full of those. She said a silent prayer and then visualized the thin carbon knife she'd taped to her forearm, underneath her long-sleeve shirt.

In a split-second she grabbed the knife and pulled it out, and then stabbed the man nearest her. Then she leapt on top of the table and slashed the blade in front of her, cutting the jugular of a second man. Blood spurted from his neck as she spun around and stabbed a third guy in the face.

Suddenly Rachel felt a blinding pain in her head and she staggered to her knees.

Then everything went black.

# Chapter 72

*The Situation Room*
*The White House*
*Washington, D.C.*

"Why are we here?" J.T. Ryan asked.

"I'm not really sure," Erin Welch replied. "I got a call yesterday from the White House and was told to come to D.C. They told me both of us will be briefed at this meeting."

Ryan glanced around the large, highly-secure room. He and Erin were the only people there. "Why meet in this room? I thought this place was reserved for National Security meetings."

"It usually is, J.T. But I met with Mike Corso in here. He felt it was the only room other than the Oval Office where we could talk without being spied upon."

"I understand."

Just then a Secret Service agent opened the door to the room and let in a thin, mousy-looking woman with frizzy hair. Ryan had met her once before. She was Samantha Lowry, the Deputy DNI. The woman looked more like a librarian than a high-level government official.

The Secret Service agent left and closed the door behind him.

After shaking hands the three people sat down at the long conference table.

"Thank you for coming on such short notice," Samantha Lowry said. She had a high-pitched, squeaky voice that seemed out of place in the top-secret room. "But I needed to brief you on an important matter."

"No problem," Erin replied.

Lowry had curly, frizzy hair and she unconsciously toyed with one of her curls. "Ever since Mike's tragic death ... things have been ... hectic ... here at the White House ...."

Erin nodded. "I can imagine. Ms Lowry, have the results of Mike Corso's autopsy come in?"

The mousy woman pulled out a handkerchief and blew her nose. "It has. The M.E. determined Mike died of natural causes. A massive heart attack."

Ryan and Erin exchanged glances.

Then Ryan said, "So the DNI's death was not a murder?"

Lowry nodded. "That's right." She put away her handkerchief. "Which brings us to why I asked you here today. As you know, we've had some very shocking developments in the last several months. The murders of the Senate Majority Leader and the Chief Justice of the Supreme Court. The Cardinal. The Secretary of State and the Secretary of Defense. And now ... Mike's death. Well, it's been a difficult time ... a chaotic time ... here at the White House ...." She played with the curls of her hair again and Ryan realized it was a nervous habit.

"We're scrambling to fill the vacancies," Lowry continued. "And all of this has happened while the president himself is undergoing impeachment hearings."

"How is that process going?" Erin asked.

"It's being debated in the Senate," Lowry said. "Endless hearings, endless speeches ... it appears it will drag out for months."

"I see."

"I met with President Harris yesterday," the mousy woman said, "and he asked me to assume the role of Director of National Intelligence. Since I have been the Deputy DNI for several years, he feels I'm best qualified for the job." She toyed with her curly hair again. "I tried to talk him out of it, but he insisted. It's a big responsibility, since it's the highest ranking intelligence job in the U.S. government. I'm not sure I'm up to the job. But the president is the president, and I want to support him in any way I can. So I accepted."

"Congratulations," Erin said. "We'll do everything we can to make it a smooth transition."

Lowry again took out her handkerchief and blew her nose. "After I accepted the position, the president filled me in on your team's investigation. Up until then, I had no knowledge of your activities. President Harris also gave me Mike Corso's files, so I now have a good idea of your progress so far. Do you have any new developments on the case?"

"Rachel West is in Norway now," Erin said. "She's trying to track down the ringleader, a woman named Angel Stone. We hope to arrest Stone soon."

"Very good. Anything else?"

Erin glanced at Ryan. "Why don't you fill her in on your part of the investigation, J.T."

"Sure," he replied. "I've been able to track down three rogue government employees. All of them worked for the NSA. The latest man I arrested was a high-level manager at the National Security Agency. His name is George McNab. He had access to the NSA's top secrets, which he sold to the criminals for large amounts of money."

"Where is McNab now?" Lowry asked.

"He's locked up at Fort Meade, still undergoing questioning."

Lowry played with her curls again. "Were you able to learn anything from this McNab person?"

"Some," Ryan said. "He worked for another high-ranking government employee who is also involved with the criminal organization. That man's identity is still unknown – but we do know his code name is number 4. Since Angel Stone runs the operation and she's number 3, we feel that catching this man known as number 4 would be a key break in the case."

Lowry nodded. "Excellent work. It appears you both are close to solving this case." She paused a moment and glanced at her watch. "I have a meeting with the president soon and I need to get ready for that. Please keep me informed, Erin, of your team's progress."

"Of course, ma'am," Erin said.

Lowry stood. "Thank you both. And may God be with you, and with us all. We're going to need his help."

***

Ryan and Erin were escorted out of the White House by the Secret Service. At the security checkpoint their weapons and their cell phones were returned. When they got back to their vehicle in the West Wing parking lot, Ryan noticed he had a message on his phone.

They climbed into the rented SUV and Ryan said, "I need to answer this call. Looks important."

"Who called you?" Erin said.

"General Kyle at NSA Headquarters."

Ryan punched in the number and the call was answered on the second ring.

"This is J.T. Ryan," he said.

"I have bad news," Kyle replied, his voice tense.

"What is it, General?"

"I went to question George McNab three hours ago. Found him dead in his cell."

Ryan gripped the phone tightly. "What? How's that possible?"

"I don't know. I had MPs posted outside his cell 24/7. It shouldn't have happened. But it did."

"How did he die, General?"

"From what the coroner tells me, McNab died of food poisoning."

# Chapter 73

*Voss, Norway*

Rachel West regained consciousness and felt a blinding pain on the back of her head. She was still in the same conference room, but now she was bound to a chair with her hands tied behind her back. Her feet were also secured to the chair.

Standing in front of her was Karl Vaasa, his tie and white shirt stained with dried blood. He was holding a gun at his side. Three other armed men were also in the room, their pistols pointed at her head.

"This bitch killed two of my men and wounded another," Vaasa spat out. "She needs to die. Now!"

Rachel heard a woman's voice from behind her. "Not yet, Karl. I get to question her first. Then you can kill her."

Rachel saw movement from the corner of her eye and a very attractive woman came into view.

The woman stood in front of her, an enigmatic smile on her face. She had long, raven hair which cascaded past her shoulders. Her exotic, model-like beauty was only marred by a small scar on her left cheek. She wore a black turtleneck and black slacks which hugged her curves tightly.

The raven-haired woman took Vaasa's gun from him and slid it into her own waistband. "Leave us now, Karl. I want to question her privately."

"Are you sure, Angel?" the man asked. "This woman is a CIA agent. She is extremely dangerous."

The woman's eyes bore into his. "What did I say?"

"Of course, Angel. As you wish." Vaasa motioned to the other men and they all left the room, closing the door behind them.

"Do you know who I am?" the raven-haired woman said, the enigmatic smile still on her face.

Rachel nodded. "I'm sure you're Angel Stone."

"You are correct." Angel laughed. "You seem smart. Even though you're a blonde." She chuckled again. "But I guess you've heard a lot of dumb blonde jokes in your lifetime."

Rachel's thoughts raced, trying to figure out the woman's strange behavior. *Is she crazy? I just killed two of her people and she's making a blonde joke?*

Rachel said nothing.

"You're going to tell me everything I want to know, Rachel West. You see, we're a lot alike in many ways. As I'm sure you know, I was a covert CIA operative years ago. Which means I've been through the same rigorous training you have. I know how to interrogate people. Your nightmare is just beginning."

Angel smiled. "I know how to put fear into people. Yes, you're going to tell me every detail you know about Operation Fireball. And more importantly, how you were able to find out about it." She paused. "But before we get to that, you and I are going to have some fun." She chuckled. "Well, fun for me, maybe not so much for you."

Angel Stone reached into one of her pant pockets and removed a thin knife. Rachel recognized the blade immediately – it was her own carbon knife, the one she'd used to kill the two men earlier. Dried blood was still on the dagger.

Angel held the tip of the blade close to Rachel's face, then moved it closer so that it touched her cheek.

Rachel flinched and tried to move away but she was securely bound to the chair.

Angel grinned as she delicately slid the sharp knife across Rachel's cheek, almost piercing the skin.

"We'll get to my questions later," Angel said. "But first I want to see what you look like. You're a pretty thing, aren't you?"

The raven-haired woman slid the knife down the front of Rachel's shirt, cutting off the buttons. Then she hooked the tip of the blade on the brassiere and cut it open. After roughly pushing away the cut garments, Angel said, "Oh, my, you are a pretty one. Well endowed, too."

Rachel thought furiously, trying to figure out how to get away from the insane woman.

"Don't look so worried, blondie," Angel said soothingly. "I'm not going to kill you. I'll let Karl do that. I just want to have some fun."

The woman cackled, then slid the blade lower, slicing into Rachel's jeans and her underwear. Then she forcefully tore off the cut clothing, leaving the CIA operative completely naked.

"You have a sweet body," Angel cooed. "Under different circumstances, I could see us becoming lovers, blondie. I prefer men, but I enjoy women almost as much. It's a pity we won't be able to become close friends."

Angel's face hardened. "Well, that's enough foreplay. It's time I make this meeting something you won't forget for the rest of your life." She pointed to the scar on her own cheek. "You see this?"

Rachel nodded.

"I got this when I was locked up in Guantanamo," Angel said. "Now I'm going to give you a scar just like it." She smiled, but it was a cold, hard grin that had no humor in it. Angel grabbed Rachel's ponytail roughly with one hand, while her other hand slid the knife closer to Rachel's face.

Rachel tried moving her head away without success. Angel was a strong woman and held it securely.

The tip of the blade touched Rachel's cheek.

Angel thrust the knife, slicing into Rachel's face.

The sharp pain was instantaneous and Rachel grit her teeth to keep from passing out. She felt blood seeping from her cheek, down her throat, and on her naked breasts.

The raven-haired woman stepped back and stared at Rachel as if admiring her handiwork.

"I think that will do nicely," Angel said. With a satisfied look on her face, she put the bloody knife back in her pocket.

Rachel tried to block out the pain as her thoughts churned, trying to figure out a way to escape from the crazy woman.

"Now that we've got that out of the way," Angel said calmly, "we can get to my questions."

"I'm going to bleed to death."

Angel laughed. "Probably. But not right now. I didn't cut you that much."

"Bitch," Rachel spat out.

"I'm sure that's true." She slapped Rachel hard across her wounded cheek. More blood spurted out of the wound and the coppery taste of gore filled Rachel's mouth.

The CIA operative saw stars, the intense pain causing her to pass out.

When she came to a minute later, she found Angel still standing in front of her, her arms folded across her chest.

"Ready to talk now, blondie?"

"Fuck you," Rachel growled.

The woman slapped her again, but this time Rachel was able to stay conscious.

"How did you find out about Operation Fireball?" Angel demanded.

Rachel said nothing, a defiant look on her face.

"Tell me, blondie, or you'll regret it!"

"I'm not talking, bitch."

Angel flashed a hard grin again. "We'll see about that." Then she removed the bloody knife from her pocket and held it in front of Rachel's face.

A stab of cold fear ran down Rachel's spine. Goosebumps rose on her nude torso. Although she was a highly-trained CIA operative, she was having trouble fighting off the terror. Then she heard a phone ringing.

Angel stepped away from her and pulled a cell phone from her pocket.

"This is number 3," Angel said after picking up the call. Then she stared at Rachel. "Yes, number 1. I have the woman here, in Voss."

After a moment Angel nodded. "Yes, number 1. I'll take care of it." She hung up the phone.

"That was my boss," Angel said. "He wants to question you himself. Pity. Since our fun was just starting."

Rachel breathed a sigh of relief for the reprieve. "He's coming here?"

Angel shook her head. "No. I always go to him."

"Where is he?"

The raven-haired woman flashed that icy grin again. "You'll find out soon enough, blondie."

# Chapter 74

*National Security Agency - Headquarters*
*Fort Meade, Maryland*

J.T. Ryan quickly read through the coroner's report, then placed the folder on General Kyle's desk.

"Pretty clear cut," Ryan said. "George McNab was poisoned."

"That's right," Kyle answered, picking up the folder and storing it in a desk drawer. The two men were in the general's office.

"The question is, General, who did it?"

Kyle's expression was grim. "That's the hard part. I had McNab's jail cell guarded 24/7 by MPs I trust implicitly. But McNab was poisoned by something he ate. Unfortunately there are over fifty people who work in the kitchen where the meal came from. It could be any of them."

Kyle slammed a fist on his desk. "Damn it! I can't believe so many NSA people are involved."

"Sir, I assume you're checking the backgrounds of each of the fifty people?"

"I am, Ryan. And when I catch the fucking bastard I'm going to choke the truth out of him."

Ryan nodded. "Whoever it was really screwed our investigation. McNab was our best lead. And now he's dead."

The general's face flushed. "I blame myself for this. His death happened under my watch. God damn it, I should have prevented this!"

Ryan didn't reply, mulling over the situation. *Is General Kyle complicit? Is he the conspirator known as number 4?* It was impossible to know. Kyle didn't appear guilty. But he could be a good actor, Ryan knew. He'd run across criminals who were smooth liars, criminals who appeared above reproach.

Pushing aside that disturbing thought, Ryan focused on one inescapable fact: McNab was dead. And McNab had been his best lead.

# Chapter 75

*Bergen, Norway*

Angel Stone was packing her suitcase, getting ready for her upcoming trip to Iceland. When she was half-way done, she heard a knock on her bedroom door.

"Come in," she said.

The door opened and Gustav, her head of security stood at the entrance.

"Your jet is fueled and ready to go," the Norwegian man said.

"Good," Angel replied. "Where's the prisoner now?"

"Tied up in the garage."

"Did you patch up her wound?"

"I did, Angel. But she has lost a lot of blood."

"She's the least of my worries. Just make sure she's on my plane when we take off." Angel glanced at her Rolex. "I want to leave in an hour. Inform the pilot."

"Of course."

Just then Angel's cell phone rang and she retrieved it from her pocket. Seeing the code number on the info screen, she turned to Gustav. "Get out. And close the door behind you."

The man nodded and left.

"Yes," Angel said into the phone.

"It's number 4," the caller said.

"You have good news for me, I hope."

"I'm afraid not, number 3."

The familiar acrid taste of bile surged up her throat. "Tell me."

"The impeachment proceedings against President Harris."

"What about them, number 4?"

"They're not going well. As you know, the president was impeached by the House of Representatives and the case was forwarded to the Senate for a conviction and subsequent eviction from the White House."

"I know all that, damn it."

"Of course, number 3. The Senate appears to be deadlocked on the issue. We don't have enough votes for a conviction."

Angel grit her teeth and her face flushed bright red. She swallowed hard, the sulfuric taste of bile in her mouth growing. "Do you need more money? I can transfer whatever amount you need."

"That's not going to help this time, number 3. We've tried bribery. We've tried blackmail. The senators we can't convince to vote with us are steadfast in their resolve."

Angel gripped the phone tightly. "You mean they're honest people."

"That's right, number 3."

"I didn't think there were any of those left in Washington." Angel rubbed her forehead, trying to will away the growing migraine.

"What do you want me to do, ma'am?"

"We need to accelerate our plans," Angel said. "Put Fireball on the final phase."

"You mean?"

"Yes, number 4. That's exactly what I mean."

"Should I do that now?"

Angel considered this for a long moment. There would be no turning back, once the final phase of Fireball was initiated. "I want to discuss it with number 1 first. But you need to get everything in place. Be ready to act on a moment's notice, number 4."

# Chapter 76

*Atlanta, Georgia*

J.T. Ryan was driving south on Peachtree Street, on his way to the FBI building downtown. Traffic was heavy and it was sleeting, a bad combination in Atlanta. The city's traffic, which was horrendous under normal circumstances, was a nightmare in bad weather. He'd already spotted three car wrecks along the icy road.

Ryan's cell phone vibrated and he pulled it out of his blazer pocket. Slowing the Ford Explorer, he answered the phone.

"It's Alex Miller," he heard the man say. "You remember me?"

"Of course." Miller was the Director of the CIA's Special Operations division. "I'm surprised to hear from you, sir." Miller, along with Ryan, was on the president's task force, but the CIA man had never contacted Ryan before.

"Are you on a secure phone, Ryan?"

"Yes, sir."

"Good. We need to talk."

"About the investigation?"

"That's right, Ryan."

"Okay. I'm driving in heavy traffic. Give me a minute to pull over." The PI slowed the SUV, and after passing the Fox Theatre, took a right off Peachtree. He found a parking spot on a side street and pulled to the curb. Shutting off the SUV, he said, "I'm listening."

"As you probably know, Ryan, I sent Rachel West to Norway to continue the investigation."

"Yes, I'm aware of that."

"Well, we have a problem."

"What problem?" Ryan said.

"Rachel hasn't checked in with me in four days. That's against CIA protocol. She's supposed to check in once a day. Especially since this is such a sensitive, high-priority case. Something's wrong. Very wrong."

A sinking feeling settled in the pit of Ryan's gut. "Where was she, last time you heard from her, sir?"

"Voss, Norway. There's a secret NSA monitoring station there. She was checking a possible connection between the people at that facility and Angel Stone, the ringleader of the criminals we're seeking."

"Sir, I'm assuming you've dispatched a CIA team to find her?"

There was a long pause, then Miller said, "No. I can't do that."

Ryan squeezed the cell phone so hard the casing almost cracked. "Why the hell not? Rachel could be in extreme danger."

"I understand that, Ryan. All too well. But we've had so many traitors at the NSA, the FBI, and possibly even at the CIA, that I'm not sure who to trust."

"Yes, sir. I hear you."

"That's why I'm calling. Because you're on the task force. You're one of the few people I can trust completely." Miller paused a moment and then said, "And there's another reason I'm calling you. One that's equally important."

"What's that, sir?"

"I know you and Rachel are involved."

Ryan recalled that Miller had warned Rachel to squelch their romantic relationship. "Sir, my relationship with Rachel is strictly professional."

"You can cut the bullshit, Ryan. I know you both are a lot more than that. I'm not an idiot. She's lied to me about this before and now so are you."

"All right. It's true. Rachel and I have become close. And I'll do anything and everything to make sure she's safe."

"I know, Ryan."

"What do you need me to do? Just name it."

"Go to Norway," Miller said. "Find Rachel. Then find Angel Stone. She's the key to exposing the Fireball criminals."

"I'll do it. You can count on me, sir."

"Excellent. I'll provide you with everything you need. Equipment, money, weapons, anything. I'll arrange transport. I'll have a CIA jet pick you up in Atlanta and fly you to Norway. I'll text you the details."

"Yes, sir."

They discussed several more items, then Ryan hung up. He fired up the Ford Explorer and continued driving to the FBI building in downtown.

After a slow, torturous drive on the icy roads, an hour later Ryan was sitting in Erin Welch's office.

"You're going where?" Erin said with a grimace.

"Voss, Norway," Ryan replied.

"The hell you are. I'm running this task force, not Alex Miller. You work for me, remember?"

"I'm going, whether you like it or not."

Erin glared and leaned forward in her executive chair. "No. You're not going. I need you working on the NSA angle here, in the U.S." She pointed a finger at his face. "I want you on the next plane to Fort Meade. We're close to finding the top conspirator at the NSA."

Ryan shook his head forcefully. "Get somebody else. I have to do this. Rachel needs me."

Erin's face flushed. Her hands closed into fists and she pounded on the desk. "I'm giving you a direct order. You will not go to Norway."

Ryan's jaw clenched and he stood abruptly. "The hell I'm not."

"You're just like every other man I know," she said, her voice shrill. "You're letting your male body parts cloud your judgment."

"That's not fair," he replied tersely, stung by her remark. "You've known me a long time. You know I'm one of your best investigators. I've helped you solve dozens of big cases."

Grimacing, Erin didn't reply. She folded her arms in front of her, obviously mulling over what he'd just said. After a long moment her features softened. "I'm not going to talk you out of this, am I."

"No."

She pointed a finger at him again. "One of these days you're going to push me too far."

Ryan grinned, in spite of the tenseness of the situation.

"But not today," he said. "Think of it this way, Erin. Angel Stone lives in Norway. Rachel's in Norway. I'll find them both and break the case wide open."

"Pretty cocky, aren't you?"

Ryan smiled. "Yes."

"That's going to get you killed one day."

He tried to come up with a funny retort, but realized the woman was right. He let out a long breath as the seriousness of the situation sank in. "I can't argue with that," he replied, the smugness gone.

# Chapter 77

*Vatnajokull, Iceland*

"Papa, it's so good to see you!" Angel Stone said as she walked into the mansion's massive den.

Viktor Papadopoulos looked away from the roaring blaze in the fireplace and gave Angel a sad smile. "Ha, you're here. I missed you, child." The elderly man was sitting in one of the wingback chairs by the fireplace.

She approached him, leaned down and gave him a big hug. "And I you."

She sat across from him. "You look sad."

The old man nodded. "Thinking of mama. Some days are better than others." His gaze went back to the fireplace.

"I know what you mean," Angel said sympathetically. "I miss her too. A lot."

"I know you do, Angel." He had a faraway look as he continued staring at the blaze.

"Papa."

The man faced her again. "Yes?"

"I brought the woman, like you asked me. The CIA agent we captured."

His eyes sparked with interest. "Good. I want to question her."

"That's going to be difficult."

"Why, child?"

"Unfortunately she's lapsed into a coma. She lost a lot of blood from an injury she suffered."

"I see. A pity. Where is this woman now, Angel?"

"Gustav locked her up in the basement. I asked your doctor to do whatever is necessary to make certain she lives. The doctor is with her now."

"Good thinking, Angel. We need to find out all she knows about our operation. This agent, what's her name again?"

"Rachel West."

Papadopoulos nodded. "Yes, you told me that before." He rubbed his forehead. "I'm getting so forgetful these days ... ever since mama's passing ...."

"Don't worry, papa. I'll deal with her. I'll take care of everything."

The elderly man gave her a sad smile again. "I don't know what I'd do without you."

"I'm just repaying you, papa. For all the kindness you've shown me over the years."

He nodded and grew silent and began staring at the fireplace.

Angel considered the best way to bring up the next subject, trying to minimize the impact of her words. "Before I left Norway," she said, "I got a call from number 4."

His head quickly swiveled back to her, his eyes fully alert. "Number 4?"

"That's right. There's been a complication."

The old man glowered. "Last time you were here you said everything was going smoothly."

"It was, papa."

"Tell me," he ordered.

"It appears the Senate hearings on President Harris have stalled."

He grimaced. "Does that mean that ...."

"Yes, that's right, papa. If the Senate does not vote to convict Harris, he will stay in office as president. He will still be disgraced in the history books as being one of the three presidents who were impeached."

Papadopoulos waved that away with a hand. "That's not enough! Not nearly enough! President Andrew Johnson and Bill Clinton were impeached too – but they stayed in the White House. So will Harris, damn it!"

The elderly man glared at her, his fists pounding the arms of his chair. "You promised me, Angel! You told me Fireball would get me the revenge I want. The revenge I need!"

She lowered her gaze and stared at her hands which were folded on her lap. After a long moment she looked up at the man. In a little girl's voice she said, "I'm sorry, papa. I'm so sorry. I'm despondent over this ... I've failed you ... please, please, papa, forgive me ...." She dabbed away a tear with her hand, then lowered her gaze to the floor.

His anger melted and he stood and approached her, kneeling by her side and putting an arm around her shoulders. "Now, now, child, don't cry. I didn't mean to be so harsh."

Angel was able to summon up more artificial tears and she acted out sobbing noises.

The old man stroked her back gently. "There, there, Angel, everything's going to be all right, you'll see ...."

She gazed at him, her eyes moist and red from the crying. After wiping away the tears, she whispered, "Do you forgive me, papa? Please forgive me ...."

"Of course I forgive you."

"Really, papa?"

"Yes, yes ...."

She hugged him tightly, holding the embrace much longer than appropriate for a father-daughter relationship.

He broke away, seeming a bit embarrassed with the long, tight hug.

"Thank you, daddy! Thank you for forgiving me!"

He nodded, gave her a sympathetic look, and then went back and sat in his wingback chair. He grew silent and began staring at the fire.

"Papa."

"Yes, Angel."

"I know of a way to still get your revenge."

His head swiveled back to her. "How?"

"Do you remember what we discussed a while back? Enlarging Operation Fireball beyond it's original scope?"

"I remember. But after mama passed away I lost interest in that."

A stab of fear ran down Angel's spine. *Is the old bastard changing his mind?*

"But don't you see, papa? If we implement the enhanced version of Fireball, you'll have the perfect revenge. And so will I."

Papadopoulos appeared uncertain. "I know. But your plan seems ... so drastic ... so catastrophic."

"We'll be safe."

"I know that, child. But still ... all those people ...."

"Please," Angel purred, her voice as sweet as honey, "please consider it."

"All right. I'll consider it." Then he went back to staring at the roaring blaze and grew silent.

# Chapter 78

*Voss, Norway*

Alex Miller had been true to his word, thought Ryan, as he drove on the snow-covered rural road. The CIA man had provided Ryan with two large suitcases full of covert equipment and virtually door-to-door transport via a private, unmarked jet.

Ryan slowed the rented Land Rover as he read the mailbox numbers along the dimly-lit, fairly desolate road. Guessing that Rachel had been captured after her visit to the NSA facility, the PI had decided a different approach would be better. And safer.

Luckily, Miller had been able to obtain the home address of the man who ran the NSA monitoring station, an address he was looking for now.

An hour later Ryan spotted the correct mailbox and took a left turn into the ice-covered road. Through the trees he could make out the house in the distance. He drove deeper through the virtually pitch-black property. It was 9 p.m. and Ryan figured the man would be at home.

Parking the Land Rover in front of the large, two-story home, he turned off the vehicle. From the looks of it, the upscale house probably cost well over a million dollars. Difficult to afford, Ryan thought, on a U.S. government salary.

The PI racked the slide on his SIG Sauer P226 pistol, set the safety, and slid the handgun into a pocket of his heavy parka. After zipping up his coat he stepped out of the Land Rover.

A frigid, icy wind hit him immediately, its howl deafening. Ryan, who was used to Atlanta's mild winters, hadn't been prepared for Norway's near arctic conditions.

Covering his face with a hand to keep the blowing snow from his eyes, he trudged over the accumulated powder. Reaching the front door, he rang the buzzer.

He heard, then saw the mounted security cameras whir toward him. Then a voice in a foreign language came over the loudspeaker.

Since Ryan spoke no Norwegian, he said in English, "I'm John Ryan, with the American FBI. I need to speak with Mr. Karl Vaasa."

The reply came back in accented English. "What do you want?"

"I need to speak with you."

"I have office hours – 7 a.m. to 6 p.m. Meet me there in the morning." Then the man read off the address of the NSA facility.

Ryan pulled out his cred pack and opened it and held it up so that the cameras could get a good look at it. "I'm sorry to bother you at night, sir. But this is an emergency."

"What kind of emergency?"

"A CIA agent named Rachel West has gone missing. I was sent to find her. If you could just answer a few questions maybe it would help us find her."

There was no response and Ryan said, "Please, sir. This will only take a minute of your time."

After a minute he heard the clicks of door locks and the front door opened. A man stood at the entrance, holding a handgun at his side. Miller had texted him a photo of Karl Vaasa and this was definitely the guy. Vaasa was flanked by two large German Shepherds and both dogs emitted muted growls.

*Damn*, Ryan thought. *I hate guard dogs. They always complicate things.*

"Let me see your identification," Vaasa said.

The PI handed him his cred pack and the man inspected it closely and handed it back.

"Come inside," the man said.

Ryan followed Vaasa into the luxuriously appointed living room, as the two large dogs warily monitored his every move.

The two men sat across from each other. Vaasa rested his handgun on a side table while the German Shepherds stood guard at one side of the Nordic man, obviously ready to leap into action. Their ice-blue eyes stared unblinking at Ryan.

"As I said before, Mr. Vaasa, a CIA agent named West has gone missing. We know she visited your office recently."

The man nodded. "That is correct. She came to our facility. She asked some questions. And she left. I do not know where she went."

"I see." Ryan knew he had to draw the man out. He sensed Vaasa was nervous, but then, most people would be when being questioned by the FBI. Ryan had to catch the man lying. "The FBI and the CIA are running a joint investigation," Ryan said. "An investigation into a murder plot known as Fireball. Have you ever heard of this?"

Vaasa's eyes narrowed. Then he shook his head forcefully. "No. I told the same thing to agent West. I have never heard of this."

"All right. We're looking for a woman who runs this criminal group. Her name is Angel Stone."

Vaasa looked away from Ryan a moment before responding. It was a sure tell. People lying usually do this exact thing. "No. I know of no such person."

Ryan nodded. "Well, I'm glad we could clear that up." Then he said, "Is there anything else you could tell me, anything at all that would help me find Ms West?"

The man shook his head. "No, I am afraid not. I am sorry I am not able to help you more. Since I work for the American NSA I want to cooperate in every way."

Ryan smiled. "Yes, of course. And I appreciate that." He faced the German Shepherds. "What beautiful dogs you have. They're so well trained."

Vaasa reached out and gently stroked the back of one of the dogs. The canines seemed to relax and sat back on their haunches. "Yes, they are. I have had them since they were pups."

The PI reached into his coat pocket and took the safety off the SIG Sauer. "Your dogs have beautiful blue eyes, Mr. Vaasa. How old are they?"

The Nordic man continued to stroke the nearest canine. "Four years old. They make excellent guard dogs."

In a split-second Ryan pulled out his gun and squeezed off four rounds at the dogs. The boom of the shooting echoed in the room. One of the canines dropped to the floor instantly, while the other yelped, then charged at Ryan, leaping into the air in a single bound.

The PI pulled the trigger again, the rounds slamming into the flying German Shepherd. He felt the warm spray of blood as the animal landed on top of him. He pushed off the dead carcass and trained the SIG Sauer on Vaasa, who was reaching for his own gun.

"One more move and you die, Vaasa."

The Nordic man froze, his eyes locked on Ryan's pistol.

Wiping blood off his face with his free hand, the PI shouted, "Lie on the floor, face down. Do it now!"

Vaasa looked ready to run, his eyes darting around the living room.

"This SIG Sauer pistol has a 15 round magazine, Vaasa. I've only fired six bullets. I'm a good shot and I won't miss at this range."

The man nodded. "All right." He held up his hands. "But what do you want? I told you the truth before."

"Bullshit. Now lie on the floor, face down. Hands behind your back. Do it. Do it now!"

The man complied and Ryan bound his hands and feet with plasticuffs. Then he dragged him across the floor and pushed him roughly onto a wingback chair.

"I am a citizen of Norway, Ryan. I know my rights. You can not do this!"

The PI smiled. "Really? I didn't know about those Norwegian rights. I'll check into that when I get a chance."

Vaasa's eyes darted around the large room, as if trying to figure a way out.

"Look at me you bastard," Ryan ordered menacingly.

The man's head swiveled back to the PI. "What do you want?"

"The truth," Ryan said. "And nothing but the truth."

"I told you before –"

Ryan slapped the man hard across his face, drawing blood from his lips. Then he stuffed the muzzle of the SIG Sauer into Vaasa's mouth.

Vaasa's eyes grew wide as more blood trickled from his open mouth.

"I want answers, Vaasa. I don't have time for bullshit answers. You talk now or you die now. Which is it?"

The man's eyes grew bigger still, now as large as saucers.

Ryan pulled the pistol out of his mouth so he could talk. "Well, Vaasa? Are you going to tell me where Rachel is?"

Sweat dripped from the Nordic man's face, but he still said nothing.

Ryan pointed his gun a half-inch to the left of the man's head and squeezed the trigger, the round cutting away part of his ear.

Vaasa shrieked and flinched away as gore spurted from his wounded ear. Ryan inserted the pistol's muzzle inside his mouth again. "That was just for fun and games. The next round goes into your mouth." Then he pulled the gun out.

Vaasa nodded furiously. "Yes ... yes!"

"That's more like it, friend."

"I am bleeding ...."

"Yes, you are. Where's Rachel West? Tell me the truth or I will kill you."

"West is with her."

"With who, Vaasa?"

"My boss. Number 3."

"She is with Angel Stone?"

Vaasa nodded. "Yes."

"That's a start. Now keep talking. Where in Norway is Stone?"

"She is not here anymore."

"Angel Stone left Norway?"

"Yes."

"Where is she, damn it!"

Vaasa became hesitant again, despite his evident pain.

"Tell me, you bastard!" Ryan shoved the pistol into the man's mouth, this time so forcefully it broke several of his teeth. Vaasa passed out and his eyes rolled white. When he came to moments later, Ryan shouted, "Tell me!"

"Angel Stone took the CIA agent to Number 1."

"Who is number 1?"

"He is a billionaire. He is the person who funds Fireball."

Ryan already knew the answer to his next question, but wanted to see if Vaasa would lie to him. "What is number 1's name?"

"Viktor Papadopoulos."

*He's telling the truth*, thought Ryan. So he asked him another question, one he didn't know the answer to. "Where is Papadopoulos?"

"Iceland," Vaasa said.

# Chapter 79

*Vatnajokull, Iceland*

"How is she doing, Doctor?" Angel Stone asked as she approached the hospital-style bed.

The physician looked up from the chart he was reading. "The same. She is still in a coma."

Angel stared at the woman reclining on the bed. Rachel West's beautiful face was as white as the sheet covering her torso. The only other sign of trauma marring her features was the bandage covering her cheek where Angel had cut her. The blonde woman was hooked up to a feeding tube and a mechanical ventilator. She was inert except for the rise and fall of her chest.

Angel shook her head slowly. "We're not going to be able to question her, are we."

"That is correct."

"Do you have a prognosis, Doctor? When she'll snap out of it?"

"I cannot determine that. Each patient is different. Some recover in days – others, years. And some die."

Angel clenched her teeth, aggravated by the CIA woman's condition. "Bitch," she muttered under her breath.

She turned on her heel and stalked out of the room. There were two armed guards posted at the entrance.

"Allow no one into this room, except me and the doctor," she snapped at them.

The guards nodded.

Using the elevator, Angel left the basement and made her way back to the mansion's enormous den. Before going inside, she marshaled her thoughts. She hadn't anticipated that she would have so much trouble convincing number 1. Despite her cajoling, the old man wasn't ready to commit to her enhanced version of Fireball. *Today*, she mused, *I'm going with a different approach.*

Angel stepped into the den and closed and locked the door behind her. As she had expected she found Viktor Papadopoulos seated by the roaring fireplace, his eyes fixed on the crackling flames. The pleasant aroma of burning wood filled the room.

The elderly man seemed moody and lost in his own thoughts.

Angel pulled a wingback chair close to him and sat down. "Papa," she said gently.

He glanced at her, realizing for the first time there was another person in the room.

"How are you feeling, papa?"

"So, so. Thinking of mama."

She reached with a hand and gently stroked his arm. "You poor dear. I know you miss her so much. As do I ...."

The elderly man nodded, the melancholy look still on his face.

"Papa, I wanted to talk to you about something."

"I hope it's not about Fireball ... I can't focus on that right now."

Angel shook her head. "No. It's about something more important. Much more important."

That seemed to spark his interest.

"I was thinking," she said, continuing to caress his arm, "about our current situation."

"Situation?"

"Yes. I really don't want to return to Norway."

"But that's your home, Angel."

"I know." She changed the inflection of her voice so she sounded more like a child. "I'm lonely there, daddy. Very lonely. I have no one there I care about, or who cares about me." She waved a hand in the air. "And you live by yourself now, after mama's unfortunate passing, in this four-story mansion. You have servants and guards, but no one close." She batted her eyelashes. "If I moved here, we could keep each other company."

The old man's face registered surprise. But after a long moment he nodded. "Of course, child. There's no reason you can't live here if you want to. We have plenty of spare bedrooms."

"Oh, thank you, daddy!" She opened her arms wide and gave him a big hug. "You're so special to me!"

While still hugging him she rested her head on his chest.

Papadopoulos began stroking her long, silky, raven hair. "And you're special to me also."

They stayed like that for several minutes, not saying anything, comforted by each other's embrace.

While still hugging him, she raised her eyes, looked at him and whispered, "Papa?"

"Yes, child."

"Have you ever thought about us being together?"

"What do you mean, Angel? We're together now."

She caressed his chest sensually. "I know that. I meant in a different way. An adult way."

His eyebrows knitted together and a perplexed look settled on his face. "I don't know what you mean."

"Now that mama's passed," she whispered, her eyes locked on his, "you must be lonely for the kind of closeness only a loving, married couple share."

"You mean sex?"

She continued to sensually caress his chest, idly playing with the buttons of his shirt. She lowered her eyes to feign shyness and demurely said, "Yes, papa, that's what I mean ...."

He laughed. "Oh, child, I'm too old for that sort of thing. I'm 85! My wife was sick for many, many years. We hadn't done that sort of thing ... well, it's been so long I've forgotten when."

Angel modulated her voice so she sounded like a little girl again. "But papa ... hadn't it even crossed your mind ... once in a while? You may be 85, but you're strong and virile."

He got a faraway look in his eyes. "Well ... I guess I have had fleeting thoughts, over the years." He paused a minute and gazed at her closely. "But it's silly to even talk about something like that. I'm sure my ... plumbing ... wouldn't be up to it."

She undid several of his shirt buttons and slid her palm inside. Then she began caressing his bare chest, her palm massaging his skin. She grinned sensually, the little girl look and tone gone now. "I wouldn't be too sure about that, papa."

Startled by her sensual touch, his eyes went wide.

"Just relax, papa. Just relax."

"Are you sure about this, Angel?"

"I'm very sure. I know exactly what I'm doing."

While continuing to caress his chest, she slid her other hand and rested it on his pants by his groin. It was soft now and she began stroking the area gently and lovingly.

After a few minutes she could feel his growing hardness.

The elderly man closed his eyes and started breathing heavy. "Oh, child ... please don't stop ...."

As she continued to stroke him sensually, she whispered, "Don't worry, papa, I'm not going to stop. Just relax and enjoy it. I know exactly how to please you. And now that I'm going to be living here in your home, we can enjoy ourselves like this all the time."

A look of contentment settled on his face.

# Chapter 80

*Voss, Norway*

J.T. Ryan closed the shades of his hotel room window and pulled out his cell phone. Punching in a number, he waited for Alex Miller to pick up.

After the second ring, he heard Miller say, "Yes?"

"It's Ryan."

"Are you on an encrypted phone?"

"I am, sir."

"Okay. You questioned the NSA target in Voss?"

"I did. I know where Rachel is. I also know where Angel Stone and Viktor Papadopoulos are."

"Where?"

"In a remote area of Iceland, sir. Vaasa told me Papadopoulos has a massive estate in an area called Vatnajokull. It's by a glacier."

"I see. Where is the NSA man now?"

"I have him tied up in the back of my SUV."

"Okay. I'll send some people to pick him up."

"That's good, sir. And I need you to locate where Papadopoulos lives so we can figure out the best way to go in."

"Will do, Ryan. I'll start working on that right now."

"Thank you."

"No, thank you. For finding out where Rachel and Stone are."

"Don't thank me yet, sir. The really hard part is next."

# Chapter 81

*Special Operations Division*
*CIA Annex Building*
*Langley, Virginia*

It had taken six hours for Alex Miller to get a clear fix on the billionaire's exact location. Using CIA satellite information, he pinpointed the mansion to its precise coordinates.

As Ryan had told him, the man's home was located in a very remote, unpopulated part of Iceland. In fact, the place was located adjacent to a national park named Vatnajokull. The snow-covered area was rugged, mountainous, and mostly consisted of glaciers and frozen tundra.

From the satellite images it was also clear that the estate was heavily fortified, including guard stations all along the only way in, a paved two-lane road. Miller estimated it would take a small army to break through the numerous checkpoints.

After spending several more hours doing research, the CIA man contacted a few high-level people at the U.S. Department of State. Having learned as much as possible, he picked up the handset of his desk phone and made a call.

J.T. Ryan answered on the first ring. "Ryan here."

"It's Miller."

"Yes, sir. You have info for me?"

"I do. But you won't like it."

There was a pause from the other end, then Ryan said, "Go ahead, sir."

"I have the exact coordinates for the mansion. It's in the middle of nowhere Iceland. From the looks of it, Papadopoulos is a total recluse. His nearest neighbors are probably fifty miles away. Although it's unlikely that he even has any. The area is mostly frozen tundra, glaciers, snow, and ice. That's why we were never able to track down Papadopoulos for all those years. He was hiding in the middle of nowhere."

"I'm with you so far," Ryan said. "So what's the problem?"

"Several, from what I can gather. The estate is ringed with heavily-fortified guard outposts all along the only road leading into the mansion. The home is even protected with an anti-aircraft missile system. You would need a platoon of tanks and a small army to break through."

"I see."

"And there's something else," Miller continued. "I talked to a couple of people I trust at the State Department. They did some checking. Based on their analysis, there's no way the government in Iceland should have allowed Papadopoulos to build such a massive estate adjacent to a national park. It's possible people in the government there were paid off to look the other way. I suspect that Papadopoulos bribed officials. Which means we're not going to get cooperation if we ask for their assistance in arresting him."

"I'm starting to see the situation, sir."

"It gets worse, Ryan."

"Worse?"

"I can't send you any help. If I insert a CIA team into Iceland and things go sour, it'll cause an international incident. Europeans aren't too pleased with Americans as it is."

"I understand, sir."

"So there you have it, Ryan. What are you going to do?"

"I need to think about this. Can you text me the coordinates of the location and any other pertinent information?"

"Yes. I'll do that right now."

"Thank you, sir. I'll call you back when I've come up with a plan."

# Chapter 82

*Voss, Norway*

J.T. Ryan mulled over the situation as he studied the map spread out on the bed of his hotel room. He'd bought the map of Iceland earlier in the day and had spent hours poring over the topographical information, matching that with the data Miller had texted him.

Iceland was basically a very large island, mostly comprised of frozen tundra, snow-covered mountains, glaciers, fiords, and not many people. The whole country only had a population of 348,000. Most of the people lived in the capital city of Reykjavik or in small towns that hugged the coastline. There was only one highway in Iceland, a road that ringed the country as it followed the coast. All of the interior roads appeared to be rural.

Vatnajokull National Park was located in the southeast of Iceland. There was only one town close to it, a place named Jokulsarion. The Papadopoulos estate was on the northern edge of the vast, desolate park, which was comprised mostly of glaciers and snow-covered mountains. The park was so remote and the terrain so rugged that very few tourists ever visited. The satellite images that Miller had texted him clearly showed the guard stations along the ingress road to the mansion. Ryan knew it would be a suicide mission for him to go in that way.

He spent several more hours brooding over the situation as he continued to study the map and the satellite images.

Finally a plan emerged.

There was only one way in.

It would be highly dangerous, probably deadly. For a moment he doubted himself, briefly frozen by the fear of death. Then his mind filled with images of Rachel. The woman he deeply cared about. *She needs me*, he thought. *No one else is going to help her.*

Pushing aside the fear, he took out his cell phone and punched in a number. It rang for a long time before getting picked up.

"Hello," he heard Alex Miller say in a sleepy voice.

"It's Ryan, sir."

There was a long pause from the other end, then he heard a yawn. "Do you know what time it is here, Ryan?"

The PI glanced at his watch, realized it was 3:05 a.m. back in Langley. "Sorry, sir. But you did give me your private number and told me to call you day or night."

"All right ... all right ... I'm in bed. Give me a minute to get to my home office."

"Yes, sir."

Ryan waited several minutes and then heard Miller say, "Go ahead."

"I may have figured a way in."

"Okay, Ryan. What is it?"

"I've studied the satellite images and the map and I agree with you. I'll be dead meat if I try to break through the checkpoints. It would be suicide if I try that approach."

"You have a better solution."

"I do, sir. I need to skip over the fortifications."

"Like with a helicopter or a light plane? That won't work, Ryan. Papadopoulos has a radar station and an anti-aircraft missile battery. Any plane or chopper would be shot down."

"I agree. I considered that approach originally, then noticed the radar facility and ABMs."

"All right," Miller said. "So what's your plan?"

"Sir, have you ever heard of a HALO jump?"

"Maybe. It sounds familiar. Refresh my memory."

"HALO," Ryan said, "stands for High Altitude Low Opening parachuting. It means you jump out of a plane at a very high altitude, like 35,000 feet, then free-fall skydive most of the way down, and then pull your parachute at a low altitude."

"I see. So radar wouldn't be able to spot an aircraft flying at such a high altitude and one man parachuting in is too small to detect either."

"That's correct, sir."

"Tell me, have you ever done a HALO skydive before?"

Ryan recalled the two times. "Yes, once in a training exercise. And on one mission. When I was in Special Forces. The unit I commanded in Afghanistan HALO'd into a terrorist held region."

"And how did it go?"

"On the positive side," Ryan said, "we accomplished the mission and killed all of the terrorists."

"And the negative?"

"I lost half my men. They were shot dead after they pulled their parachute at low altitude."

"I see, Ryan. So you're telling me you only have a 50/50 chance of success?"

Actually, Ryan knew his odds of a successful HALO skydive were even lower. He'd be dropping into frigid, arctic conditions. The snow and ice and incredibly cold weather would probably kill him before he reached the billionaire's estate. And skydiving from 35,000 feet meant there wasn't enough oxygen at such a high altitude. He'd have to parachute in with an oxygen tank.

"Sir, I'm very confident I can do this successfully," Ryan lied.

"Well, it's your funeral. But to tell you the truth, I can't see any other way to get into that mansion."

"I'm going to need your help to pull this off," Ryan said. "I'll need a transport plane to drop me off over the area, and I'll need the HALO parachute equipment."

"Whatever you need," Miller replied. "Just name it."

"I still have contacts at Fort Bragg. That's the Army base where Special Forces Command is headquartered. They handle all covert military operations for the U.S. military. Delta Force, SEAL teams, the Green Berets, are all there. They can arrange for everything I need, including the C-130 transport plane and the HALO equipment. I'll text you the information."

"All right," Miller said. "Is there anything else you need?"

"You can wish me luck, sir."

"I think you're going to need a hell of a lot more than that, Ryan. I'm a religious man, so I'll say a prayer for you."

# Chapter 83

*Vatnajokull, Iceland*

Angel Stone was ecstatic.

Everything she ever wanted in life was hers.

Ever since she and Viktor Papadopoulos had become lovers a week ago, the old man had become incredibly agreeable, pliable to any of her wishes. He had showered her with jewelry, and furs, even given her his Rolls Royce. He'd even added her name to all of his financial accounts.

*Men are so weak*, she mused, as she stared at the roaring fireplace in the den of the mansion. Give them sex and you have them eating out of the palm of your hand.

Angel gazed around the enormous, beautifully-appointed and furnished room. It was all hers now. Along with the rest of the mansion. She loved being a billionaire's mistress. She smiled as her gaze went back to the cracking fire.

*But I want more*, she thought. Being his mistress was just the first step. She wanted it to be official. *I want the fancy ring and the marriage certificate. Not a problem*, she mused. *I'll convince him soon enough.* She had already hinted at it and he seemed agreeable.

*The marriage can wait, though.* She wanted something else just as much.

Revenge.

The revenge only Operation Fireball would deliver. And like all her other wishes, Papadopoulos had said yes. He'd finally agreed to her enhanced version of the operation.

Angel glanced at her Rolex, calculating the local time back in the U.S. It was 7 a.m. there. Pulling out her secure cell phone, she pressed one of the preset numbers. The call was answered on the first ring.

"This is number 3," Angel said.

"Yes?"

"Are you on an encrypted phone, number 4?"

"I am."

"The final phase of Operation Fireball is a go."

"Is number 1 on board with this decision?"

Angel recalled the exact moment she'd asked the old man. It had been just a few minutes after they'd had sex. "Oh, yes. Number 1 is in full agreement."

"All right, number 3. It'll take me a few days to initiate implementation."

Angel smiled. "Excellent. The sooner the better."

# Chapter 84

*Flying over the Atlantic Ocean
at 35,000 feet*

J.T. Ryan was strapped tight into one of the jump seats of the transport plane.

He was the only passenger in the C-130. Sitting next to him was the jump master, an NCO Ryan had known from his days at Fort Bragg.

The sergeant tapped Ryan's helmet and yelled, "Fifteen minutes to drop zone!"

The PI barely heard him over the roar of the plane's four turbo-prop engines. Ryan gave the sergeant a thumbs up, then began adjusting his gear for the HALO jump. Strapped to his back was his main parachute and his smaller backup chute. He was wearing a full body suit, one designed for arctic conditions. Strapped to his front was a Heckler & Koch MP-5 assault rifle, a pack with additional combat gear, and an oxygen tank.

Over his high-tech ski mask he wore a breathing cup. He adjusted the oxygen level, getting ready for the jump. Then he tightened the strap on his combat helmet and calibrated the night-vision goggles he was wearing.

Ryan felt a tap on his helmet and turned to look at the NCO.

"Ten minutes to drop!" the man yelled.

Ryan nodded, feeling the butterflies in his stomach. He hadn't skydived in over two years and hadn't HALO'd in much longer. To tell the truth, he'd always hated jumping out of planes. It scared him half to death. Ryan feared very little in life. But he dreaded parachuting. He much preferred dodging bullets on the battlefield. But Airborne training was a requirement to get into the Army Rangers and later into the Green Berets and Delta Force. It was an unavoidable fact that parachuting was an intrinsic part of being in Special Forces. So he had swallowed his fear, closed his eyes, and took that last step, the step into weightlessness as you jumped out of a plane. Luckily he'd been trained by the best instructors when he completed the Military Free Fall course. That training had taken place at the JFK Special Warfare Center in Yuma Proving Grounds, Arizona.

He vividly recalled his last skydive – the blast of wind buffeting you in every direction, the roar of the gusts, the onrushing ground below, coming fast. He swallowed hard and sucked in more oxygen. Then he crossed himself and said a silent prayer.

The sergeant unstrapped himself from his seat and went to the wall-mounted control panel. A moment later the back door of the transport plane creaked open.

Ryan unstrapped himself from his seat, then stood up clumsily, since he was carrying over 120 pounds of gear. He then adjusted the various packs a bit to better distribute the weight.

His boots trudged over the plane's steel floor, as he shuffled forward toward the huge back door.

The sergeant held up two fingers, signifying two minutes to the drop zone.

Ryan nodded and stepped closer to the door. He could see the nighttime scene below, all of it highlighted in green from the night-vision goggles. He saw puffy clouds and beyond that the irregular peaks of snow-capped mountains. He could also make out the blinding white of the frozen tundra. The roar of the plane's engines was deafening as it competed with the noise of the turbulent wind.

Ryan sucked in more oxygen as he shuffled forward again, closer to the open door.

The NCO was standing next to him and the man held up one finger. The PI nodded.

Then the sergeant slapped his shoulder and yelled, "Go! Go!"

Ryan took the last step and dove out the door, trying to recall his training. But the feeling of weightlessness, the blast of arctic air, and the roar of the plane's engines overwhelmed and disoriented him, his body tumbling uncontrollably through the air.

He fought the panic as he sucked on the oxygen tank, his thoughts a jumble of fear.

A moment later his training kicked in and he spread his arms behind him and widened the stance in his legs. Forcing his head down he dove toward the ground in the classic skydiver's flying position.

After what felt like an eternity but in reality was only seconds, his new body position smoothed out and he began to successfully skydive toward the green-tinged whiteness below.

Checking his altimeter he realized he was now at an altitude of 32,000 feet. He needed to pull his parachute at 4,000 feet, so he would literally be flying down for the next 28,000 feet. That was a distance of approximately six miles and he had to make that count. As he sucked in more oxygen he checked the GPS device on his wrist. Although the C-130 had dropped him over the target as best as possible, his awkward tumble out of the plane had taken him off course.

Ryan twisted his torso and readjusted his arms, changing course as he continued skydiving at 120 miles per hour. He was far from the plane now and all her heard was the screaming of the wind.

Moments later he broke through the clouds to an incredible sight below.

The black nighttime sky was now a riot of colorful lights. Greens and reds and blues and purples. It confused him at first, then he realized what it was: The Aurora Borealis, the nighttime lights common in arctic areas of the world like Iceland during the winter months.

He ignored the fantastic light show and instead focused on his GPS. Adjusting his arms and legs, he corrected course again. Then he checked his altimeter. He was at an altitude of 15,000 feet. He had 11,000 more feet to go.

A minute later he was through the Aurora Borealis and the snow-capped mountains and frozen tundra were visible below. He squinted through his night-vision goggles, looking for the Papadopoulos estate. At first he saw nothing, just the irregular drifts of snow and ice.

Suddenly it came into view, a two-lane road leading toward a very large mansion.

As he skydived lower more details emerged – the guard stations by the road, a plane hanger and a runway close to the estate, and the anti-aircraft missile station.

Glancing at his altimeter he realized be was at 6,000 feet. Two thousand to go. He made a final correction to his stance, one that he hoped would drop him behind the mansion, far enough away from it to be undetected.

He slid his hand toward the ripcord as he studied the altimeter.

Pulling the ripcord, he felt his body jerked sharply upward as the parachute billowed above him. Once the chute fully deployed he grabbed the handles and steered himself toward his intended drop zone.

He was at 1,000 feet now and all of the mansion's details were visible. Lights shone from several windows and the whole property was lit up by floodlights. He could even make out the tiny figures of guards patrolling the grounds. By the casual way the men were patrolling, it was clear that Ryan's arrival so far was undetected.

Ryan steered himself further away, toward a dim, snow-covered ridge at the far rear of the property. He knew he'd be hitting the ground in seconds and he tensed, recalling his training: *Hit the ground and roll immediately to break the fall.*

It came faster than he expected and he rolled clumsily into a snow drift, which luckily softened his landing.

With his adrenaline pumping, he quickly unsnapped his parachute and took it off, then un-slung the MP-5. Pointing the rifle forward, he waited silently as he scanned the horizon. He saw no movement or flashing of lights. Realizing he was safe for now, he slung his MP-5 over his shoulder and rapidly gathered up his chute and buried it in the snow drift. Then he removed his oxygen tank and his secondary parachute, and strapped his combat gear pack on his back.

That done, he studied the scene in front.

He was about a football field away from the massive, four-story estate. To the left of it was the airplane hanger and a long airstrip. To the right of it was the anti-aircraft missile battery and a large satellite dish.

He could also make out at least four guards patrolling the grounds, their rifles slung over their heavy parkas. Ryan knew they would be his first priority. And he had to take them out quietly, so that the home's residents and the guards inside were not alerted.

Ryan breathed in the frigid air. For the first time since he'd landed he noticed the arctic, harsh conditions of the landscape around him. He had been so focused on landing alive and undetected that he had ignored everything else.

He pulled off one of his gloves, reached into his pack and removed the suppressor. With his bare skin burning from the icy-cold air, he screwed on the suppressor to the muzzle of his rifle. Quickly putting his glove back on, he extended the bipod of the rifle and pointed the MP-5 toward the mansion, while he lay prone on the snowy surface.

He took off his night-vision goggles and peered through the weapon's scope, which was also equipped with night-vision optics. He focused on one of the guards as the man made a circuit of the airplane hanger.

Ryan put the crosshairs over the man's torso as his finger closed around the trigger.

He squeezed gently.

The MP-5 coughed.

The guard dropped to the ground.

One down, three to go.

Ryan immediately scanned the whole area and saw no movement. No new lights came on. No shouting. No alarms went off.

The PI breathed a sigh of relief. He moved his rifle and bipod to a different part of the snow drift. A second guard was patrolling the area directly ahead of him. The area appeared to be a patio, but Ryan figured it was rarely used in the arctic conditions.

He focused the scope again.

He caressed the trigger and gave it a light tug.

The assault rifle emitted a thud and the guard fell, face forward. But this time the crumpled body moved and Ryan squeezed off another round. Then the body was inert.

No new lights blazed and no alarms sounded.

Ryan turned his attention to the last two guards, who were leaning against the anti-aircraft missile battery. With their rifles slung over their shoulders, they were smoking cigarettes. The guards were facing away from the house, gazing out toward the back yard, talking as they smoked.

Through the scope Ryan could clearly see the men's eyes. The PI hated this part the most. It was always better to do a kill without seeing the face clearly. But this time it was unavoidable. Taking a life was never easy, even for a highly-trained soldier like himself. He briefly thought of Rachel and his resolve rushed back instantly.

Ryan trained the crosshairs on the chest of one of the guards and quickly pulled the trigger.

The rifle coughed and the man dropped to the ground.

The PI immediately focused on the second guard. He fired, the high-powered round slamming into the man's chest. The guard staggered back and fell to the snowy ground.

Quickly folding the bipod of his rifle, he slung the weapon over his shoulder. After putting his night-vision goggles back on, he pulled out his SIG Sauer semi-automatic pistol, racked the slide, and took off the safety. A suppressor was already attached to this handgun. Getting up from the ground, he advanced forward in a crouch, his combat boots sinking into the white powder.

As he trudged closer to the mansion, his head was on a swivel, scanning the whole area. Luckily he was able to use the large snow drifts that covered the whole back yard to conceal his movements. He noticed a snow-tractor parked next to the mansion, which he figured was used often.

Ryan was now about 100 feet from the back of the home. He squinted through his night-vision goggles trying to locate any other guards he hadn't seen previously, and luckily saw no others.

The PI knew that the estate was too far from civilization to be connected to a municipal electric grid. Which meant the home was powered by an electric generator. Probably several.

As he scanned the back of the home he listened closely for sounds. Other than the whistling of the wind he heard nothing. Crouching, he moved forward another twenty feet. He dropped behind a nearby snow drift and burrowed into the powder. Slowing his breathing, he ignored the sound of the wind.

Then he heard it.

The hum of electrical equipment. A power generator, he was sure.

Glancing over the mound of snow he spotted it: A large rectangular metal structure to the left of mansion. Painted white, it blended in with the rest of the of the icy landscape.

He trudged toward it, his boots sinking into the powder, his weapon trained forward.

Suddenly he saw movement out of the corner of his eye, a blur of motion as a man in a heavy coat stepped out of the house.

Ryan froze, his heart pounding in his chest.

The guard spotted him instantly and the PI aimed and fired. The SIG Sauer coughed twice, the guard's rifle dropped and the man staggered back. His eyes wide, he clutched his chest.

Ryan fired again and this time the guard collapsed. Expecting alarms to ring, the PI raced to the power generator and crouched behind it. He heard nothing except the purr of the electric generator. Glancing toward the large estate, he noted that lights shone from five different rooms. But he was relieved that no other guards came out of the home and no alarms sounded.

Slowing his breathing, he removed his backpack and reached inside. He took out two cell phone size devices and turned them on. The explosive devices were magnetized and he stuck one of them to the power generator's metal housing. Striding around the large generator, he searched for a backup generator, figuring an estate as large as this wouldn't rely on just one. As he expected, he found the backup unit close by. This one was smaller than the main unit and was not operating. Obviously the backup would only kick in if the main unit failed. He attached the second explosive device to this generator and moved away, closer to the estate's back entrance.

From a pocket he removed the detonator and, as he hugged the home's back wall for cover, pressed the trigger.

Nothing happened for a moment and Ryan feared the explosives had malfunctioned.

Then he heard two muted booms and saw sparks fly from the generators. The machine stopped humming and the mansion's lights went dark. Simultaneously the floodlights that had lit up the outside area also went dark.

# Chapter 85

*Vatnajokull, Iceland*

Angel Stone was sitting in the mansion's den staring at the crackling fireplace as she reminisced over her very satisfying and productive day.

She and Viktor Papadopoulos had been married in a civil ceremony that afternoon in a hastily-arranged wedding. Within minutes she and Viktor had signed several key documents, giving her total control of his vast wealth. The old man was fast asleep now in the master bedroom, totally worn out from an hours-long sexual interlude.

Angel smiled, musing that if she kept up the frenetic love-making, the 85 year old man would die soon of a heart attack.

Suddenly the overhead ceiling lights shut off and the stereo went silent.

Angel continued gazing at the crackling fire, unconcerned about the power failure. She knew the home's backup generator would kick in momentarily.

But when that didn't happen, she stood abruptly and stared around the now dim room. *What the hell's going on?* she thought, irritated by the inconvenience.

# Chapter 86

*The Oval Office*
*The White House*
*Washington, D.C.*

The Secret Service agent opened the door to the Oval Office and escorted Erin Welch inside.

Erin noticed President Harris was already in the room, seated behind his desk.

The president stood, walked around his desk, and gave her a tired smile. "Thank you for coming on such short notice," he said, motioning her to the nearby wingback chairs in the room. "Let's sit over there."

"Of course, Mr. President," Erin replied.

They sat opposite each other and Harris turned to the Secret Service agent. "That'll be all."

The agent nodded and left the room, closing the door behind him.

Erin studied the president closely, noticing that he seemed to have aged a decade since she'd seen him last, which was only a few months ago. His previously jet-black hair was now graying at the temples and his face appeared haggard and worn out. His blue eyes were blood-shot and his shoulders sagged. The impeachment, the multiple murders, the treason by deep-state government employees, and the riots across the country, had taken a heavy toll on the man.

"As you know," the president began, "I've been getting regular progress reports on your team's activities from my DNI. But since the stakes are so high and since time is of the essence, I wanted to have you brief me personally."

"Of course, sir."

"Where are you with the investigation?"

"We've made a lot of progress," Erin said, tucking her long brunette hair behind her ears. "J.T. Ryan has been working closely with the CIA. They've been able to track down the location of the ringleader, Angel Stone, and the billionaire who's funding the conspiracy."

"Where is that, Erin?"

"Iceland."

"I see. Is Ryan there now?"

"Yes, Mr. President. I talked to Alex Miller of the CIA just before I came to this meeting. He informed me that John Ryan was flown over the billionaire's estate and he parachuted in. I don't have any more information beyond that, but we hope to make an arrest soon."

"That's good news, Erin." The president rubbed his weary face with a hand. "Very good news. Something that's been rare around here."

"Would you like me to give you the details of the investigation, Mr. President?" She had brought a folder with her and she opened it now.

Harris waved that away. "Not necessary. I'm only interested in the results."

Erin closed the file. "Of course, sir."

The president leaned forward in his seat. "Once your team arrests the ringleaders I want them interrogated thoroughly. It's imperative we find all the U.S. government people involved in the Fireball plot."

"Yes, Mr. President. That's exactly what we're planning to do."

"Excellent."

Just then there was a knock at the door. A Secret Service agent opened it partway and peeked around the jam. "Sorry to disturb you, Mr. President. But Ms Lowry is here. She needs to speak with you. She says it's urgent."

Harris nodded. "Send her in."

Samantha Lowry, the Director of National Intelligence came into the room, carrying a briefcase. As usual the thin, mousy woman was wearing a frumpy dress that made her appear more like a librarian than a high-level intelligence official.

The DNI approached them and President Harris said, "What is it, Samantha?"

"Mr. President, we have a national security crisis. It needs your immediate attention."

Harris frowned. "Crisis? What kind of crisis?"

Erin watched as the DNI placed her briefcase on the president's desk and opened it. Lowry removed a thick stack of 11"x14" black-and-white photographs from the case and spread them on the desk.

Harris and Erin walked over to the desk and scrutinized the pictures. Then the president looked at the DNI. "What are these?"

"Sir," Lowry replied, "these photos are from NSA satellites." She pointed to one of the pictures. "This one shows ICBM missile silos have been opened on the Russian base in Derazhnya." She pointed to another photo. "And this one clearly shows a battalion of Russian tanks surging at the Russia-Finland border. And this other photo shows a Russian submarine base in Vladivostok. There are no nuclear subs docked there. They're all at sea. And this picture here is of the Russian bomber base near Alaska – the base is in the process of launching its planes."

"Why is this happening, Samantha?" Harris said, his voice agitated.

"There can only be one reason, Mr. President. The Russians are planning a nuclear first strike against the U.S."

Harris's face turned beet red. "But why, damn it? We haven't provoked them in any way!"

"I agree, sir," the DNI responded. "We haven't provoked them. There can only be one explanation. It's because you've been impeached. And because of the riots across the United States. The Russians know you're not focused on national security issues. You're distracted by these other crises. Don't you see, Mr. President? The Russians feel we're weakened and we won't respond to their attack."

President Harris nodded. "That sounds plausible. Have you confirmed this information with multiple sources?"

"I have, sir. I checked with the CIA and the DIA, the Defense Intelligence Agency. They confirm what these NSA satellite photos show. The Russians are planning a nuclear first strike."

Erin tensed. Her heart was pounding, knowing the situation was critical. There could only be one response to a Russian threat like this. It would be for the USA to preempt it with a nuclear attack of its own.

Harris rubbed a hand over his tired face. "Damn it all! I can't believe all of this is happening on my watch!" He sagged onto the executive chair behind his desk and pressed a button on his intercom. "I need the SecDef, SecState, and the CJCS in my office," the president ordered. "Now!"

The president, the DNI, and Erin waited anxiously in the Oval Office, silent for the next few minutes.

The Secretary of Defense came into the room first. He was followed soon after by the Secretary of State, and the four-star general who was the Chairman of the Joint Chiefs of Staff.

Erin knew that each of the men were new at their positions. This was due to the recent murders of the Secretary of State and Secretary of Defense. The general who had been the previous CJCS was currently in the hospital after being involved in a severe car crash.

President Harris turned to the DNI. "Brief everyone on what's happening, Samantha."

"Yes, sir," Lowry replied. She went on to explain the crisis, once again pointing out the details of the Russian forces that were poised to mount a nuclear first strike.

When she was done, Harris said, "There you have it, gentlemen. It's clear what the Russians are intending to do. What's your opinion?"

The SecDef, SecState, and the CJCS glanced at each other briefly. Then the Secretary of Defense said, "I agree, Mr. President. The Russians are poised to launch a first strike."

The Secretary of State nodded. "That's my opinion also, sir."

Harris turned to the Marine general. "What about you. What do you think?"

"Yes, Mr. President," the CJCS said, "it's clear what they intend to do."

President Harris, a grim expression on his face, said nothing for a moment. Then he stood. "All right, then. I have no choice. If Russian ICBM missiles hit the U.S. first it will be catastrophic. Tens of millions of Americans will die in minutes. Large parts of the country will be wiped out." Then in a forceful voice, he added, "I'm declaring a national security crisis. I want our nuclear arsenal on full alert, ready to launch at my command. ICBM missiles, bombers, and nuclear submarines. All of it. Go to DEFCON 1."

# Chapter 87

*Vatnajokull, Iceland*

J.T. Ryan hugged the rear wall of the mansion as he scanned the dim interior of the home through the French doors. He was still using the night-vision goggles and the interior was visible in hazy green.

Ryan saw no people in the enormous kitchen by the rear entrance. He was fairly sure he hadn't been detected yet, but knew that wouldn't last long. Quickly ejecting the half-empty clip in his SIG Sauer, he snapped in a fresh mag and racked the slide of the pistol.

Then he turned the knob on the door. As he expected the entrance was locked. He elbowed one of the glass panes, it shattered, and he reached inside and unlocked the door. The mansion's alarm system was powered by the generators, he now realized, otherwise the broken glass would have triggered a piercing alert.

Ryan stepped inside and closed the door behind him. He was tense, his pulse racing, expecting more guards at any moment. When none came into the kitchen, he advanced past a large dining room and into a wide corridor.

Like the rest of the home, the hallway was also dark. He heard loud voices calling out from other parts of the house.

He saw movement in the corner of his eye and then saw a beam from a flashlight.

Crouching, he squeezed off two rounds.

The suppressed pistol found its target and a man carrying a submachine gun collapsed to the floor.

The PI sprinted to the man and checked his pulse. He found none and he continued forward, deeper into the mansion. Suddenly a flashlight beam blinded him and he heard the boom of gunfire.

Ryan instantly dropped to the marble floor. From a prone position he fired his handgun, spraying the area in front of him. He heard screams of pain but the incoming gunfire continued, whistling over his head.

There was an open doorway to his right and he rolled his body inside the room. Reaching into his backpack he took out a grenade, pulled the pin, and lobbed it around the door jam into the corridor in the direction of the gunfire.

The grenade exploded, the roar of the blast momentarily deafening him. Even though he was sheltered in the room he still felt the concussion sensation of the powerful explosive. The earsplitting boom of the grenade echoed throughout the mansion.

It was quiet in the corridor now and he peered around the door jamb. Through his night-vision goggles he could make out four prone bodies at the far end of the hallway. Once the smoke from the blast cleared he saw that the bloodied men were silent and inert.

With his gun pointing the way, he crouched and advanced toward the crumpled bodies, lying in a pool of blood. The stench of gore and gunpowder hung in the air. After confirming the four guards were dead, he continued deeper into the estate. He passed several dim rooms, including a massive den-like space with a burning fireplace. All of these rooms were vacant so he continued further.

Soon after he reached a marble staircase which led up to the upper floors.

He approached the first step of the staircase and stopped. Glancing up he noticed the second floor was dim, although he could make out flashlight beams.

Suddenly he heard the piercing voice of a woman calling out from the second floor. "What's going on down there, damn it?"

Ryan froze and crouched by the banister. Using the side of the staircase for cover he listened closely for other sounds.

"What the fuck is going on?" the woman screeched.

The PI said nothing. *Is that Angel Stone?* he wondered. *Possibly. But where's Rachel?* He felt a momentary stab of fear. *Is Rachel dead?*

Pushing that thought away, he refocused on the situation. He had to get up there. Listening closely, he heard whispers from the second floor. It was obvious there were several people there. *Was Papadopoulos up there with Angel?*

He hoped so, but that wasn't his immediate concern. There were probably more armed guards on the second floor. He had to eliminate that threat first before he could deal with Angel and find Rachel.

*But how?* He couldn't use another grenade and risk putting Rachel in danger. Then he remembered something Master Sergeant Lewis had placed in his backpack before getting on the transport plane.

A flash-bang grenade.

"You never know when this may come in handy," the sergeant had said. When flash-bang grenades exploded they blinded you with a brilliant light, deafened you with an earsplitting sound, and generally disoriented the hell out of criminals without killing them. The devices were primarily used by police SWAT teams and by military Special Ops soldiers.

Ryan reached into his backpack and removed the flash-bang. Pulling the pin on the grenade, he lobbed it with all his might up to the second floor. The metal canister rolled on the upstairs corridor floor and exploded with a deafening blast. The flash of the explosion was so bright it briefly blinded Ryan himself although he was on the floor below.

With his ears ringing from the blast, the PI charged up the stairs while holding his gun with both hands in front of him.

He reached the second floor and spotted a Nordic-looking man on his knees. The man appeared dazed but was still holding a submachine gun.

Ryan fired two rounds and the Nordic man collapsed to the floor.

The smoke created by the flash-bang was dissipating and through the haze Ryan saw two other inert bodies lying at the end of the corridor. He advanced cautiously toward them, half expecting them to open fire.

When he was a few feet away he realized both people were unconscious from the explosion. One of them was an elderly man with white hair. Dressed in sleepwear, he looked to be in his eighties. Viktor Papadopoulos, Ryan guessed.

Lying next to him was a stunningly beautiful woman with long raven hair. He recognized her immediately. It was Angel Stone, the same woman he'd arrested years ago. She was dressed in a tight black turtleneck and black slacks. Although she too was unconscious, she was still holding a Glock pistol in her hand.

Ryan pocketed her pistol, then searched Stone and Papadopoulos for other weapons. That done, he used plasticuffs to bind their hands and feet. Taking a roll of duck tape from his pack, he taped their mouths.

He continued searching the rest of the massive home, looking for other guards. He found none, although he did locate nine people huddled in one of the rooms. It was evident they were hiding there, frightened by the gunfire. None of them were armed and by the way they were dressed, eight of them appeared to be servants, maids, or cooks. There was also a man wearing a white lab coat who was possibly a doctor.

Ryan tied them all up and continued searching the four floors of the house. He didn't find Rachel and began to panic, thinking she'd been killed.

Going back to the first floor, he found a staircase leading down to a basement level. With his SIG Sauer trained forward, he cautiously descended the steps. When he reached the basement he scanned both sides of the corridor. There was no one around and he heard no sounds.

One by one he searched each of the rooms off the hallway. Most were storage areas for food, equipment, and supplies.

Going to the last room in the corridor, he tried opening the door and realized this one was locked. Ryan tensed, thinking more armed guards were holed up inside. He holstered his handgun and un-slung his MP-5. Aiming the assault rifle at the door lock, he fired off a three round burst. The door knob shattered as did part of the wooden frame. Ryan kicked in the door and charged into the room, his finger on the trigger, ready to blast away.

Surprised by what he found, he lowered his weapon. Instead of armed men he spotted a hospital bed. Along the wall of the room were numerous medical scanners and equipment. There was a woman lying on the bed and although the room was dim he realized the woman was Rachel West. He took off his night-vision goggles, pulled out a light-stick from his pocket, and turned it on.

Rachel's eyes were closed and she appeared to be unconscious. Her long blonde hair was matted and tangled, and her face was extremely pale. A bandage covered one of her cheeks.

He raced to her side and felt for a pulse. It was weak but she was alive.

Relief and elation flooded his senses. His eyes watered a moment as he said a silent prayer of thanks to God for his help in finding her alive.

He caressed her pale cheek. "Rachel," he said.

Rachel's eyes remained closed and she didn't respond. With a hand be brushed some of her tangled blonde hair off her face. "It's me, Rachel. Can you hear me?"

After a long moment her eyelids fluttered and then opened and he saw her vivid blue eyes.

"J.T...," she murmured hoarsely, "... you ... found me ...."

Ryan took hold of one of her hands and squeezed it gently. "I did."

Her blue eyes sparkled and she gave him a weak smile. "I didn't ... think ... I'd ever ... see you ... again ...."

Ryan chuckled. "I'm like a bad penny. You can't get rid of me."

She squeezed his hand, the smile not leaving her face. "Always ... the wiseguy ... aren't you ... you'll be cutting jokes ... at your own funeral ...."

He laughed, elated the woman he cherished was alive.

Then her smile faded, replaced by a panicked look. "The guards ... J.T.... they're ... everywhere ...."

He caressed her face. "Don't worry. I took care of them. They're dead."

"Even the ones ... at the sentry points? ... there's over twenty guards ... at the entrance gates ... leading to the mansion ...."

Ryan tensed, his adrenaline pumping again. *That's right*, he thought. He recalled the sentry checkpoints all along the road leading to the house. The ones he had skydived over. Those guards were all still alive and by now were probably racing toward Papadopoulos's estate.

"I have to go," he said. "But I hate to leave you here by yourself."

She gave him a wan smile. "Go ... take care of business ... I'm not going ... anywhere ...."

Ryan grinned. "When I get back, we'll get coffee, or have dinner, or whatever."

Even though Rachel was pale and weak she must have remembered their shared joke because she said, "I like ... the whatever ... best ...."

He nodded, kissed her gently, and left the room.

Ryan turned off the light-stick and put on his night-vision goggles again. He sprinted up to the first floor and exited the house by the back entrance. As soon as he set foot on the snow-covered patio he heard it.

A low rumble coming from far away. The sound was distinctive and he recognized it immediately. A diesel truck engine.

With his boots trudging over the snow, he raced toward the side of the house and scanned the horizon through his goggles. He noticed twin light beams coming closer. Headlights from a large truck. A truck full of armed men. Rachel had said there were about twenty of them at the various checkpoints. Obviously the guards had noticed the power failure at the mansion, and not getting an answer to their calls, figured there was trouble at the estate.

*Twenty to one*, he thought. *Bad odds. Very bad odds. Even for a well-trained Special Forces guy like me.* He racked his brain trying to figure a way out, all while watching the truck lights get closer and closer to the mansion.

Then in a flash it hit him.

Ryan sprinted to the other side of the home, his combat boots sinking into the white powder as he ran.

There it was in front of him.

The anti-aircraft missile system. As he studied the complex missile weapon, he realized his problem right away. He'd never fired anything so sophisticated before. And he didn't have the time to read the operating manual, if he could even find it. Not to mention, he would not be shooting at a stationary target – he'd be aiming at a fast-moving truck.

He circled the missile battery and noticed a smaller weapon sitting next to it.

It was a GAU-19/B Tactical System, a Gatling-gun type of machinegun. Much less high-tech than the missile system, the GAU-19/B was usually mounted on military armored personnel carriers to repel enemy infantry. It was also mounted on military helicopters to strafe enemy troops. It was the largest and most deadly machinegun ever made. It had a firing rate of 2,000 rounds per minute. Luckily Ryan had previously used this type of weapon.

He climbed into the turret and pointed the huge three-barrel machinegun toward the road. Then he turned on the diesel-powered control panel and checked the ammunition level. The weapon was loaded with a full armament of .50 caliber armor-piercing rounds. He turned off the GAU's safety and removed his night-vision goggles.

Looking through the GAU's viewfinder, the snow-covered road came into view. Like his goggles, the weapon system was also outfitted with night-vision optics. He began tracking the racing truck as it rumbled closer and closer to the mansion.

Ryan's finger caressed the trigger mechanism while he adjusted the crosshairs with his other hand.

The headlights grew in size until they completely filled the viewfinder.

With his heart pounding, Ryan knew the time had come. He had to make his move and make it now.

Holding his breath, he pulled the trigger.

The huge Gatling-type machinegun howled like a jet engine as the multiple barrels spit out .50 caliber rounds at the rate of 2,000 per minute. Ryan gripped the handholds tightly, feeling the recoil of the powerful weapon.

As the blaze of high-powered rounds fired from the GAU, its tracer bullets lit up the pitch-black night sky.

Seconds later the gunfire reached the speeding truck, the .50 caliber rounds shredding the grillwork, the cab, and the rear compartment.

The now-flaming vehicle veered off the road and crashed into a large boulder.

The night sky lit up as the truck exploded, sending fiery fragments in all directions.

# Chapter 88

*Vatnajokull, Iceland*

Ryan raced back into the mansion.

Once inside he made sure Rachel was still safe in the basement, then he climbed the stairs to where he had tied up Angel Stone and Viktor Papadopoulos.

The PI turned on his light-stick and saw that the old man was still lying on the floor, unconscious. But Angel Stone was fully awake, her dark eyes blazing with hate. She had maneuvered herself to a sitting position, her back leaning against the wall.

He removed the duct tape from her mouth.

"I know who you are!" Angel spat out, venom in her voice. "You're the bastard who put me in that hellhole Guantanamo!"

Ryan shook his head slowly. "Where you belong. I still can't figure out how the hell you escaped. No one else has ever done that before."

"It wasn't that difficult," she replied sarcastically. "Men are weak when it comes to sex. Spread your legs for them and they give you everything." She flashed a cold, hard grin. "Untie me and I'll show you how good I am in bed. I'll fuck your eyeballs out!"

"Save your breath, bitch. I'm arresting you for multiple homicides, bribery, treason, and money-laundering."

Angel frowned, obviously realizing her ploy hadn't worked. After a moment she said, "If you let me go, Ryan, I'll pay you. A kings ransom. One hundred million dollars."

Ryan shook his head. "Forget it. But that is a lot of money, I'll grant you that. Tell me, how can you get your hands on so much cash?"

She pointed her cuffed hands toward the unconscious man on the floor. "The old geezer. Papadopoulos. I'm his wife now. I have access to his billions."

"I guess I should congratulate you," Ryan said with a chuckle, "on your marriage. And on your new found wealth. Unfortunately for you, you won't be able to spend it where you're going. I'm going to recommend they put you in the Supermax prison in Colorado. No one has ever escaped from there. I figure you'll get a life sentence. Multiple times over."

Angel grimaced. "I'll give you 200 million dollars."

"There's only one thing I want from you and it's not money."

"What is it, Ryan? Whatever it is, you can have it. Just let me go!"

"Information."

"What kind of information?"

He squatted across from her and stared into her coal black eyes. "I want to know all the details of Fireball. I want the names of all those involved, both inside and outside the U.S. government."

She gave him a hard look. "What do I get in return? You'll let me go?"

He shook his head and laughed. "Hell, no. But I'll make sure you get a better prison cell at the Supermax."

Angel scowled and spit into his face. "Fuck you, Ryan! That's a crap deal. I'll just get the best attorney money can buy." She laughed a cold, mirthless chortle. "I bet I never spend another day in prison."

His anger boiling, he wiped the spittle off his face. "Then again, maybe I won't arrest you. Maybe I'll just interrogate you. And after that I'll beat you half to death." His voice dropped an octave. "Your pretty face will look like hamburger meat after I get through with you."

Angel's eyes bulged. But after a moment her features relaxed. "I don't think you'll do that. I remember when you arrested me years ago. You said you always treated women with respect. Some bullshit code of ethics you have."

Ryan ground his teeth. She was right. There was no way he would beat up a woman, no matter how evil she was.

He let out a long breath. Then anger surged through him as he recalled Rachel's condition.

He slapped Angel hard across her face and blood seeped from her lips.

"That was for kidnapping Rachel," Ryan snapped.

Angel's eyes grew wide again, shocked by the PI's action.

After a long moment she grinned. "Oh, I get it now. You and that blondie bitch have a thing going. I should have killed blondie when I had the chance!"

Ryan shook his head and stood. "Since I'm not going to get answers from you, I'll find the information some other way."

"I'll give you 500 million dollars!" Angel shouted.

"Forget it, lady. You're wasting your time."

"A billion dollars! Think of it, Ryan! One fucking billion dollars. Just let me go!"

Ryan pulled out his roll of duck tape, tore off a piece, and slapped it across her mouth. "That's better," he said, enjoying the respite from her shrill voice.

That done, he began a methodical search of the mansion, looking for any information about the criminal plot. He inspected the bedrooms first, and later moved on to the other rooms, checking for files, reports, notebooks, diaries, and computers, anything that might contain details of Fireball. He found nothing of value in any of the rooms, indicating Papadopoulos probably kept records at another location.

Frustrated by his lack of progress, he searched each of the rooms again looking for clues. In the massive den there was an antique roll-top desk. It looked very expensive and from the lack of files inside it he realized it was a decorative piece of furniture.

But after searching the roll-top desk a second time he located a locked, secret panel at the back of the cabinet. Prying open the panel, he found a laptop computer inside. A label on the bottom of the laptop said: *Number 3*. Clearly this was Angel Stone's personal computer.

Instantly intrigued, he set the computer on top of the desk and flipped open the lid. He booted up, but was immediately faced with a dilemma. The computer was password protected and he had no clue as to the password.

Ryan began inputting possible passcodes, such as '123456789', 'password', 'Angel', 'AngelStone', and 'Fireball' with no success.

"Damn," he said out loud.

He kept at it for another fifteen minutes, but all of the letter and number combinations he guessed at were incorrect. Staring at the screen, he racked his brain trying to figure out what she would use.

Then, just as he was about to give up and continue searching the mansion for a third time, he mulled over what Angel Stone would hate most in life.

It came to him in a flash.

Guantanamo.

The place where she'd been imprisoned for years.

Ryan methodically typed in: 'G-U-A-N-T-A-N-A-M-O' and hit the enter key.

The previously black computer screen turned a kaleidoscope of colors: vivid greens, and purples, reds, and blues. He recognized it immediately – the screen saver was a photo of the Aurora Borealis. The Aurora was a common sight in the night sky of arctic places like Iceland and Norway.

He studied the screen closely and saw file folders arranged on the left side of the screen. Quickly reading the names of the files, he noticed several were labeled 'Operation Fireball'. Two of these were Excel files, meaning they were spreadsheets of numbers. The third file was a Word document and he clicked on that one.

The file opened. It was a narrative, an electronic diary of sorts where Angel wrote the details of the operation. The file was lengthy, over 500 pages long. Knowing he had no time to waste, he quickly scrolled past the first 490 pages and began reading the last ten. That entry was dated with today's date and in it Angel described her hastily arranged wedding to Papadopoulos, then some notes on kinky sex practices she had performed on him in the afternoon. The implication of this passage was clear – she hoped that the intense sexual activity would cause the elderly man to die of a heart attack from the excitement, leaving her in total control over his billions.

Ryan skipped over these sordid details and focused on the next part, which continued to describe the operational details of Fireball.

Five minutes later he was done.

Shocked by what he'd learned, his mouth hung open. *Damn*, he thought. *It's worse than I could have ever imagined. Much, much worse.*

Alarmed by the nightmarish scenario of Fireball, and by the people involved, he abruptly closed the lid on the laptop and stood.

Taking out his satellite cell phone he punched in Erin Welch's number. It went to voice mail. He left an urgent message and hung up. Realizing it was critical he talk to her immediately, he called her again several times. But each time it went to voice mail so he left several more messages.

Angry and frustrated at not being able to connect, he called Alex Miller.

The CIA man answered on the first ring.

"It's Ryan," the PI said. "It's urgent I get a hold of Erin. But when I call her all I get is voicemail. What the hell's going on?"

"Calm down, Ryan. Erin's at the White House. The president wanted her to brief him personally on the task force's progress. As you know, personal cell phones aren't allowed inside the White House."

Ryan recalled this detail from his previous visits to the place. "I understand what's happening now, sir."

"Where are you calling from, Ryan?"

"Inside Papadopoulos's mansion. I'll skip over the details of what happened, but the important thing is I've arrested the billionaire and Angel Stone. And, thank God, Rachel's alive. She needs immediate medical attention, but I think she'll be fine."

"That's great news," the CIA man replied. "Have you been able to piece together what the conspiracy is all about?"

"Yes. And it's worse than we thought. Much, much worse. Catastrophic." Ryan went on to describe Operation Fireball.

"Oh, my God!" Miller said. "That is a nightmare scenario."

"I agree, sir. That's why I need to get a hold of Erin. She has to warn the president."

"Yes, yes, you're absolutely right. I'll call the White House, see if I can to talk to the president myself."

"Good idea, sir. And I'll keep trying to reach Erin. And there's one other thing."

"Yes?"

"Sir, there's an airplane runway on the mansion's property. I've disabled the anti-aircraft missile battery that Papadopoulos had installed. Can you send a jet to pick us up? I want to get Rachel the medical help she needs, and I want to put the criminals behind bars."

"Of course. I'll organize that right away."

"Thank you, sir."

Ryan hung up and punched in Erin's number again.

# Chapter 89

*The White House*
*Washington, D.C.*

Erin Welch strode to the West Wing's parking lot and got in her sedan.

She rubbed her forehead, trying to massage away a throbbing headache. The recent meetings in the Oval Office had left her dejected, exhausted, and afraid. It appeared that President Harris had no viable options. It was clear the Russians were intending a nuclear first strike. The evidence was irrefutable. The satellite photos clearly showed what was about to happen. It was just a matter of time before the DEFCON 1 alert turned into a nuclear war. The Russians were forcing the president's hand. He had no choice but to strike first.

Since Erin's expertise was not required for military decisions, she'd been asked to leave the Oval Office. Only the president and his military advisers had remained in the room, huddling over the details of when and how to proceed.

Just then Erin felt her cell phone vibrate in her pocket. Taking it out, she realized she had at least five voice mails, all from J.T. Ryan. She was about to listen to the first message when her phone vibrated again.

"Yes?" she said.

"It's J.T.," the man replied, his voice tense. "Thank God I reached you!"

"What is it? I see I've got several messages from you."

"You've got to talk to the president, Erin! You've got to warn him right now. I found out the real purpose of Fireball. And the name of the key conspirator."

"Really? You found out?"

"Yes! I captured Angel Stone and Viktor Papadopoulos. I read Angel's plan. She wants to start a nuclear war with Russia! She's trying to trick us into thinking the Russians are mounting a first strike!"

"But it's true, J.T. The Russians are planning to do exactly that. I saw the NSA satellite photos myself."

"It's all a lie! It's phony evidence. The NSA information is fake!"

"Are you sure about this?"

"Absolutely sure, Erin. I read all of the details. It was all there in black and white. Angel hated the U.S. because the government imprisoned her at Guantanamo. A nuclear war will destroy America and Russia both. She would get her revenge. To quote a line from her notes, she says, 'the United States will be destroyed in a fireball of death'. And since she and Papadopoulos live in Iceland, they would survive a nuclear holocaust. Iceland is a very remote place. One of the most remote countries in the world."

"I've got to warn the president!" Erin said, her adrenaline pumping. "He's planning on launching a preemptive first strike himself, before the Russians attack. We're already at DEFCON 1. But answer me this, J.T. How could the NSA satellite photos be falsified?"

"Because I found out who number 4 is," he said. "The top-level person in the U.S. government involved in the plot."

"Who is it, J.T.?"

"The new Director of National Intelligence. Samantha Lowry."

"She's number 4?" Erin replied, amazed at the revelation. The mousy woman was the last person she'd suspect as a traitor to the United States.

"Yes, her."

"Now it all clicks, J.T. Lowry was the one who showed the president the NSA satellite photos. She's been secretly working with NSA employees who were part of Fireball. But why did she do it? What's her motivation?"

"Greed," Ryan said. "Angel was going to pay her 100 million dollars when it was all complete. And that's in addition to the money she'd already been paid while the plot was in the works."

"But Lowry would be in jeopardy herself. A nuclear war would likely wipe out Washington D.C., where she lives."

"Angel and Lowry had figured out that part too, Erin. I read the file. Angel sent a private jet to pick up Samantha Lowry at Dulles Airport in D.C. I'm sure that plane is there now. You've got to stop all of it! Before it's too late!"

"I'm in the White House parking lot. I'll go back to the Oval Office and warn President Harris. I'm hanging up now!"

Not waiting for a reply, Erin threw the phone on the seat of the car, jerked the door open, and raced back to the entrance of the West Wing. Pulling out her FBI cred pack she held it in front of her. As she approached the entrance, she saw that the same Secret Service agent that had escorted her out of the building was still posted at the door.

"Erin Welch, FBI Assistant Director, I've got to see the president," she said in one long breath. "It's urgent! It's a matter of national security!"

Sensing her alarm, the Secret Service agent nodded. "Of course, Ms Welch." He opened the door, spoke to the other agents posted inside, and turned back to her. "Follow me, Ms Welch. I'll take you back to the Oval Office."

As she trailed behind the Secret Service man, she noticed he spoke into his lapel mike and listened to his ear bud.

Two minutes later Erin was admitted into the Oval Office by the agents posted at the door.

She rushed in and found almost the same group of people who were in the room a short while before. President Harris was there, sitting behind his historic wooden desk. Standing nearby were a group of men. The Chairman of the Joint Chiefs of Staff, the Secretary of State, the Secretary of Defense, and three other military generals. And there was someone new in the room: An Army colonel in uniform carrying a large, black metal briefcase. Erin had never seen this briefcase before, but had read about it. Referred to as the 'nuclear football', the case was the device used by the president to input passwords authorizing a nuclear strike.

President Harris looked up from his desk, which was still covered with the NSA satellite photos. "What is it, Erin?"

"Mr. President," she stated, almost shouting, "the photos are fake! They're altered images. It's all a hoax!"

Harris stood abruptly. "What the hell are you talking about?"

"Sir, she did it!" Erin replied. "She created the false evidence! The Russians aren't planning a nuclear attack."

"Who are you talking about? Who did it?"

Erin scanned the Oval Office, frantically looking for Samantha Lowry. But the woman wasn't there. "Mr. President, it's your Director of National Intelligence, Samantha Lowry. She's number 4 in the Fireball plot."

The president shook his head. "Are you crazy, Erin? She's my trusted aide. She's worked at the White House for years. She was the Deputy DNI for a long time. Are you certain of this information?"

"I'm positive, Mr. President. John Ryan arrested Angel Stone and Viktor Papadopoulos. He read their secret files." Erin glanced around the room again. "Where's Lowry?"

"She went home," Harris said. "She suddenly came down with the flu. I'll have the Secret Service go there now and bring her back here. We'll interrogate her. If we confirm what you say is true, we'll arrest her."

"Samantha Lowry won't be at home," Erin replied, her voice tense. "Angel Stone sent a private jet to pick her up at Dulles Airport. My bet is Lowry is there now, boarding that jet. The plane is taking her to Iceland."

An alarmed expression settled on Harris's face. He pressed the intercom device on his desk. "This is the president. I'm invoking a National Security Emergency. Immediately stop all flights going out of Dulles Airport. In fact, I want a lock down on all Washington D.C. airports. Got it?"

"Yes, Mr. President," came the reply. "I'll do that right away."

President Harris turned to the Army colonel carrying the 'nuclear football' briefcase. "Thank God, it doesn't look like we're going to need that today, Colonel."

The president crossed himself and turned to Erin Welch. "Have a seat, Erin. Tell us everything, and I mean everything, you've learned about Fireball."

Erin breathed a sigh of relief, realizing a catastrophic nuclear war had been averted. "Of course, Mr. President."

# One Month Later

## Chapter 90

*The Situation Room*
*The White House*
*Washington, D.C.*

J.T. Ryan, along with the rest of the task force, was in the Situation Room waiting for President Harris to arrive for today's meeting.

The last month had been a blur, J.T. Ryan thought, recalling what had happened after he'd captured Angel Stone and Viktor Papadopoulos in Iceland.

As Ryan had hoped, those two people had been charged under the Patriot/USA Freedom Act for treason, terrorism, and murder, and had been incarcerated at the Supermax prison in Colorado. They were joined there by Samantha Lowry. Based on the treasure trove of information Ryan had obtained from Angel's computer, dozens of other people had been imprisoned as well. Most of these were NSA employees, but there were also employees of other government agencies. And although trials would be held sometime in the future, all these people would, Ryan was sure, die of old age in the maximum security prison.

In addition to that, Angel's financial transactions had revealed that large sums of money had been paid to congressmen and senators for bribes. Some of these officials had already resigned and others had been charged for a variety of crimes and would be brought to trial. And now that the payoffs had stopped, the nationwide riots had come to a standstill. The *Overthrow* movement had collapsed. Likewise, the stalled impeachment hearings had been called off in the Senate.

Ryan glanced around the Situation Room as they waited for President Harris to arrive.

Sitting next to him at the conference table was Erin Welch. Next to her was the CIA's Alex Miller and Rachel West. Rachel had fully recovered from her injuries and when she noticed Ryan looking at her, she gave him a radiant and slightly mischievous smile.

Ryan smiled back, looking forward to spending time with her.

Just then the door to the Situation Room opened and President Harris strode in, followed by General Foster, the Chairman of the Joint Chiefs of Staff, who closed the door behind him.

Ryan stood, as did Erin, Alex, and Rachel.

The president walked around the table and stood in front of them.

"Normally we would hold this ceremony in the Rose Garden," the president began. "After all, receiving the Medal of Honor is a great achievement. It's the highest commendation the country can bestow for protecting the United States." He paused, a serious expression on his face. "Unfortunately, this ceremony has to remain secret. I wish I could tell the world the incredible courage and selflessness you four people have shown in destroying Fireball. But your involvement must remain a secret, since I, or a future president, may need to utilize your skills again."

President Harris turned to General Foster. "Let's proceed, General."

"Yes, sir," the four-star replied. The general was carrying a briefcase, which he set on the conference table and opened.

Harris reached into the case and removed one of the medals. Each of the prestigious medals hung on blue ribbons. He walked over to Erin Welch and after shaking her hand, draped the Medal of Honor on her neck. "Thank you, Erin, for leading this team. I'm deeply indebted to you, as is the whole country."

"You're very welcome, Mr. President," she replied.

Harris repeated the process twice more, awarding the Medal of Honor to Alex Miller and to Rachel West.

Then the president turned toward J.T. Ryan. "I did some research on this, Ryan. And I found out that only 19 other people in the history of the U.S. have been awarded two Medals of Honor. I know you received one years ago for your heroic service in Afghanistan. So this one today will make your second."

Harris reached into the briefcase and removed the medal. "From what I hear, Ryan," the president said, "you're a cocky son-of-a-gun. So getting this today will swell your head even more."

Ryan almost chuckled at this, but Erin, who was standing next to him, jabbed him sharply with an elbow.

The president draped the Medal of Honor over the PI's neck. "Thank you for your service, Ryan."

The two men shook hands.

"You're welcome, Mr. President."

# Chapter 91

*The White House*
*Washington, D.C.*

After the brief ceremony in the Situation Room, the task force was escorted out of the White House. Erin Welch and J.T. Ryan walked to the West Wing parking lot and climbed into their sedan, while the two CIA people got in their car.

Erin turned to Ryan. "Now that the Fireball plot is behind us," she said, "I've got another case for you."

"That's great," the PI replied. "But I'll need a few days off first. This Fireball thing has worn me out. Mentally and physically."

Ryan visualized the gorgeous woman he cared about so much. Rachel West. Her sparkling blue eyes and her slightly mischievous smile. Her sense of humor, razor-sharp mind, and never-give-up attitude. Not to mention her long blonde hair and stunning curves.

"On second thought," Ryan said, "I'll need a week off."

Erin gave him an amused look. "This wouldn't have anything to do with a certain CIA operative by the name of Rachel, would it?"

Ryan laughed. "No wonder you're an Assistant Director of the FBI. You have excellent detecting skills."

Erin chuckled as she started the car.

His interest piqued by Erin's mention of a new investigation, he said, "What's the new case about?"

"Well, it has nothing to do with national security or Washington D.C."

Ryan glanced out the car's windows. "That's good. I'm sick of this city. It's a swamp of dirty dealing. And no matter how many times good people try to drain the swamp, the bad stuff always creeps back in."

"I agree. I'm sick of this city, too," Erin replied. "This new case involves a series of mysterious deaths that have taken place in Atlanta and several other cities."

"Sounds intriguing, Erin. Tell me more."

As Erin drove out of the White House parking lot, she continued describing the details of the new case.

By the time they got to Pennsylvania Avenue, Ryan knew he definitely wanted to investigate the mysterious murders.

# END

\*\*\*

# About the author

Lee Gimenez is the award-winning author of 14 novels, including his highly-acclaimed J.T. Ryan series. Several of his books were Featured Novels of the International Thriller Writers Association, among them FBI CODE RED, THE MEDIA MURDERS, SKYFLASH, KILLING WEST, and THE WASHINGTON ULTIMATUM. Lee was nominated for the Georgia Author of the Year Award, and he was a Finalist in the prestigious Terry Kay Prize for Fiction. Lee's books are available at Amazon and many other bookstores in the U.S. and Internationally.
For more information about him, please visit his website at: www.LeeGimenez.com. There you can sign up for his free newsletter. You can contact Lee at his email address: LG727@MSN.com. You can also join him on Facebook, Twitter, Google Plus, LinkedIn, and Goodreads. Lee lives with his wife in the Atlanta, Georgia area.

\*\*\*

# Other Novels by Lee Gimenez

**FBI Code Red**
**The Media Murders**
**Skyflash**
**Killing West**
**The Washington Ultimatum**
**Blacksnow Zero**
**The Sigma Conspiracy**
**The Nanotech Murders**
**Death on Zanath**
**Virtual Thoughtstream**
**Azul 7**
**Terralus 4**
**The Tomorrow Solution**

**FBI CODE RED**, a J.T. Ryan Thriller
is available at Amazon and many other bookstores in the
U.S. and Internationally.
In paperback, Kindle, and all other ebook versions.

**THE MEDIA MURDERS**, a J.T. Ryan Thriller
is available at Amazon and many other bookstores in the
U.S. and Internationally.
In paperback, Kindle, and all other ebook versions.

**SKYFLASH**, a J.T. Ryan Thriller
is available at Amazon and many other bookstores in the
U.S. and Internationally.
In paperback, Kindle, and all other ebook versions.

**KILLING WEST**, a Rachel West Thriller
is available at Amazon and many other bookstores in the
U.S. and Internationally.
In paperback, Kindle, and all other ebook versions.

## THE WASHINGTON ULTIMATUM,
### a J.T. Ryan Thriller
is available at Amazon and many other bookstores in the
U.S. and Internationally. In paperback, Kindle, and all other
ebook versions.

Lee Gimenez's other novels, including
- Blacksnow Zero
- The Sigma Conspiracy
- The Nanotech Murders
- Death on Zanath
- Virtual Thoughtstream
- Azul 7
- Terralus 4
- The Tomorrow Solution

are all available at Amazon and many other bookstores in the U.S. and Internationally.
In paperback, Kindle, and all other ebook versions.